Desperation Lingers

Anthony Paull

Cover Design: John Greske
Photography: Matthew Holler
Illustration: Van Jazmin
Cover Model: Kirsten Sponseller

For T. Cronin Moore

Hear to sea.

Table of Contents

CHAPTER 1

IF I COULD speak to my daughter I'd say there's a story here. They might not see it, but I'm certain that somewhere under the blanket of Miami Beach stars the locals would recall my life as something other than a tragedy, but the tale of a mother who longed for a family.

With my daughter I had that – a family. But I lost that long ago, and then I lost myself, somewhere in the clouds.

Still, that won't be the headline in the Herald. They'll merely print the facts. Desperation Lingers, age fifty, plunged from her eleventh floor condo in an apparent suicide. They won't know why I did it, or care. They'll flip to the next page or skip the article altogether. Who can blame them? There's enough sadness in the world, and I consider the idea of diving into a sidewalk maniacal too. But sometimes life makes one do crazy things.

Once I had it all – a chest that would chin up and smile, a pearl of a pet cat, and a husband who'd wake to warm me with a kiss. Now I can't get a text to wink.

Still I persist. With a bit of pip and a lot of pizazz, I go on even if my career is a bust. Counselor – that's my title. Guidance – that's what I offer. That's me, 'here to help' except I have no clients; at least, none seeking advice of their own volition.

The administrators say I can't relate – I'm too removed from the hooligans at Horizon Institute. I'm a wicked soul to whom only the janitor will speak. Can't they see my talent? I love the children in a way. Why won't they allow me a classroom? I'm too highfalutin, too proud to meet the students halfway. That's what they say. I'm scared to get my feet wet, afraid to take the plunge. I'll show them.

Setting down my fourth martini for the night, I take to my balcony and call, "Look out below!" Then staring over the edge I prepare to take the greatest jump of all.

Be quick, I think. Don't look back. Be brave like the citizens of Pamplona. Outwit the hooves of the bulls. That's all behind you – hooves, thorns, pricks, cuts. And who can forget the promises, the empty promises of every man who stabbed an inch deeper than the one before?

Behind you, think of the knives, the razors that threatened you, the taunts you endured as a girl. Think of your acerbic mother, the sting of her tongue. You were never good enough, not smart enough, never stylish enough, and oh Little Miss Mess, how you always had to work on manners and etiquette. Remember: address adults as sir or ma'am. Add a please and a thank you. Place the salad fork to the left of the dinner fork. Raise your spoon to your mouth, not your mouth to your spoon. Don't slouch. Never wear Lycra. Don't substitute a cocktail onion for an olive and call it a martini. It's a Gibson. Yes, the ghost of your British mother, Beverly, is behind you, providing instruction. Not that you've learned.

After all, no true lady would think to throw herself from a building.

How crude and messy. How uninspired.

Nevertheless, I leap on my balcony railing, questioning if my life matters. It's a blur – the Mediterranean condos across the way, painted pastel pink. I look down and the street shines with glittery fountains and sugary rides. I grow dizzy, hearing the call of the Atlantic.

I blink my eyes and a crowd gathers. Down below each person is no bigger than a drop of water. Forming an ocean, they call out in waves, inviting me for a swim. I see myself falling. I picture worker bees rushing to the scene in red trucks with flashing lights. Below the blaring sirens I hear screams of my name.

"Ms. Dee! Ms. Dee!"

Do they know me? Do they...care?

The voices ring with concern. But is it real?

The faithful say everything happens for a reason, that

people are disjointed pieces of a puzzle. We're part of a whole, and that the whole equals God.

Then dear God, fill this hole.

Why was I born? What have I contributed? Grant me one clue, one reason why I should live.

Thzzzzzt.

Why does it hurt to breathe? Why does it have to... hurt?

Thzzzzzt.

What is that? That buzzing?

Thzzzzzt.

Why, it's my doorbell.

Someone is ringing me. But why?

Wait. Maybe it's....

Hector.

No! Stop it! Don't say that.

But....

No. It couldn't be him. Just last week, he informed me that 'we can never do whatever it is we're doing again.' After two years his heart can't take it. His pastor warned him that turbulent affairs poison a man's soul. Well, that's lovely. I never wanted a man who couldn't devote time to me anyway. I don't understand. He claims to be separated but never separates himself entirely. So why is he here? Is he hungry? Does he want me to prepare another burrito for his bloated belly? Oh good heavens! At this late hour, can I give him another chance?

Oh, I'm so fed up with this life, this puzzle. Still, I'm ashamed to admit the opportunity to see Hector warms my heart.

Maybe he'd finally like to offer me that teaching job he's been holding over my head. Or perhaps he'd merely like back his belongings.

Well, if that's the case he can take his antacid pills and that silver ring he places on the base of his penis and dispose of them as he sees fit.

Thzzzzzt.

"Leave me alone!" I call. Though truly, I want to hear it again, just once to feel connected.

Thzzzzzt.

"Well, fine!" I say, retreating from the railing.

You see, I don't really want to die. I just don't want to make the mistake of living another day. But if I do, think of it as a habit. After all, we're each entitled to make one or two precious mistakes in life. That or a million. The truth is, when you reach fifty, every step forward feels like two steps back. Still, a lady can't get ahead in a man's world walking in reverse. So those like me, we do what we can, marching under painted faces while clowning around with the notion that we're fabulous even if no one agrees. Ta-da!

I press the intercom button. "Hello?"

"Mr. Chengs."

"Mr. what?"

"The moo goo gai pan," a boyish voice utters.

My dinner. I forgot! But didn't I place that order hours ago? What day is it? Oh yes! My birthday! Oh dear, I must resist these martinis. They make me so forgetful. Thank God.

"It's open," I say, ringing the boy up.

Then in a mirror I powder my nose, flick my chicken chin. What happened? Once, my face was a thing of beauty. Blood rushed to be there; men rushed to be there. Hence these days it's somewhat trampled, transformed from fine porcelain into an eggplant. I'm a Big Bird of a lady – that's always been the case. Tall and thin, with spaghetti arms and legs skinny as a hambone.

I could have been a model. That is, if my nose agreed and didn't make me the spawn of a Great Blue Heron. Mother (*not mother, please, call me Bev, dear!*) called it a strong nose, which is the English equivalent of being equally polite and critical. "It commands attention," she'd say. "It has a way of saluting people when you enter a room."

Bev Dear had to be the most beautiful one in the family. And she was. Even on the morning of her death, planned the day I set off for college, she was breathtaking. I remember she fashioned herself in the brightest diamonds and a red sequined dress. Only Bev Dear could make a pill overdose glamorous. My one advantage in terms of aesthetics is my radiant long black hair. I fluff and puff it now. Poof, poof. Grimace. Then I answer the call of the bell.

"That'll be \$12.95," the chubby boy says, as I open the door. He hands me a brown bag with a menu stapled to it. A baseball cap covers his eyes.

"Running late?" I ask.

"Someone quit."

"An apology would be music to my ears. I could've starved." He lifts his cap, revealing chubby cheeks and a thin black mustache. He can't be more than a teenager. I tap my foot. "I'm waiting."

"For what?"

I fling up my arms. "Why do I try? Please. Come in." He listens, remaining by the door. "So you know," I mention, heading to the kitchen, "when addressing a lady, the term ma'am is appreciated, particularly if you haven't been formally introduced." Sipping a martini, I return with my red sharkskin purse, taking note of the ill-fitting jeans hanging from his waist. "Oh dear," I say, taking note. "Does your supervisor approve?"

"He hasn't said nothin'."

"Well, allow me to say it for him. Pull them up. You're not in prison. You're not that dangerous." Oh, I should stop drinking. It drowns my filter, allowing me to utter the most unspeakable things. "Tell me. Do you like the idea? Prison? Hot showers with indiscriminate men?"

He flinches. "What?"

"A little oopsie in your poopsie?"

His face coils in anger. "A little what?"

Oh dear. Have I gone mad? This is vile, unladylike. If mother were alive, she'd say I picked up this language from our driver Rose.

I sway and he catches me.

"Whoa. You ok?" He studies my eyes and I blink, finding temporary sleep. Then waking, I shake off the dizziness and hand him the money. His head seems to spin like a sun-warped record when he holds me. "You cool?"

"Cool? What is cool these days?" Befuddled, he stalls for a reply. "Suicide, is that cool? I hear the popular kids try it at least once." He looks at me in confusion and I wonder if he's loved and lost yet. Has he felt emptier than a hollowed tree? His youthful eyes tell me no.

"You better sit down," he says, leading me to the couch. Its red cushions feel cold as ice. On the wall, I lock eyes with a painting, one of Lichtenstein's heroines. The distraught girl's face arrives and departs on waves of dots. Kissing a man she cries. She's weak. She welcomes it.

"You're not my Hector," I mumble. "What's your name?"

"Cici," he offers.

"Sissy?"

"CI-CI," he replies. He props me up.

"Oh Sissy," I toy, resting my head on his chest. "Don't think you're the first sissy who's had me in his arms. Back in the day, men would flip me over and pretend." I chuckle, reflecting. "Gay men were once so charitable."

He tucks a pillow behind my head and from the balcony I hear the call of Miami nightlife – conga music coupled with the screams of excitable girls.

"You comfortable, ma'am?"

"Ma'am?" My eyes grow with delight. He smirks, balancing my head. "You have learned something." I smile from the thought. "And they think I can't teach. Hmph." I close my eyes and see Hector, along with the men who've cared for me before him – my father St. Clair and my four husbands, for better or worse. I think of my black cat Flippy and smile. "You may not believe it but I was caring once. I was good." Reflecting, I recall father teaching me the benefit of helping others, how it siphons the coal in the soul. Father was the owner of HL Mining Company but was never too big to join the workers underground. To them, he was a hero. To me, he was dad. That was enough.

Cici sets my dinner on the coffee table and stands. "All right. I have to go."

My eyes rush open. "Already? But I was enjoying our talk. I don't get many visitors."

"I can see that," he says, with a grin. "How about I just grab my money?" He bends to reach for my purse and his pants sag, revealing white boxer shorts.

"Great. Another man who can't stay long enough to pull up his pants."

He takes his cash. "Can I add a tip?"

"Sure. I have a tip." I summon him with a finger.

He views me with caution, setting down the purse to backtrack. "Forget it. Get some sleep. Ok?"

"Tip numero uno," I declare, rising. "Never leave a desperate woman at a desperate hour."

"Sure. Great tip." He continues to the door.

"Hey Superman!" I call, as he grips the door handle. "You fly out that door, I fly off that balcony." I hear a moped coasting on Collins, the whisper of a warm wind catching its tail and then silence.

He sighs. "C'mon. Why you gotta talk like that?"

I view him intensely. "Would you rather I sing it?"

He remains calm, controlled. "You should call 911 or someone. How 'bout that Hector guy?"

I laugh. "Hector doesn't care. I'm just filler, beans for his burrito." I search for a mental escape. It's a trick I learned from Bev Dear; close your eyes to quiet the world, ear to palm. Squeeze 'til you hear the sea and breathe.

So I do. I breathe, taking down sweet air as my palms fill my ears with the ocean like the call of a conch shell. I envision placing my head underwater. Below, I imagine the current taking me to God. I envision a classroom of children who no longer run at the sight of me. Instead, they see me for what I once saw in myself – something pure, loving, warm.

"You alive?" Cici asks. He nudges me and I waken, overcome by sadness. I panic and stand, setting into a run. Alcohol troubles my balance and I ask myself, why should I live? I have no loved ones on earth. Even my cat Flippy is gone. So what if the pavement cracks my spirit? I'm already split in two. In heaven, I'll see Flippy. I'll see Felix, my true love. Now, all I see is the balcony, the perfect black night – so perfect one little jump can't stain it.

"Whoa! Hold on!" Cici says, wrapping his muscled bicep around my chest. Capturing me, he pulls me back inside.

I struggle in his arms. "Let go!"

"Calm down."

"I miss Flippy. I miss my cat! I heard him barking the other night. I heard him from heaven. He wanted his mommy and a bowl of milk." I reach for a vodka bottle on the wet bar.

"No! No more of that," he says, pulling me to the couch.

I flail my arms but fail to maneuver my body out of his grip. "You think I'm mad. I heard Flippy bark. I did. He misses me."

He lowers me to the couch. "Let's call Hector."

"No. He can't see me like this. He's my boss." Catching my breath I pat the cushion beside me. "Please. Sit." He hesitates, grumbling before switching on the tele. Then flipping to a sports update he sits beside me, basking in the bright colors on the screen. Soon I nod off, dreaming of swimming in an ocean with no floor. It's night, and I try not to panic, gliding on rolling waves. From a distance I see another. Is it Hector? No. It's mother, clutching a lantern on a raft. Draped in white pearls she raises a martini glass of sand, the way she likes it – dry, very dry.

"Mother!" I call. "You're here. You came to save me."

She takes a drink and sets down her glass to toss me a life jacket. "Oh Dee. Don't be silly. No one can save you."

"But...you're my mother."

Her green eyes dull, withdrawing. "No. I'm Bev, dear."

She drifts away, her hair the color of a bonfire. And wading in the darkness I realize she's right. She's too beautiful to be related to me, and technically I don't know who my real mother is.

CHAPTER 2

THE NEXT DAY, I wake with a headache and a heavy heart, reminded there's work to be done. As a child, that's what parents forget to tell you. Being an adult comes with responsibilities. Like now, I'd love nothing more than to bury my face in a feather pillow and turn off the world, but I have a job. Therefore, I've no time to inquire why there is a strange man snoring beside me on the couch. Long ago I learned it's best not to ask questions so I simply shower and cover myself with a white robe and attend to the stove. There, I prep a mushroom and Swiss omelet. I may be a headcase but I'm still a good host.

"Hello?" the man calls, with a cough. I hurry into the living room to find him removing the plunger I'd placed on his chest. He tosses it like it's infected. "Nasty! What the heck is that?"

"A plunger," I casually state.

"I know that," he says, sharply. "Why's it on my chest?"

I'm too embarrassed to tell him the truth, that Hector managed to clog up my love life and my toilet. He must be the only Cuban unable to digest spice. The master bath has been out of order for over two weeks, since his last visit.

"There are certain tasks in life a lady does not perform," I say, grabbing the plunger off the floor. I hand it to him and he refuses it. I set it next to him on the couch. "Remind me your name again?"

"Cici."

"That's right. Sissy." I head back to the kitchen to sprinkle his omelet with paprika. "Glad you're here. Now, go on. Find your way to the loo off the master bedroom while I prepare your breakfast. Try not to splash water while you work."

"Work? What time is it? I got school." He stands, finding me in the kitchen, where he searches his pockets. "Where are my keys?"

I grin, jiggling them in my hand. "Fix the toilet. I'll give them back."

His face contorts. "You stole my keys? Damn! What's wrong with you?" On the street, voices arise, the sound of a truck backing up. He rushes to the balcony, clipping a potted orchid. "My scooter!" he shouts.

I set his plate on the dining table, returning to the kitchen. "Is something wrong?"

He ignores me, dialing his cell. Entering a conversation, his voice remains low, yet hard. He lights a cigarette, pacing on the balcony. I remain busy, cleaning the frying pan and sipping coffee. A minute later, he returns to demand his keys.

"After you unclog the toilet," I state.

"Yo, I'm not playing games. There's a U-Haul down there about to crush my scooter."

That's right. I heard a tenant was moving in. My chatty eleventh floor neighbor Ms. Hallstein had caught word, feeding my ear in the elevator after complaining about a rash of graffiti she discovered on the side of the bistro just down the road. I jokingly told her it was an original Banksy and she took it on herself to paint over it to save the city money.

"Don't worry. I'll buy you a new scooter," I say.

"I don't want your money."

"The toilet," I insist, pointing toward the loo.

"You know what lady? You're nuts, you and that barking cat." I don't argue. Instead, I stand firm, folding my arms, refusing to give up. Grumbling, he hesitates before returning to the couch for the plunger. "Fine. I'll do it. Then I want my keys."

I agree then pack two lunches: one for Cici and one for my friend Trixie.

In the bedroom I decide on an ensemble. Bright colors resonate on my tan palette so I opt for a red business suit.

For extra flair, I top it with a large-rimmed hat bearing pink pompom balls. Cheetah beads mark my neck. Marvelous. If only my coworkers would agree. I hear the talk.

Just who does she think she is? She's too loud. Her clothes point out what students can't afford. What kind of example is she setting?

They don't understand I'm teaching the importance of appearance. That's the one thing Bev Dear taught me. Not that Cici cares. Handing him his keys, I try to convince him to shower but he flees without so much as brushing his teeth. I don't say a word about it considering he did manage to unclog the toilet. As we ride the elevator down, I thank him right before the door opens to the lobby.

"Morning Ms. Lingers," Archibald says. Tall and reserved with thick black glasses, he's been the doorman at the Savoy since I was a little girl. He never has to say much. His eyes do the talking, particularly when Cici tosses his lunch in the gold planter containing a palm near the entry.

"Well Archibald. I'm glad you still have manners," I utter. He opens the glass door and Cici escapes to the outside. "These days, so many men seem to forget."

"Some remember," Archibald assures me. In a navy blazer and barbershop tie, he grants me a wink, as a tall lady enters, struggling with two creatures in her arms. She nearly trips, launching into a fit of laughter reminiscent of a caged monkey at the zoo. Archibald saves her from a fall.

"Lordy, thank you, thank you!" she says, steadying a hand on his shoulder. She releases the two tiny critters – a cat and a dog – from her grasp. Whizzing by, the cat vanishes behind a potted cactus by the elevator. "No Tacky! Come back to momma!" the woman calls. Meanwhile, the dog – a Chihuahua without hind legs, yaps at Archibald's feet.

"They really are friendly. They're just not used to transition," the woman says, picking up the dog. His butt is anchored to a pink cart with wheels. "They won't be a bother. Right, Taser?" She kisses him on the nose, eliminating his bark. "Oh, where are my manners?" She extends a hand. Each finger is coated in gold rings. "I'm Cathy Fritter, just moving in. Friends call me Kitty."

"Dee," I reply, with a firm shake.

"And you've met the lil' munchkins." She speaks in an easy breezy country tone. "Tacky and Taser. I got them in the divorce."

I perk up. "Divorce? Lucky you. My first husband left me a bill."

"Oh, that's no good," Kitty says. In the awkward silence that follows I study her features. Her face is peculiar, narrow like a V, veiled in white pancake makeup. Her nose is pronounced, bearing no resemblance to a beak but a duckbill. She has the broadest nasal septum I've come across on a lady or a man for that matter. "I'm sorry your husband was so unkind, but there are a lot of good men out there. I just know it." She flips her blonde locks as Taser pees. "No!" she cries, removing the pink handkerchief tied around her neck. She bends to clean the spill. "That's my biggest problem with him. Since he doesn't have back legs I never know when he's going to lift one." She playfully pokes at him and I flash to having a family, to singing my daughter to sleep in my stomach. Pain riddles my chest.

"Archibald, remind me," I request. "Isn't there a rule regarding pets at the Savoy?"

"A rule?" He ponders the question. "What do you mean?"

"I mean...*a limit*."

He emits a subtle gasp. "Why, now that you mention it. We do have a limit. One per unit."

Kitty's green eyes fill with fear before she switches gears, laughing it off – a clever ploy. "Oh, I don't own a unit. I'm poor. I'm just leasing." She bats her eyes. "Does that count?"

"I'll let Archibald do the math. I'm not good with numbers," I say. But the truth is I have Ms. Fritter's number down. I've seen her kind before: the type who feels privy to a free pass by pretending the rules don't apply if she winks. Look at the sad woman. She's ready to take on the world in a frayed jean miniskirt and no man, including Archibald, will get in her way, granted she keeps it hiked up.

"I'm certain we can work out something," he tells her.

I exit in a huff, rushing down the stairs to the sidewalk. The valet Salvador is engaged in a conversation with a friend.

"Salvador! My car!"

"Sí madam." He jogs off, and I look for my homeless friend Trixie in her customary spot. Wrapped in a raggedy rainbow shawl she sells day-late flowers and palm fronds fashioned like crosses from a shopping cart.

"What's this?" she scowls, taking a container of blueberry yogurt from the bag.

"I'll have you know, the antioxidants in blueberries are better for your skin than any cream on the market." She groans, caressing her leathery face. "Tell me. Do you have enough clothes?" She nods a firm yes, pointing to one of the black trash bags in her cart. The bag is brimming with designer dresses I donated last month. She refuses to wear them. She just pawns them when she needs cash, stating the impoverished look gets her more attention.

"Miss, I mean, uh, ma'am," Cici calls. I turn to find him attempting to start his scooter, which is wedged between a U-Haul and a pickup truck. He dismounts and approaches. "My scooter's buggin'. Can I hitch a ride to school?"

"Who is *that*?" Trixie asks. With her thin arm, she blocks Cici from coming closer. She doesn't trust men, not since her husband gambled their savings in a house-flipping scheme that landed him in prison, where he began emailing other women.

"I'm Cici."

"I hate you," she says.

"Daaaamn. What's your problem?"

"She only likes me," I explain. The valet approaches in my purple Jaguar.

"Whatever," he says. "You need to help me. I fixed your toilet."

"And in return, I fixed you a ham and brie sandwich, which you tossed in a planter in the lobby."

"The lobby?" Trixie says. Before I can reply she makes a dash to the Savoy entrance, retrieving it. Shedding Salvador a few dollars, I rush to my car.

"Look at you, high and mighty, talking etiquette and shit," Cici says. "What does your etiquette book say about turning someone out?"

Turning someone out? Who does this boy think he is? I've been known to aid a fellow man or woman in distress. Look at what I've done for Trixie. She's the only homeless person in Miami with a Prada clutch.

Still, he did fix my toilet and taking him to school shouldn't take too much time. So why not give him a ride? It could give me a chance to teach him how to dress.

"You are aware, baseball jerseys are meant for baseball stadiums," I inform him, crossing the Venetian Causeway. Falling asleep he shrugs me off, and I turn my head to marvel over Biscayne Bay. The water is glassy and serene, settling me like the thought of being surrounded by family. I wonder where everyone has gone. How did lonely happen so fast?

It's funny how life works. As a child, I was so determined to grow up that I missed getting there. Bev Dear made me desire adulthood before my time. Crawl? There wasn't time. For mother, infants were no more than ankle biters waiting to stink up the night.

From day one she began to school me on what is most important.

Poise. Presentation. Perfection.

Yes. Mother was full of wisdom when she wasn't polishing off martinis and prescription pills. At first, the pills would ward off terrible migraines. Only during adolescence did I learn father and I were the cause.

The other P: privacy.

Privacy lent hand to mystery, and mother always said those make the most fascinating reads. I suppose that's why she held things close, including the truth about me. It was only after mother's cremation that I first learned of my adoption. Sealed in a manila envelope in mother's lock box, it was not the loving voice of a parent, but the cold, printed word that passed along the truth about my lineage. Still, the holes ran deep, due to mother, who was wise enough to clip the names, dates, and other identifying information.

"Mr. Cici, wake up," I say. Clearing my head, I nudge

his shoulder. "Where am I dropping you? Little Havana?"

With a stretch, he nods. "Horizon Institute. Just stay on Flagler, and then take a left on...."

"Horizon? You attend Horizon?"

"What? I ain't like them," he defends.

I hesitate. "I work at Horizon."

He grins, getting a rise. "I knew you looked familiar. "Ain't you a, uh...." He snaps his fingers. "A secretary?"

"Counselor."

"Yeah, that's it," he says, his voice growing grave. "Yeah, I ain't been to you, but I heard you can be a b...." He resists.

"A what?"

He laughs it off, turning to the street, where a colorful line of people waits for the bus. Standing beside a red bandana-headed punk, an old woman in a pink muumuu pulls curlers out of her hair.

This is the real Miami: no supermodels or rap stars, just working-class citizens in the midst of life. I arrived as a preteen, summering in South Beach after father purchased our unit at the Savoy. Our driver Rose was the first to give me the tour. Back then Horizon Institute didn't exist. It was founded seven years ago: a dozen beige portables resembling a second-rate Stonehenge. This is where I see clients. Their crimes, punishable by law, restrict them from attending traditional educational facilities. Horizon gives them a second chance.

"I'm out," Cici informs me, reaching the school parking lot. Exiting the car, he holds up his baggy pants, running off. There you have it. No thank you. No 'see you later.'

No clue.

Oh, if only there was someone to teach the children manners. Not that the adults are better. I'm seated in my office no more than ten seconds when Vita, my administrative assistant, rushes in without knocking.

"Oh. Ms. Lingers. Isss no good," she says, with a heavy Latin accent. "I say prayers but I see it coming." She fans her sweaty face, clutching a string of rosary beads. Her breasts pour out of her sparkly blouse when she plops down in a seat.

A voluptuous woman, age sixty, her tears are more artificial than her blonde wig. "Isss Ms. Macomber. She loves fried chicken. I say no. Isss no good." She uses the strands from her wig to dry her eyes. "I say no. Now she's dead."

"Dead?"

"Sí," Vita says. "Heart attack."

I gasp. *"Lucky thing."*

Vita appears confused. "Qué?"

"I mean, lucky in an awful way. Dreadfully awful."

Her horrified expression says she's not convinced. And she's right. I don't see this as a tragedy, but as a woman who found freedom. She wanted to die. She told me. She was sixty-five and weighed 350 pounds. She lost seven toes to diabetes and had to navigate campus on an electric cart. She was a wonderful soul who I will miss. But she was done.

"Isss so sad!" Vita bellows.

"Terribly sad," I agree. "I'll be sure that Principal Rivera sends flowers."

She casts me a knowing look. "Sí. He knows a florist. I gave him a number last week to order flowers for Anna." My heart burns from the news. "This week, they celebrate twenty years."

"Counting the last two? The years they've been separated?"

She bows her head in silence, knowing all too well about my relations with Principal Rivera. Yet God forbid she speaks of it. She doesn't like to talk of things like separation, marriages that don't work. She's been married to the same man for thirty-two years. He hogs the TV and only gifts her with sex on her birthday. She cries about it in the office sometimes. Last year we cried together over a hot tea on Lincoln where she held my hand on the anniversary of Felix's death. She's the only one who remembered.

Vita is good about dates, specifics. She can be a snoop though. That's why I ask for time alone, finding my resume, stored in a locked filing cabinet holding student records among other things. One binder contains information regarding my adoption. A water bottle contains vodka. Frida Kahlo is the only soul to know, her face framed in a portrait above my desk. I smile at it before heading off to see Principal Hector Rivera.

He's just a skip ahead, down the hall, past the administrative bullpen – a series of cubicles littered with cat calendars and dying plants. Sadly, the burden of paperwork has led most office staff to a manic state where every last woman is out for herself. I get along by keeping quiet, my only trouble stemming from Noni Harper, the other half of the guidance department. This month, she's been particularly caustic since suffering a lower back injury on a trip to Maccu Pichu. Competitive by nature she thinks I'm too honest with the children. Heavens be if I talk about anything other than rainbows and butterflies.

"You gave a condom to a student?" she asks, lifting her neck from writing a note as I pass her office. Her long face is tan, raisin-wrinkled. Her gray hair hangs in a rigid tail. "You can't assume these kids are having...." She refuses to say the word 'sex.'

I smile. "Yes, of course. The sulfur in the water fountains caused the recent outbreak of pregnancies on campus. So salty."

Her face coils in disgust, as I knock on Principal Rivera's door.

"Yes?" he calls.

"It's me."

He hesitates. "Come in." It sounds more like an obligation than a welcome. I bite my tongue from commenting about the clutter on his desk. He's not in a playful mood. I can tell by his stiff demeanor, the way he fails to take his eyes off the computer when I sit across from him.

"Yes?" he asks, keeping it simple.

"Have you sent flowers to Ms. Macomber's home?"

He waits to answer. "I thought she was divorced."

"She was. She lived with her mother." He looks up, deep in thought. "The elderly lady she'd bring to the holiday parties." He doesn't follow. "The one who baked you brownies."

"Right." He clears his throat, adjusting his red

checkered tie. He hates being reminded of things, particularly by me. "I'll send flowers. That it?" He looks down, typing on his keyboard.

"Actually no." I hand my resume across the desk. "I'm here to help."

He skeptically eyes me, snatching it and leaning back to read. "You want Macomber's position."

"That is correct."

He chuckles, tossing the resume on the desk. "Not this again." Clasping his hands behind his neck, he leans further, grazing his black curls against the Cuban flag hanging on the wall behind him. He grins, inflating his bearded baby cheeks. "Macomber taught American History. What do you know about that?"

"Enough to know that men claim to be solely responsible for it. At least the good parts."

He shakes his head like I'm absurd. He had the same response on the night I told him that I wanted more than an occasional text and a ghost of a boyfriend that went bump in the night. Yes, I wanted that at first. So what if I had second thoughts and began to want more?

"You gotta stop. Why do you want to teach so bad?" he asks.

"Because I do. Why does it matter? Simply say yes, and we'll call it a day."

"Dee, the kids...."

"Will stand and applaud."

"Are-afraid-of-you."

I flinch, choking on his words even if they contain a morsel of truth. Fine, I admit it. Certain children turn the other way if they see me coming. But afraid? I should be the frightened one. These kids are no more than criminals waiting for a plea bargain. I offer guidance and they barely take it. They go to Noni because she tells them life is a patch of posies. So I tell them the truth. So what? They should be grateful.

"Look at you," Hector says. "The dress. The hat."

I tap a fuzzy ball atop my head. "Splendid. I know."

"These kids don't know when their next meal is

coming."

I take a breath. "And I'm sure that's my problem."

He leans in, whispering. "If you want to teach...yes." He shakes his head as if I'm oblivious. "Remember, I was one of them." Hector often reminds me of this.

At sixteen he was sent to detention for robbing a Quickie Mart with a scalpel during a stint with a Cuban gang. But that was ages ago. He's a redeemed man. One must not drown in what *was*. "These kids need someone who can relate," he says.

"No. They need manners. Then they need a grammar lesson."

"You don't get it."

"Get what? What would you like me to do? Go to the thrift store and buy a frumpy dress like Ms. Harper? Tell them abstinence works?" I exhale calmly. "I'll have you know the children relate to me quite well."

"Yeah? When was the last time you had a student come to you *willingly*?" I turn to stone. How dare he snake me after two years of intimacy? Look at him, smiling like he's clever. Those burritos he loves, I wish him a thousand with no toilet in sight. Still, I won't show him I'm mad, that his words cut like crystals. As he knows, I'll bite my tongue until it bleeds before I show weakness to a man, though it can be hard at times. For instance, when Vita steps in to announce that Anna's on the line, I'd love to crumple, but I refrain, satisfied that Hector doesn't take the call – a clear indication he *does* think of me. Sometimes. At least I like to think he does even though I just found out he ordered flowers for Anna last week. Why would he do that? He never sent me flowers.

Oh heavens. He must know I'm upset because he stands and approaches, stirring the air with his woodsy scent. The first time we kissed, the aroma left me reeling. I wanted to lick his skin, sample every bit of his furry body. That day, he told me his wife no longer saw him; that's why they parted. The sight of Hector, a beautiful view to me reflected mediocrity to Anna. She felt he could be more, rise above a less-than-average paying job – one that totaled half her salary as a corporate accountant. Eventually, being the breadwinner made her take charge in regard to the bills and the bedroom. That led him to feeling like half a man. That's why he came to me. I gave him control. I surrendered myself, landing here today, powerless. *When was the last time a student came to you willingly?*

"I shouldn't have said that," he says, helping me stand. He sets a finger on my chin, guiding my face. "I want to give you the job. You know that."

"Do I?" I consider diplomacy but the words spill like lava. "Why don't you think I can do it? I'm not perfect, but I have good intentions. I try to prepare the children the best I can. Isn't that enough?" He hesitates and I grab the resume. "It was for you when Anna left. I cared for you... your stomach."

"Shh." His eyes reference the door.

"They're not stupid. They know about your irritable bowels. You can hear your stomach growling from the moon." He shakes his head, irritated. "You won't give me the job because you love to tease, holding something I want. It's all about you."

"Oh mena, mena, mena," he says, trying to calm himself. It's a relaxation technique: 'amen' with an 'a' at the end for additional support. He learned it from the pastoral counselor who advised him to clear his head, be single. He repeats it, beginning to pace. He doesn't ask me to leave though. He loves the fight. He gets off on it. I see him growing in his pants.

"Why did you send Anna flowers? You said it was over years ago."

He snaps, throwing up his hands. "It is!"

I can barely contain myself. "Don't lie. You just ended it with me last week. You're already sending her flowers?" The thought stabs at my heart. "I told you I wouldn't get involved if you were trying to make it work with Anna. I know what it's like to be cheated on. I could never cause another woman that pain."

"It was her birthday. I was stupid." He takes a breath, figuring out a way to explain. "You don't walk from twenty years of marriage and not care."

I smirk. "You walked from two years with me and seem perfectly fine." He looks off in shame, and I cover my face with my hand, humiliated that I let him get the best of me. "That's all right," I say, waving it off. "I found someone to unclog the toilet you left behind." I note a flicker of jealousy in Hector's brown eyes. "And at least he was man enough to spend the night."

With that, I turn, reaching for the door, and he grabs me, locking his arms around my chest. "Don't!" he begs, squeezing me. His breath is hot and torturous against my neck. It's the same as every time before. He doesn't want me. He can't be with me. Then along comes another man and he can't do without me. "I miss you."

I struggle in his grip. "It's not enough."

He spins me to face him. Kissing my neck he scratches at my chin with his beard as he works up to my lips. I give in, taking his tongue; it wrestles mine to a win. Below, his manhood hardens on my leg. "I'm fucking crazy, baby," he mutters. He pulls away to gaze in my eyes. "I want to fix this. We have fun, right?"

I don't want to believe him. Even if my heart warms my heart has wronged me before. I gain my composure. "I thought you couldn't do this anymore."

"I thought," he begins, hesitating. "I don't know what I'm thinking half the time. It's the divorce." The morning bell rings and he pulls me in for another kiss. I try to resist but drown in the rhythm of his heartbeat against my chest. It soothes any thought of uncertainty, hypnotizing me.

His grip loosens, and I pull away.

"I know I'm a bit prickly," I admit. "I act tough. I'm not good at this game."

"Game? Is that what you think this is?" He laughs it off, becoming serious. "Ok then. What do you want?"

"A date," I admit, before I can stop myself. "A night out. Just once."

"Done," he says. And before I second-guess him he quiets me with another kiss and I'm washed over, welcoming the allure of the undertow.

CHAPTER 3

L ATER THAT EVENING I'm accessorizing a flirty look when Hector texts me to say he's sorry. There's no explanation, no excuse in regard to why he's not coming. He keeps it short and sweet. That way I won't read into it. I won't be that woman who thinks there's more to this than what we really are. I won't think about snipping his testicles even though all I can think about is clip, clip.

Nudge. Nudge.

Wink. Wink.

Is that bad? Is it awful to think there'd be no game to play if the player lost his balls? I don't want these grim thoughts in my head, but they magically appear like dreams. I can't direct them so I simply watch in awe, wondering if it's normal to imagine a man becoming a eunuch and finding him beautiful as a unicorn.

I shouldn't be drinking. One martini sparks two before I uncork a bottle of wine. Then I'm fuzzy but fine. Granted, depression will set in. But who can be sad while recalling a time of being in love?

I'm speaking of true love, the kind that grows in tall tales where mothers convey the notion that life would be unlivable without it. So their daughters run, chasing it. And those who catch it, may they hold it forever, because those who lose it will feel as if they've wasted their entire lives pursuing their own demise.

I married four times but *truly* loved once. His name was Felix Seetried. My final 'I do', he taught me once you marry for love you have no choice but to seek something equal or greater if ever you marry again.

How slippery love can be. Only when sliding a foot over

a railing, destined to take that final plunge, does one realize its implications. Take Felix. My life with him is something I keep hidden and sacred in fear I'll lose his memory to others if I share too much.

Felix is dead; that's the main thing. There was a malfunction in his heart – a detail he forgot to share when he asked for my hand in marriage. I would have said yes, regardless. When he dropped to one knee on our six-month anniversary trip to Isla Mujeres, I couldn't imagine life without him. I held more love for him than anyone in the world. An artist by heart but dealer by trade he was the perfect blend – a visionary with a head for business. That was the purpose of the trip. We were to make a purchase by an artist said to be creating masterpieces in the same vein as Kahlo. Felix brought me on all of his excursions, claiming I was his muse. He found me at a Hopper exhibit in Manhattan. He bought me green tea. He said I appeared uptight.

He was right. Before Felix, I was guarded, reserved – always wondering what the world thought of me. Bev Dear painted me into a life of poise and perfection, a platform from which Felix allowed me to jump.

Like tonight, I could bore Miami with a black dress but how many women would I replicate on Lincoln Road? Miami created the little black dress, shedding a few inches for appeal. I'd rather not be a clone. Felix would have none of that. He opened the closet door to a life of color. Tonight's result: a lime miniskirt with a coral tulip top. But will it matter? I haven't a date. So I sit with a drink until I hear a knock. Is it Hector? Is he late? It can't be him. He would need to be buzzed up.

I use the walls for support, opening the door.

"Lordy, did I wake you?" a tall odd woman asks, greeting me with a crazed smile. I should remember her name, but I barely remember mine. I shift my eyes 'til she reminds me. "I'm Kitty, your new neighbor." I flinch, and she pretends her fingers are legs, walking them down. "I live on the fourth floor. We met this morning." She clutches a kitty litter pan. "Remember? In the lobby?" I shake my head negatively but I *do* remember. How could I forget the lady in the jean miniskirt? She's still wearing it this evening, coupling it with an acid wash denim coat and a cat broach with diamond whiskers. "Well, let me reintroduce myself. I'm Kitty Fritter." She extends a hand and I shake it. Her smile is charming enough to light a ballpark. "Now don't think I'm nuttier than squirrel dunk, but I thought I'd stop in for a good old fashioned housewarming party. That's what us Southern gals do best."

I blink to ensure she's real. "But...I've been residing here for years."

"Not for you, silly. For me." She wiggles past me, inside. "I figured it would be good to clear the air. You know, after what happened this morning."

"This morning?"

"You know, Taser and Tacky." She removes her clogs. "Now, I know. I know. I'm not supposed to have more than one pet but we can keep that our little secret? Just between us gals?" Rather than respond, I hang silence over her head like an anchor. "We all have secrets, right? One or two?"

"Of course." I close the door.

"So what's yours?"

I don't skip a beat. "I'm suicidal."

Tilting her head her face remains neutral like her brain refuses to absorb it. With a sweeping smile she dusts it off and heads to the kitchen. "My Kitty Litter Cake will take care of that. Where do you keep the knives?"

I follow behind. "Excuse me?"

"The knives," Kitty repeats, going through my kitchen drawers. "Beautiful place, by the way. I just love the picture hanging by the sofa. It's like a comic book. Is that where you got it? The comic shop?"

"It's...a...Lichtenstein."

"Really?" She emits a monkey laugh. "I should have known. He's French, right?"

"German."

She pays no heed, continuing to blabber. "I've always wanted to be French. They're so sophisticated. I love the way they smoke and eat baguettes. It seems fun." I raise a brow to illustrate a clear distaste for whatever the hell she's going on about. She catches on. "Lordy," she says, discovering the knives in a drawer. "Where are my manners? I walked in here without permission, didn't I?" I nod. "I'm sorry. At home, we're so set on the 'what's mine is yours' mentality. Tell me you won't hold it against me."

I surrender. "I'll get the dishes." I can't expect anything more from a farm girl. I figure, the faster she eats the faster she'll leave.

"Good lord, being up so high, my knees feel weak," she says, making more small talk. "I don't know how you city girls do it. I can't imagine living above the fourth floor. Do you like being up so high?"

"Of course. All the more room to jump."

"Oh, there you go again." She tick tocks a finger and emits a laugh. I hand her a dish, and the stoic expression on my face signals I'm serious. "Ooh, oh." She clears her throat. "You shouldn't do that." She cuts into the cake. "Because, if you do, you prove them right. *They* want to be right."

"*They?* Who are *they*?"

"Don't be silly. You know who *they* are. Everyone hears *their* voices." She shivers at the thought, brightening when she licks cake off her fingers. "Here, you have the first piece." She hands me a plate of powdery crumbs.

"Thank you, but my diet consists mainly of liquids."

"Oh. You must be one of those juicers, right?"

Crossing into the den I smile dully, pouring another glass of Pinot. Taking a sip, I become nauseous. Perhaps I've had too much or it's the company. "I, I need to sit," I state, locating the sofa. It's devastating. An hour ago, I was on the verge of a date.

"Did I do something wrong?" Kitty asks. Fast footing it to the den, she sits beside me. "I was just making chit-chat. That's what I do when I'm nervous. This talk of you hurtin' yourself, it's not sittin' right in my stomach."

"Then join me for a drink."

"A drink? No. That'll make it worse."

"Worse? Please. As one divorced woman to another, you should know, life can't get much worse."

She becomes quiet. "Divorced? Who said I was divorced?"

"You did. This morning." She lightens, realizing I remember our encounter. "You said the pets were part of the divorce."

"Ohhhhh." She laughs. "I meant the divorce from my parents. I took them because I thought they'd make the move easier. I've never been married or divorced. I've barely been with a man."

Oh dear. How did I end up with this woman? What happened to Hector? I rest my head back in a daze.

"Dee, are you ok?" Kitty asks.

My tongue is heavy. I lift my hand, motioning to the door. "I...want...to go out."

"Out?" She smiles, twitching her lip. "Of course you do. You're all dressed up and pretty as a flower. Oh well." She sighs. "I have to learn the city somehow." She momentarily resists before standing to help me up. I don't accept the charity. The alcohol awakens my spirit and I dash to the loo before I get sick.

If only Bev Dear could see me now. *Never hold a drink that can take hold of you.* It's something she learned during a rehab stint in the Rockies. Father said she was at a spa. For him, it was better to lie than to admit how much she was drinking. He didn't want to lose his wife. The truth is scary but change, that's downright terrifying.

Take Ms. Kitty. She's walks fast, shaking in her clogs on Collins. *Where are we? Is it safe? I should have brought Taser.* She's a bundle of nerves. Therefore, I opt for a low-key setting – a patio bar on the end of the strip where we hide from foot traffic behind potted palms. Kitty eyes jeweled patrons in fascination. Large fan blades twirl overhead.

I order a pear martini, informing the young waiter Kitty will have the same. He moves on before she can refuse.

"A martini? Are you sure?" she asks.

"It will calm you."

"But I don't know if I can drink one. Doesn't it burn going down?"

"The best things in life often do." She winces, covering

her mouth. "Oh, it's simple. Part your lips and swallow." I raise a brow. "Something a true southern *gal* should be familiar with."

She blushes. "You make it sound sexual." Her eyes scan the cigar smokers: old Latin men in pastel coats at the next table. She loosens when the drinks arrive. "Truth be told, I was never one of the *gals*. Growing up, they didn't like me. They called me Conch Fritter."

"Conch fritter?"

"Kitty Conch Fritter," she says, inspecting her martini. She tastes the diced pear. "It's no big deal. I never fancied myself as a gal back home anyway. I always felt like a seed in the wrong soil." For the first time, sadness lines her tone. I drink, nodding for her to do the same.

"So here you are," I cheerily state.

"Here I am."

"And now that you're here what will you do?"

She takes a drink, clasping her martini glass with both hands – the largest I've seen on a woman. She winces. "First, I need a paycheck."

"Of course. Your field?"

"Retail," she boasts, before gritting her teeth. "Fast fact. I don't have much experience. Just the time I spent at Dottie's Discount. I loved it." Taking another drink, she smiles. "To get paid to compliment people all day, well, that's payment itself."

Peculiar. I wonder how she can find happiness in flattering others. I'm not used to such an individual. It's a hard to follow. Still, I won't be hard on the naïve girl. She's new to the big city, green. So I simply listen, ordering another round of drinks as she informs me about the agreement she made with her mother Gladys. For two months Gladys will cover Kitty's living costs. But if Kitty can't make it on her own by then she'll be forced to return home.

"Ma doesn't think I'll last two weeks," Kitty confesses, finishing her second martini. At first, she'd barely sip it; now she downs it like a pro. "I should stop but it's cooler than Kool-Aid." She calls on the waiter, ordering one more. "I'm sinnin'. I know it. But I'll say an extra prayer tonight." She zips her lip. "Our secret."

Yes. Our secret. But little does she know, secrets bloom into flowery tales at the bottom of a martini glass. For instance, she reveals, at the ripe age of forty-five, she's never been kissed. Well, unless you count her uncle, who fed her his salty tongue on Christmas Eve twenty years ago.

"Don't get me wrong. I'm not an advocate for incest. I'm not from *that* part of the woods," she says, laughing. "But an uncle...I don't think most people would consider that family."

"The courts might."

She snorts. "Oh, you stinker." Her shoulders shake like maracas. "Like you never made out with a hot uncle."

The martini buzz hits and I drift. She continues to ramble, her face fuzzier than an old tele. She mentions her ailing father James Fritter who is hooked up to a ventilator back in Arcadia. They never got along but she loves him and wants him to see her succeed. I struggle to focus when she turns the spotlight on me. "Where are your parents?" she asks.

"Dead."

She clutches her heart. "I'm sorry."

"Don't be..." I trail. "It's life. I've grieved enough."

Kitty casts me a worried look, taking a sip of her martini. It spills down her chin. "Oh shoot. I don't know what I'm doing." She battles to balance the glass in her hand. "Will you teach me?"

I scoff at the thought. "To properly drink? Oh, that would require weeks of rehearsal." I sigh. "I wouldn't make a good teacher anyway. At least, that's what I have been told."

Her eyes fill with dismay. "Who said that?"

I signal the waiter for the check. "Certain individuals at the school where I work."

She sticks out her tongue. "Phooey. You don't need them or a school to be a teacher. You can teach *anywhere*."

Anywhere? I give her a curious look, imagining a row of desks in my home. Each chair holds a student, desperate to listen, to learn. I envision myself at the chalkboard, the thought warming me before I snap out of it.

"No matter. It's hogwash. I'm not a teacher," I say. "I'm a counselor at Horizon Institute. It's for children who need a second chance."

"That's wonderful!" she says, as a busboy with a Mohawk clears our glasses. "Kids need guidance. Adults too. Look at me. I don't know what I'm doing. I don't even know how to go on a date. I've never had anyone teach me. Ma and pop never could see me as a *woman*."

"Let me guess. Daddy's little girl?"

"Not exactly." Drunk, she bites her lip. Her eyes are in a watery glaze. "You know what I mean." Her eyes close and she nearly drops her drink.

On the walk home she leans on my shoulder. Beyond the sidewalk, behind art deco hotels, I hear the crash of waves and picture one pulling me under when she begins talking of her uncle again.

"You think I'm silly for kissing him," she says.

I pat her back. "No dear. We all have skeletons in the closet."

Her heel catches the sidewalk and I grab her arm, pulling her close. "I wish my skeletons were bold enough to dance," she sadly admits. "I want better stories but men don't see me. Or when they do they run." A passing taxi creates a breeze. "Oh, why am I talkin' 'bout this?"

"It's all right. Neither of us will remember in the morning."

With a hiccup, she trips over her feet, wrapping her arms around my neck. "Do you know any nice men?"

I pull a strand of hair from her mouth. "A few."

Her eyes grow wide like a child. "What do they want?"

I struggle to keep balanced, tugging her along. "Oh dear. I've been married four times and have yet to know that."

She looks up to the stars and I follow her lead, watching the way they wink. Could they be listening? I wonder if love is a universal joke and people the punch line.

"Maybe men just want someone to help them smile," Kitty suggests. "That's what friends do. Like you and I. We're friends, right?"

Friends? I smile but avoid the question, pushing on to the Savoy. Ahead, its white walls are backlit, striped in ivory. I change the topic. "You really don't have a clue how men operate, do you?" I ask.

"No I guess not. But you'd think I would." She sniffs, climbing the entrance steps. "It's only been six months since I had the body of a man. It hasn't been that long since the operation."

CHAPTER 4

INTERESTING HOW THE world works. Just when you think you have the grand design down, finding continuity in the chaos, the most unsuspected events occur as if the universe intentionally foils you for being too keen.

Yes, I had all the answers at the age of eighteen. I was to attend Vassar to major in international business but I'd never require the degree because I was also expected to graduate with a husband. That's what Bev Dear wanted. Prior to her untimely death she had scouted a number of elite campuses, hoping to pass off her parental duties to a potential suitor.

"No daughter of mine graduates without a ring," she said, paying my first year's tuition. "We're not here to waste good money."

Thankfully, Bev Dear didn't live to see the end result. She would have been in search of a refund because while Vassar had manicured lawns, formal gardens, and a crenulated gothic library – it lacked men. Females greatly outnumbered them.

Now, had I been born with beauty instead of brains I certainly would have made the radar of a successful campus man. However, I was blessed with distinct attributes such as the beak of a Great Blue Heron. That's what my first husband Walter liked about me. Spotting me freshman year he said it lacked convention. It set me apart. I should have known he was a loser.

Yes, Walter Woody – the first of my four husbands – was a twin, actually. Yet he never told a soul because his brother Timothy was the more successful of the two.

A Harvard man, Timothy was on the road to be a U.S. diplomat, whereas Walter hadn't a clue what to do with his life. After graduation his only plan was to sell beef burritos to Grateful Dead fans from the back of a VW.

Still, Walter's zest for adventure and uncertain nature is what attracted me to him. One day, he'd arrive to Women's Lit in a tie-dye tee and pajamas pants. A day later, he'd gel his blond bangs and sport a tailored white jacket. I'd never met such a man. While Vassar girls found him odd I thought he was exciting. I liked how he challenged the norm. That is, 'til we married and I discovered his norm included introducing new women, including a mannequin, into our bed. I learned of his true nature upon returning from holiday just five months after we wed. He forgot to hide the Polaroids. In the pictures even the mannequin seemed to blush. That's when I learned the tedium of the courts, initiating my first divorce.

Who was I to know better? I was young. I had only graduated a year prior, and Walter was the first man to pay me any attention. It was only during the divorce proceedings that I realized the marriage was never about love but the ring. And to think, standing at the altar, I imagined I'd never worry about another thing again. Life can be tricky. Just like people.

Take Ms. Kitty Fritter. That deceitful little thing is lucky I didn't leave her alone last night after revealing she had once been a man. Who does she think she is? In my day, there were no men slicing off parts; they were too busy trying to double what they had.

Who knows? Perhaps this is the whole 'less is more' look everyone is going on about. I buy into it too; look at my condo. I plant a sad twig here, a muted vase there. Minimalism has appeal. There's less confusion, no abstract expressionist vomiting squiggly lines on a canvas above a toilet. Above mine: a modest piece by Mondrian where lines create color squares with understated authority. In the end, that's the essence of life, each of us hoping to leave a simple impression.

Still, even a hard-nosed minimalist has a limit.

If everything in art and life is reduced to nothing it shall eventually return to the world of abstract, will it not? Ms. Kitty, this alien being from the male dimension, she snips it away with a wink and thinks life will be easy? Well, I hate to inform you, but being a woman isn't a garden, honey. The grass isn't greener on this lush side of the earth. There is a lot in the way of manicuring. Pluck this. Tweeze that. There isn't enough time in the day to perform the necessary maintenance.

Kitty will find out but she won't hear it from me. In fact, the next morning, I turn my nose up when she attempts speaking to me in the lobby. Not to be rude. I'm simply running late, and admittedly, not in the greatest mood, thinking about Hector.

Thank heaven traffic is favorable. In Little Havana, it's business as usual. Within the gates of Maximo Gomez Park the elderly members of the domino club gather while local hat-maker Javier sets up his shop.

I lower the passenger window, allowing in the sweet scent of Cuban pastry. Tempting aromas lift the heaviest of spirits, just like the arrival of an anticipated phone call. And that's what occurs when I pull up to Horizon. I receive a call from Jerry Rich, a world-renowned private investigator.

Eight weeks ago, I hired him to locate my birth mother. I spotted him on a crime show. His face was blurred. He's too famous to reveal his identity he states. But I've come to believe he suffers from a slight case of agoraphobia served over a large heap of grandiosity. He works exclusively by phone or email, and his hourly rate is costly – enough so that I've spent a fortune doing business with him. He tells me the 'find' would have happened if Bev Dear hadn't provided so many roadblocks. She bought off certain players in the world of private adoption and in return, my birth record had not only been altered but also duplicated. Six days ago, Jerry sent me a note stating he'd uncovered two birth certificates under the name Desperation Lingers – the first stating Richmond, Virginia as my birthplace, and the second – Ocala, Florida. To further complicate matters, the rightful names of my birth parents were replaced with St. Clair and

Beverly Lingers. Each certificate has a different birthdate.

If only I could remember something about that day.

That's the funny thing about birth; no one can recall her own. Therefore, it remains a mystery. Yes, you may be in a photo fussing over the switch from the boob to bottle, but where's the evidence that you belong to the parents who claim you? *What hospital was I born in? When did I first smile? Why aren't there any pregnant pictures of you?*

"You just want to see me fat!" Bev Dear would snap, offering a shadow of a reply. However, my birth certificate – that's black and white, and though she may have grayed certain areas she was still required to have a professional third-party certify her unlawful behavior.

For most, the witness is a medical doctor or hospital administrator. But for this occasion, each certificate obtained by Jerry had been signed by a midwife named Roberta Smith. But is she truly a midwife? Had Bev Dear doctored her up as well?

"Don't ask so many questions," Jerry says as I turn down the radio. In the school parking lot my car is parked in front of two male students in black hoodies. Smoking, they look down to their phones instead of each other. "Be happy I found the broad."

"The broad?" That's the thing about Jerry. He's far from tactful. A rags-to-riches New Yorker, he has the voice of Woody Allen without the articulation. "You found Roberta Smith?" I can hardly contain my excitement.

"Yeah. She's in a nursing home right outside Valdosta."

"What did she say?"

"She knows everything. Beverly, St. Clair. She even remembered you." He laughs. "She said who could forget that nose."

I cough, recalling kids who badgered me growing up. A honker, that's what they'd call it. "What did she tell you about my birth parents?"

"Dead. Your mother, I mean."

"Dead?" My chest feels hollowed out. My throat becomes constricted. "What do you mean?"

"I mean dead," he says, as I stare off in a daze, unsure

if the sun is blinding me or if I'm blind with rage. "Hey, you there?"

"Yes."

"Look. You wanted the truth. I don't sugarcoat it."

"I understand." My chest falls, heavy as lead.

He moves on. "Roberta said your mom's name was Elise. Died years ago. Roberta never met your pop. Never got his name either. He ran off, some kind of musician. He could be alive."

I utter my mother's name. "Elise." That's all I manage. The universe stops, exploding into a million shades of red. That's what happens when a dream dies. Not once had I considered that either of my birth parents was dead. Quite naïve. But if you're brave enough to dream, even for a second, why fog the inside? I sit up in my chair to focus and sharpen my tongue. "I'm sorry. This isn't acceptable." I'd cry but I'm too angry. I'm always angry. I don't want to be. "How do I know what you're telling me is true?" There are so many questions. Is Roberta Smith legitimate? Are there any aunts, uncles? What's Elise's last name? How'd she die? What about siblings? Do I have siblings?

"Relax. Roberta's legit," he says. "I know you want more but that's all I got. She won't quack anymore without a little dough."

"Pardon me."

"What? You think she's some upstanding citizen?" He laughs. "Look. Good people don't assist in falsifying birth records."

I groan. "How much does she want?"

I listen to his reply, but it doesn't matter. There isn't a quote too high when it comes to learning the truth about my past. Still, the number spoils my morning, and that's usually Vita's job.

I enter the office to find her in idle chat with the day nurse Martha Ferrera. Vita turns her head to greet me. "Buenos días Ms. Lingers. Just who I was looking for." Martha uses the opportunity to sneak out for a cigarette, one of twenty a day. "That dress is nice," Vita says, approaching with her bullying breasts. She pets the white carnation on the hip of my red Betsey Johnson dress. "Is it new?"

"I wore it once in Spain." She oohs and ahs, and I prepare for what else she has to say, knowing Vita's compliments are conditional. I cut to the chase. "How can I help you?"

"Oh, isss just...we still need chaperones for the Fall Mixer." Presenting me with a sign-up sheet, she clutches the cross on her neck. "It'll mean sooo much to the children."

I smile but pass. "I don't have time."

"That's too bad." She bunches her lips. "You know, Mr. Rivera isss going to be there." This is Vita's technique – laying out the bait if it serves her best interest. Then later she'll judge me for taking a bite, praying for my soul. But this has been going on since the advent of the Bible. I don't take insult. Rather, I indulge in the festivities, taking the mind games to a new level.

"Mr. Rivera can manage fine without me. He only seems to need me on my back anyway. I can't imagine what use that would serve at the mixer." Vita gasps, covering her mouth. Her eyes are white like twin moons. "Now, excuse me. I must have a private moment with Mr. Rivera."

"He's in a meeting," she says. Regardless, I march on fully aware meetings usually consist of him stuffing his face with a beef burrito while playing solitaire on his desktop.

"Knock, knock," I say, opening his door. He doesn't deserve the courtesy of granting permission to enter. Not after he stood me up last night.

"Ms. Lingers," he calls, with a guilty tone. He has a guest. Her perfume fills the room like flowers.

"Hello," she utters, standing.

"Dee, this is Miss Robb," he offers. Rushing his words, he pops up from his chair. "Dee is in guidance."

"*Miss* Robb?" I repeat.

Clutching a shiny blue purse, Miss Robb eyes me, then him. A pale redhead, her face is a mix of chastity and youth, her freckled skin smooth as milk. "Pleased to meet you," she states. She anxiously shakes my hand.

"I'm in guidance," I state. "You?"

Bemused, she takes back her hand, tucking a lock of

hair behind her ear. "I'm sorry. What?" She laughs, blushing. Her blues twinkle as she looks to Hector. He hesitantly nods. "Oh. Right. I've been hired to teach history." She follows the news with a child-like laugh that makes me shatter.

It happens fast. First, my chest tightens. Then I hear voices, but they're not clear, as if every skipped heartbeat equals a skipped word. The voices are youthful, calming, telling me to breathe. Hector says Miss Robb comes highly recommended but all I hear is, "Graduates...honors." The room spins.

I deserve that position. How can he fail to see that? I'm good enough. I've waited so long.

Careful, I think. Don't fall. A lady needs to remain collected, particularly when a man is watching. If one should require a moment to explode, simply lift off to the loo. That's what Bev Dear would say.

So I turn from Hector, holding out my arms for balance. If I can make it to the ladies room I won't have a spill. I'll be in the clear.

I push past the wastepaper basket filled with Coke cans and aluminum burrito wrappers. I gasp. Hector's sour cream, how could I swallow it? How could I think he'd advocate for me? He doesn't think I have what it takes and perhaps he's right. Who am I to think I'd be a good teacher? Can I make a difference? Can anyone? Oh, I'm befuddled, but I refuse to tumble on my heels as I take to the hall.

Rising, Vita shows concern. "Isss everything all right?"

"Peachy," I say. Then shadowing my face I depart, heading to the restroom prior to the first bell. On the sidewalk, I bypass clusters of saggy-panted students. Spotting me, they hoot, holler, offering a 'whoop whoop.' To them, I'm Ms. Puta. I'm Beastwoman. Bitchface. They laugh and scatter like mice when I near.

Luckily, Mr. Brady offers a smile. Pulling a trash can on wheels, he removes his hat, pausing from his janitor duties. "Spare a moment?" Tall and slender with a swimmer's build and a 007 tan he'd be a looker if it weren't for his lack of confidence. He started saying hello after his wife died in a car accident two years ago. Last month he found the courage to ask me on a date.

I ran then like I do now, smiling and pointing to the loo as if having an emergency. His lips dip down and I note the bundle of flowers in his hand, figuring they're for me. Too bad I'm thick in the weeds with Hector and unable to savor the moment. I charge to the ladies room: a cement box scented by cigarettes. I see smoke in the windows and girls in wait. I cut to the front of the line, where Cici blocks the door, pressing his face to it. "C'mon. Give me my phone back, Lisette. This ain't funny," he says.

I tap his shoulder. "Grammar, grammar."

The gold chains on his neck clink when he turns. "Damn. You?" He laughs to himself. "What? You want me to plunge this stinky ass toilet too?"

"I'd rather you plunge that mouth." Female students snicker behind us. "Now move. I need the loo."

"Nuh uh. Not until my girlfriend comes out." He places his baseball hat on backwards and backhands the door. "Lisette! Don't make me look stupid." After no response he continues, growing louder. "Ain't no good gonna come outta being up in my business. Hear that? See? This is what you get."

Someone punches the door from the inside, releasing an ear-piercing howl. Glass breaks, exploding on the interior wall. Concerned, I push Cici aside to enter.

"Yo wait!" he says. "She's got no more chances. Get her to chill before they call security." He removes his hat. "Please ma'am."

"Ma'am?" I grin. "Color me impressed."

"Just take care of my girl. She don't listen. She's all fists with me."

"I'm certain she has reasons." He glances down and a scar on his forehead catches the sun. I sigh. "I'll see what I can do."

Stepping inside, I'm immediately pelted with spit in my left eye. I cage a scream, removing the watery fluid when I hear the sound of breaking glass. My heel hits a wet spot and I begin to slip before being tackled to the ground.

"Stop Lisette! You'll hurt her," a girl calls.

"Cállate!" Lisette returns. Standing, she pokes at my stomach with her foot. On my back, I groan. My body jolts, pinched by glass. "Get up, puta! You want to take me to jail? Let's go. I'm not scared of this fuckin' school."

Pulling myself up I open my eyes to a fuzzy array of smoke and movement. My right calf burns. I stand to discover a trail of blood running down my ankle. A broken bottle had cut me. My back is soaked, reeking of beer.

"You gonna call security?" Lisette asks. I raise my chin to the tiny girl. She can't be more than five feet tall – a ball of pimples held down by the grease of her curly dark hair. She wears a black tee so large it could be mistaken for a dress. Taking off her silver cross earrings she looks as if she's ready for a fight.

I don't entertain it. Heading to the sink I kindly ask two other girls to move. They scatter as I look in the mirror. My face is a multitude of red blotches thick with sweat. It reminds of another time – how I looked the morning Bev Dear passed. I turn on the faucet to wet my face. The two girls smoking near the sink quietly eye me, as I stand stiff, waiting for Lisette to pounce.

A bathroom stall opens. A hand touches my shoulder, and I quickly turn to see a Haitian boy with the palest blue eyes. He sports an off-the-shoulder half tee. His body is skinny enough to see through.

"Here," he says, handing me toilet tissue. "You don't want your eyeliner to run."

"Leave her alone, maricón!" Lisette says. I dab my eyes. "She doesn't need your pity. Whose side are you on?"

"The winning one," he calmly says, setting a cosmetics bag on the sink. A spindle of red sewing string falls out. He sizes me up and down. "I wouldn't mess with this lady," he advises. "She's tall, even if it is those heels."

"Do I look scared?" Lisette reveals a butterfly knife. "I don't care how big a bitch is. I will flatten anyone who tries to get with my man."

"I beg your pardon," I say.

"Oh. You don't think I know?" she asks. She advances toward me. "I know what you did."

I clean my leg. The stinging warmth of the cut aches when I pat it. "I don't know what you're talking about."

"The night you spent with Cici," she explains.

Thinking back, I ponder what the confused girl could be referring to. "You think I've done something with Sissy?"

"CICI!" she hisses. She points to the Haitian boy. "Jasper's the sissy." He shrugs, lining his mouth with silver lip shine. "Now, cut the shit. What did you do?"

"I thought you knew."

She raises the knife. "You're not funny."

"Oh, get over it, Lisey," Jasper interferes. "You think she wants your roly-poly man? Look how she dresses. She doesn't want some delivery boy spilling fortune cookies in her bed. Let it go."

"I'm not letting shit go. I'm gonna constipate this bitch," she says, pebbling me with her eyes. She turns to Jasper, lowering her chin. "Yo. Why are you kissing her ass anyway? You're my best friend. You think she cares about us?"

Jasper hesitates, and I consider the question. True, I often wander the campus, wondering if the students and I are of the same species. I try to reach out but they eye me with such disdain. Still, I wouldn't be here if I didn't care.

"I DO care," I mutter.

"Huh?" Lisette says, wrinkling her nose. "Speak up."

"I said I do care."

She laughs. "Yeah, you care so much you sit in your office all day, looking down your crooked nose at us, giving out bad advice."

I press on the hook of my nose, as the other two girls nod and say 'mhhhm' in support.

"You think you can relate?" Lisette says, her Spanish accent growing thick. "Shit. All you can do is steal our men. I know you slept with Cici." She removes a cell phone from a pocket on her black jeans. "Which number is yours?" Her hand trembles. "Come on bitch. You give a shit so much. Tell me!"

Before I can utter a word, she slams the phone against the wall, breaking it in pieces. She leaps at me, raising the knife to my chin. I flinch, and the door opens, allowing in a shaft of smoky light. Noni enters, followed by a brawny guard.

"What's going on?" she says. "Dee! Is that you? Are you ok?"

"I'm fine," I say. Lisette freezes. "We're having girl talk." The other girls drop their beverages in the trash before stomping out their cigarettes. "It's nothing to be alarmed about."

Jasper laughs. "Yeah, normal girl stuff. You know. Booze. Knives."

Shivering, Lisette drops the knife.

"Nothing happened with Cici," I assure her. "I hope you believe that."

Her beady brown eyes dim, filled with grief and confusion. "I don't have to believe nothing," she says. Then with a swift slap, she makes contact with my chin. I call out in terror, bringing my fingers to the burn.

"Everyone out!" the guard says, taking Lisette by the wrists. She screams as he brings her body to the floor, pinning her down. "I said out!" he shouts again.

The first to react, Jasper tells Lisette he'll wait outside before gathering his things, dashing off. I search for him but he melts in the crowd like a sugar cube in tea. Why can't I be invisible? I take to the sidewalk and the sun melts me – the heat of judgment burning my back as the student body surrounds me in suspicion. I remain quiet, following Noni who escorts Lisette's two girlfriends back to the office for smoking.

I nearly gag.

Noni will probably go down as a decorated hero for my rescue while I'll go down as counselor zero – the slutty cougar with a taste for young skin. Oh, if only I had that good of taste in men I wouldn't go crazy over these old clunkers.

Cici pushes through the spectators, reaching me. "What happened? Damn, you're bleeding." The glimpse of concern is soon trumped by his personal needs. "Hey, you get my cell?"

"Why? So you can call your girlfriend with more lies?"

He does a double take. "What are you talkin' about?"

I'd elaborate but not with blood running down my leg and Hector and Mr. Brady within eyeshot. A fifty-year-old lady must keep up appearances. I break away toward the library, wiping my cut with toilet paper as the two men approach from opposite directions. From my left, Mr. Brady calls out my name, clutching the same flowers as before. From the right, Hector makes use of a megaphone, determined to win the battle of the male egos.

"Ms. Lingers, can we talk?" Hector calls. Braking to step off his golf cart he seems in high spirits. If only he had a brain to realize his actions started all of this. How could he favor Miss Robb over me? She's just a girl. "I got an emergency call on the walkie. Are you all right?" I turn my neck to see Mr. Brady has fallen back, keeping a watchful eye. "You gotta be careful," he says, lowering his gold-rimmed shades. "You're a fighter. I get it but some of these kids have weapons." Smiling, he makes light of the situation like I should be used to the lashes. "Let's get you to the nurse. Your leg is bleeding," he states.

"So is my heart," I mutter.

"Huh?"

"I said so is my heart, Hector." Looking up to him, I battle tears. Don't cry. Just don't. He isn't worth it. Then why do I admit it? "I'm bleeding inside."

"C'mon," he says, growing irritated. "Is this about the position? Be serious. You don't want that job."

"Don't tell me what I want."

"Get in the cart," he forcefully says.

"No."

"Dee. You smell like a bar and you're bleeding."

"Typical night on the town!"

"Don't make me put you in the cart."

"Please. You can barely put me into an orgasm."

Stepping toward me he reminds me how intimidating his size can be. His torso is wide like a linebacker. "People are watching," he says, grabbing my arm. I strain from enjoying the safety of his grip.

I slip away. "Touch me again and I'll smack you."

48

"Oh, mena, mena, mena." Flipping his tie behind his shoulder he does his best to remain calm. "Don't do this in front of the students, Dee. If you don't stop I'll...."

"What?" I interrupt. "Clog my toilet?" I wipe the beginnings of tears from my eyes. "Wait. I have an idea. How'd you like to be clean of me once and for all? We need to keep things professional, right?"

He keeps his voice low. "You're mad 'cause I told you no. Is that it? It that something your rich daddy never told you. Well, let me be the first to say it. NO. You're not qualified to teach." Taking me by the arm he pulls me toward the cart.

"No!" I say. Lightheaded, I fall to my knees and close my eyes. In my mind I picture Christina Olson in the famed Wyeth piece. Inflicted with polio, she drags her body along a bed of grass toward a ranch house on the horizon. Her frail arms are tired but undaunted, as if a true lady can never be counted out if there's but a hint of air left in her lungs.

I strive to locate such bravery.

I wonder where is it buried inside?

I open my eyes to see Mr. Brady approaching from a distance. He's a good man – that's why I don't desire him.

I don't feel worthy of proper love. Not since Felix.

"Stop this," Hector demands, lifting me. "There are other jobs."

"You think that's why I'm upset?" Tugging free, I grow dizzy, hearing the buzz of gathering students signaling one another to check out the Beastwoman. "If you're such a smart man why are you so naïve when it comes to me? I'm a fool to believe you care the first thing about me. If you did, you'd know I lost my mother today."

Is that what has me enraged? Jerry's revelation happened so fast. I barely had time to taste it, swallow it. I lost my birth mother. We never met. I think her name was Elise. Elise is dead. That's what Jerry said. How could he be so matter-of-fact about it? How could I hold love for a woman I never met?

"Your mother?" Hector's voice softens. "I didn't know she was sick."

I dust dirt from my legs. "That's because you don't

know the first thing about me. You never ask."

He takes the hit, bidding me to join him for a ride on the golf cart. "Please. Let me help you."

"I'd rather walk."

"Why?"

"You don't believe in me."

"That's not true. You're my second best counselor."

"I'm one of two!"

He huffs, his eyes gauging the proximity of the students, assessing their audible range. "Let me take you to the nurse."

"No!" I flail my arms. "You don't...." I begin to explain but the sour look on his face says it all. None of this is his fault. I'm merely a crazy woman who wants more than she once led him to believe. It was magical then. He could have his way with me without the added expectation. He could enter me without threat. When did it change? Why do I need more from love, from life? Bev Dear said I could never be selfless. It's not in my genes. "You don't see it, but I'm good. I have a heart, big as any," I say. Perplexed, Hector searches for an explanation in my eyes. "I can teach anywhere. I don't need you."

Mr. Brady approaches with flowers still in hand, smiling. "Is everything all right?"

I spin on my heel and a brilliant idea forms. "Actually, I need a gentleman to escort me to the nurse." I extend my arm and Mr. Brady latches on. "Shall we?" We begin walking and I don't look back, figuring it's best to leave Hector basting. Perhaps then I'll have time to cook up a plan.

"You've been a busy bug," Mr. Brady comments. His southern drawl seems plucked off a plantation. I've been trying to get you all morning. I heard you were in a ruckus in the bathroom. Are you sure you're ok?" Before I can speak he offers me the small white flowers, clustered together at the end of long green stems. "Those are October flowers. Usually, people don't notice them because they only bloom three weeks a year. But when they do they sure sparkle."

I bring them to my nose and my heart settles. "Thank you. They're lovely."

"I found 'em near a portable out back and thought of you. Can you imagine something that pretty being ignored?"

I squeeze his arm. "Mr. Brady, do you know where I can locate some spare desks?"

"Desks?" He scratches his chin. "How many?"

"Two or three. Maybe a chalkboard." The morning bell rings and students part from their circles, calling out goodbyes. "Could you bring them to my house? You still have that old pickup, right?"

"Yes ma'am." He swats a fly circling the flowers. "But if you don't mind me asking – what are you planning?"

"I can't say yet," I admit. But seeing students align in formation, headed to their respective classrooms, stirs something in me. If only I had enough influence to make a change. I could prove Hector and Bev Dear wrong. I could live for more than the threat to die. I could teach myself to care again. So that's where the plan shall start. And if it involves me, my house, one thing is for sure – it shall include a bit of *class*.

CHAPTER 5

LATER THAT DAY Lisette remains in a foul mood, casting me the old stink eye, slouching in the cherry wood chair that faces my desk. Moments before, Principal Rivera had sentenced the poor girl to six weeks of daily therapy sessions, which I jumped to administer. She had no idea that I had an ulterior motive. I reveal that after I explain the rules of counseling and she calls me a stupid boyfriend-stealing puta.

"Well, with a mouth like that you may need more intensive services," I say, with a smirk. "Luckily, I'm beginning a class from home to fine-tune kids just like you."

She purses her lips, exhaling from her nostrils. "Hmph."

"Does that mean you'd like to enroll?"

She eyes me dully. "Look lady. I don't need you or anyone else teachin' me nothing. All I gotta do for the rest of my life is be Puerto Rican and die." Chewing a thumbnail she spits it on the floor. "Can I go now?"

I stiffen in my seat – my wound freshly cleansed and bandaged from Nurse Ferrera. "No, you may not."

She folds her arms. "Fine. But I'm not taking your stupid class."

I glance at the guard, who waits beyond the door and straighten my yellow, cashmere scarf – the perfect compliment to the black cat suit I changed into after the bathroom brawl. "I don't think you understand. You don't have much choice. Not after your behavior earlier today."

"Whatever." She yawns. "Mr. Rivera already disciplined me for that. I have to sit here and stare at your Gonzo nose for six weeks. That's punishment enough. I don't need to go to your home too. He didn't say nothing 'bout that."

"I see." Tapping my fingernails on the desk, I realize kindness might not be the best tactic. Therefore, I opt for a rockier road, nodding to an innocuous white note pad on my desk. "Do you know what I have here?"

"No. Sorry. I can't see anything with your nostrils sucking up the ozone. Can I go?" She turns to check on the security guard who sharply grins, tapping his walkie-talkie.

"It's a list," I state, as she sulks, returning her attention to me. "You know, it's amazing how much one girl can accomplish in such a short time on this planet. Don't you think?"

She wipes her runny nose on a sleeve of her baggy black tee. "What are you talking 'bout?"

"Your rap sheet," I marvel. "Or should I be specific and say record of arrest and prosecution?"

She perks up. "Who gave you that?"

"A little birdie." In a flash she reaches across the desk, trying to snatch the list, but I grab it. "Now, now. A true lady never reveals all her secrets." I grin. "But let's have a look, shall we?" I scan the list. "Criminal mischief, trespassing, battery on an officer, petty theft...."

"Like that says shit about me."

"It seems to say a lot."

All five feet nothing, she stands – her angry face dotted with red pimples. "Fuck this. You think I'm tryin' to entertain you? Go on. Read your note. But you don't know who I am."

"A great reason to take my class."

"Take your class?" Her hands begin to violently shake. "Here's what I think 'bout your class." She lets out a scream, wiping a hand across my desk. My papers and ceramic coffee cup take flight, falling to the floor as I stand. Immediately, the guard enters, pulling Lisette's hands around her back.

"You want to apologize?" he asks. Again she screams, spitting on the desk. He restricts her face by wrapping a muscled arm around her neck.

"That'll be enough," I instruct him. "I can handle this."

"No ma'am. She's going to the self-contained room," he says.

"Please," I insist. "Let her go."

He sighs, loosening his grip.

She escapes, falling to the ground and choking. "I'll sue you," she tells him. "Ain't no man gonna touch me if I don't say it's ok."

"All right, enough with the theatrics. I'll take it from here," I say.

The guard shoots Lisette an intimidating glance before leaving.

"That bitch. I'll cut his face," she says. Kneeling on the floor she tries to catch her breath. "I'll mess him up."

I take a seat to clear my throat. "Your probation officer Oscar wouldn't like hearing that." Her eyes flash red. "Yes. Oscar and I had quite the severe chat this morning. Seems you're out of second chances. Is that right? Another mishap and you're off to lockdown?" Lisette's breathing grows heavy. "Lucky for you, I failed to mention this morning's assault. I told Oscar I was merely keeping tabs on you." She groans and stands, balling her fists. "I think assault with a concealed weapon would qualify you for a year in kid prison. What would you say?" She seems ready to leap across the desk. "I could still make the call."

"What's stopping you?"

I smirk. "The luxury of holding it over you."

She tilts her head, listening, as if respectful of the truth. Still, anger divides her forehead, shifting her pimples to a fresh page of connect the dots.

I write my home address on a bright yellow sticky, handing it over the desk. "I'm certain you won't have trouble with transport Saturday. Cici knows the way. Nine a.m. sharp."

Now, if only she'll show. If not, I suppose I'll be satisfied I made it through our first therapy session without a cut or bruise. Who knows? Perhaps she's taken a liking to me. She doesn't utter another nasty word before she leaves. She simply groans an otherwise pleasant goodbye and stomps off in her dirty white sneakers. Progress, right? I can't tell. I don't recall much about kids and pleasantries, not since father was alive to remind me of the happiness contained in the right hello and the hell of its opposite. Still, I'll consider the meeting with Lisette a success – the first in my new career as a teacher, or shall I say, professor? Professor Lingers. Oooooh, I like that; it tickles my tongue like the mint in a mojito. There's a sense of power in that title. With it, people will no doubt take heed in what I have to say. Long gone will be the day of sitting alone in the office, sharpening pencils thick as Lincoln Logs and staring at distorted birth documents.

My portrait of Frida Kahlo will look down on me with quiet discontent no more.

I am ready for a new world.

Still, I will need more students. But where can I find such likely candidates? I can't blackmail just anyone; my diabolical plan could be leaked. If Noni, Vita, or Hector caught wind of it, I'd most certainly be fired. I can't imagine inviting these children into my home would be seen as anything but unethical, but how else can I prove I'm more than a counselor in need of therapy.

Puta! Beastwoman! Bitchface!
Husband stealer! Boyfriend stealer!

The cracks take their toll and I'm off to the filing cabinet, cracking it open for my stash of vodka. Just like Kitty Fritter said, we ladies have secrets, not that he or she will *ever* be a lady.

Hector's nonverbal apology, a yellow spray rose bouquet, arrives on my desk an hour before the school day ends with no card, no signature, no way to trace it. Is it his way to guarantee a win over Mr. Brady? He's never bothered to send flowers before.

No matter. It won't work. I'm more than a prize. So I place the bouquet on Vita's desk and leave for the day.

Moments later, I'm a bit buzzed, surveying the campus for more students to enroll. Doing so, I note how most avoid me; others point, heavy in disgust. I've seen it before. Yet today, I can't let it slide. Sunshine and alcohol won't shield the truth – I'm a monster. The children don't like me. Therefore, giving up, I head to my car as students on buses call out farewells to friends.

In the parking lot, I turn my nose down and quicken my pace, when I cross paths with several students breakdancing on cardboard. Fingering my tote, I find my sunglasses – round like a bumblebee – and hastily place them on.

"Let me guess, too fabulous for a hello?" a voice calls. I ready the car key in my shaky hand. I've heard that voice before. But where?

I turn my head and see the Haitian boy from the girl's bathroom. Is it Jasper? He winks, slinking toward me with what seems to be a garbage bag purse. Before he speaks a Ford truck passes, hauling two Latin boys in the back. One boy with a blue headband stands to grab his crotch. He yells to Jasper. "Hey maricón! You swallow?"

"Not with herpes on the straw. You're out of luck!"

The truck speeds off, the boy howling in laughter.

"Jasper!" I say. "Such language."

"Sorry," he says, covering his mouth. "You know how it is around here. A girl's tongue needs to be sharper than her blade."

"You could try a more mature approach."

"Oh, come on. You witnessed it this morning. It's survival of the bitchiest." He leans on my car, styling his cropped hair with an orange comb. "So this class? Does it include breakfast?"

Breakfast? I never said anything about that. How much talk about my class is going around? How far has it spread? I brace myself, carefully choosing my words. "I don't know anything about a class."

"The-one-at-your-house," he slowly says. His eyes go buggy like I'm insane. "The one with you and Lisette. She told me about it. She said she'd wreck my face if I didn't enroll." His eyes tick tock like he should explain. "She meant it in a loving way."

"I'm sure she had the best intentions."

He enthusiastically nods. "So can I join?"

Hm. Perhaps I don't have to recruit after all. I can employ Lisette to bully others into signing up for me. What a wonderful, hassle-free turn of events except I'll have to feed the class now, the little locusts.

"You can be in the class," I offer. "But any more language, and I'll be forced to soap your throat. I'll need you to demonstrate proper etiquette."

His bright blue eyes glow with excitement. "Is that what we'll be learning? Etiquette?" He flutters his lashes. "I've always wanted to be proper."

"Yes. Well...." I begin to correct his assumption but Jasper's breakdancing crew calls him over to perform. Blowing a kiss to the wind he's gone and I take to the wheel, wondering what I have set in motion.

What do these children expect – for me to teach them manners?

Well, I don't feel I could do the topic justice. Sure, Bev Dear instructed me on the necessary basics, Etiquette 101, but she never felt I could graduate to the next step. She took me for stubborn, too opinionated and caustic – a semiformal girl rather than a lady with the deference to handle a black-tie affair. "Etiquette's primary function is to ensure the comfort of others," mother instructed. "It's the ability to make a guest feel completely at ease. Often, that requires keeping your mouth shut and putting the guest first."

Dee, you've never been that considerate of others.
You can't see beyond your nose to care.
How could you? It's such an unsightly nose.
Care to have it fixed?

Yes, Bev Dear was all about manners, the art of saying the right thing at the right time, but she never turned away an unkind word when it came to me. For mother, I was a project, a work-in-progress, rather than a child. Daily, I was schooled on the proper manner to communicate, participate, celebrate, but it was never enough. I was never enough. Neither was father. We always managed to do something that would ruin her entire day, such as leaving a dirty dish in the sink. She would be devastated.

Bev Dear's behavior became more severe during my prep school years – a thorny time where she would sharpen her incisors on me before nightly feuds with father. I suppose even she knew how bad the violence had become, sending me to study for a year abroad in England after I witnessed her end an argument by shattering a wine glass on father's temple. I still remember that dreadful night. On the stairs I clung to the banister in utter fear, overhearing the feud was about her growing interest in Miami Beach. She had slowly begun residing there on a full-time basis and father was growing suspicious of her outings with local Cuban men. Bev Dear said the men were merely investors in a business scheme to flip small, high-end resorts on South Beach, but when the men began phoning our home in Richmond, it became obvious that real estate wasn't the only thing on the market. The callers would fight with Bev Dear like scorned lovers.

"You summer with your mother in Miami. Have you met these investors? This Luis or Raphael?" father once asked.

I hadn't, but I couldn't tell him. It would have broken his heart. Therefore I made excuses, while knowing that if mother's relationship with these men had been legitimate, she would have introduced me. I wouldn't have been banished to daily excursions with her driver Rose. One summer I gained physical evidence of her affairs through a discarded Polaroid in the master bathroom. Having fallen behind a plunger, the photo consisted of mother – tan and topless – on a rainbow beach blanket with a strange muscular man nuzzled up to her back.

"This is a piece of art!" mother snapped when I brought it to her attention. "I would expect a smart girl like you to understand."

That's the problem – I understood all too well. Still, I kept silent, careful to avoid being sent to summer in some third-world country.

Truthfully, I'd grown fond of Miami and had begun to find a friend in Rose. With Rose, there was never a care for poise or appearance. She had cropped black hair that always appeared mussed and never wore makeup. Bev Dear said Rose was a regular person. That's why she had permission to do unladylike things like burp and eat burritos with her hands. "It's ok to speak with your mouth full if you can't wait to say how great it tastes," Rose would say with a laugh. She was inquisitive, cared about my thoughts. I never understood why since I was rarely asked for my opinion. In fact, I was skeptical of her enquiring mind until won over by her kindness and ability to keep a secret. She had the funniest tongue, never sharing what she considered to be a bad word. To substitute, she'd rhyme invented words. I still remember the time Bev Dear sent Rose to buy my first bra. Rose acted as if she was dabbling in drugs or black market goods. Driving, she quietly slipped me the plastic bag without taking an eye off the road. "Don't tell anyone. It's a tee-tee for your ta-tas."

Once, after my period, she took me to purchase yoo-hoos for my hoo-hoo.

I expected chocolate milk.

The childishness drove mother mad, especially if she heard me engaging in Rose-speak. Still, I found the juvenile humor refreshing, and over time, I learned it was healthy to laugh. Rose made it safe; eventually I began to reveal more.

On one drive I admitted to Rose that I longed for the kind of mother who would kiss me goodnight on the cheek and tuck me in bed. The thought made me cry.

"Oh Desi, don't let that upset you," Rose said. "Each mother shows love for a child in her own way." She handed me a tissue from the front seat. "Sometimes you just can't see it. That's the thing about love. It comes in all shapes and sizes but it never comes in the package you expect."

Rose refused to speak ill of Bev Dear. She never spoke of her own family either. In fact, she only opened up once, stating she left home in high school, never to return. She didn't say why. She simply stared off in discomfort and told me the key to life is staying busy. It keeps the ghosts at bay.

I suppose that's why I should be grateful that Jasper expects me to feed him. It gives me reason to stop at the market in search of breakfast items for the class. I toss blueberry muffins and orange juice in the cart before feeling a bit swindled. Is it not enough to teach? Now I have to be a mother too?

Oh, tsk tsk. Why am I surprised? Nothing in life is free. Take that thieving midwife Roberta Smith. Another call from Jerry while shopping reveals she still won't talk, even after payment.

"She's no dumb broad," Jerry shares. "She knows what you're worth. She's holding out for more."

"How *much* more?"

"Baby, relax. I have it under control." His nasally voice is more irritating than usual. "Pull the right string, the puppet will talk. She needs to be nudged."

"Or pushed. Perhaps there's a balcony in her room?"

He laughs. "Nah. No threats. I just need money. And time."

Time. Yes, today I can't seem to get a minute of it. I hang up the phone to find Hector has sent me five texts about the flowers. Do I like them? Am I happy? I'd be happy if he used correct grammar.

I wuz wrong.

I need u.

I luv u.

Oh why must I have feelings for a man who can only utter the word love on a machine? Is that what I'm worth? Granted, I may not be the freshest hen at the market but my expiration date hasn't hit yet. Men still find me appealing.

On the ethnic food aisle I search for such men, only to find elderly women, desperate for a new recipe to bring meaning to their lives. Then I hear my name.

"Dee, is that you?" I turn and Kitty greets me with a smile and a wave. The poor girl must have forgotten the temperature of my cold shoulder this morning. Therefore, with the swift push of my cart in the opposite direction, I remind the dear, only to spot her again, minutes later in the freezer aisle, where two teenage boys trail her cart.

"Nice dress, mister. I mean, miss," says the thicker one. A silver nose ring matches the hoops in his ears.

"Knock it off," his friend says. "Let *him* get his groceries."

Attempting to outpace them, Kitty fidgets, steering a cart that tugs her in a slanted line due to one derelict wheel. Her pink heels tap, tap, tap the floor.

"Please leave me alone," she tells the boys.

"I was just giving you a compliment," the nose-ringed punk says. "You like compliments, right?" Stopping in place, Kitty takes a few breaths. "Sorry dude." The kid passes her, smirking with a mouth of checkered teeth. "I didn't mean to piss you off, sir."

Rattled, I intervene. "No worry. It's not your mouth that pisses off people," I call to him. "It's your face."

"Huh?" Turning, his smile fades, and he looks to his mate. "Dude, what did that old bag say?"

"This OLD bag said your face pisses me off." Removing my earrings, I set them in my purse. The boys look to each other in amazement. "Would you like me to say it again?"

Kitty covers her eyes.

The thick boy slaps his forehead. "Oh. Let me guess. You got a dick too?"

"No," I laugh. "I divorced each of them." In my purse, I locate the knife I'd confiscated from Lisette. Revealing it, I dance it in my hand, aiming at the kid's face. Kitty shrieks. "What can I say? Sometimes when a woman isn't being treated right she needs to cut her man at the root."

"This chick's nuts," the other boy says. "Let's get outta here."

"Forget that. I'm not scared of this bitch. I wanna get sliced," the thick one says. His blue eyes glimmer and the world goes silent except for the electronic beeping register – the sound of products being scanned. "Cut me," he challenges.

His friend tugs him away. "No man. We're out."

The thick one laughs maniacally, calling me 'killer.' The two disappear, laughing it off.

"Well...that was odd," I state, frozen in place. Dazed, Kitty clutches her cart for support, and I return the knife to my purse just as a manager, in shirt and tie, rounds the corner, searching the aisle for a threat. "Good day," I tell him, pushing off. I make it to the frozen foods where Kitty finds me.

"What was that?" she asks.

"Pardon."

Frazzled, she struggles for words, sporadically blinking

her eyes. "You, you refuse to acknowledge me. Then you pull a knife to protect me?"

I stand firm. "Knife? What knife? I was filing my nails."

At a loss, Kitty painfully laughs. "I don't get it. Maybe I'm a hick from the sticks but I thought we had fun the other night."

I tighten the yellow handkerchief on my neck and fluff my hair. "Yes. Well. Funny, I thought you were a woman. Appears we were both misled." I navigate around her cart but she corners me.

"I *am* a woman," she defends.

"Ha!" Anger chars my bones to the point where I feel steam rising from my shoulders. "If you were a woman you would have cut that punk yourself. It takes balls to be a woman. And you...you had them cut off." I tap her chest. "You don't know the first thing about being a woman." I head down the aisle.

She clears her throat. "Back home, they made fun of me," she calls. "All the kids, even my cousins. But at least they acknowledged me."

I turn to find tears in her eyes. "They treated you like dirt. Called you Conch Fritter," I say. "I'd rather be invisible."

"You wouldn't say that if you knew what being ignored was like."

"Actually, I've known for some time." I feel it every time a younger, prettier version of me passes by, catching the eye of every man in the room. Did I mention, sometimes I see a gorgeous man and toy with the idea of faking a heart attack just for mouth-to-mouth? That started when Hector began to insist on making love to me from behind. He said it was due to my amazing ass, but even that compliment felt like a smack to the face. "I just refuse to be a victim of it," I explain.

"Is that why you're mean?" Kitty asks.

A short blonde Stepford wife picking waffles from a freezer pauses to listen.

"You think I'm mean?" Leaving behind my cart, I approach Kitty with sheer astonishment mixed with a teaspoon of malice. She grips her cart, careful to keep it between us. "You haven't seen mean. Mean is a mother who has no time for a daughter. Mean is a husband who promises to protect his wife then gives her a black eye."

Her chin quivers. "I know that type of mean."

"No. You don't. You've never been with a man unless you count your uncle, and I wouldn't." Tears stream down her face. "Go on. Cry. You think that's going to help? You think that's ever helped me?"

"No."

"Look at you." I nod to her denim skirt – the dirty, frayed thread hanging down her legs. "What came of the job hunt? Have you had any luck?" She frowns, shaking her head. "Of course not. Look at what you're wearing. This is Miami. It's about face value. Poise. Presentation. Perfection."

Suddenly I gasp.

Dear God, I sound like Bev Dear.

Tell me I'm not a monster – I'm meant for better things.

Kitty looks to me. Her bottom lip shakes. "Dee? Have you been drinking?"

"What?"

"I smell alcohol."

"So?"

"You pulled a knife on a stranger." The frozen waffle woman takes her cue to flee. "Is everything ok?"

"Everything is fine." But is it? What am I doing? There's too much clutter, too many memories of relationships gone wrong. Where am I? At the market? Oh yes. I'm purchasing food for the students. "I'll have you know, I'm teaching. This Saturday. I'm holding class for a very selective group of teens."

Kitty brightens. "How wonderful. What subject?"

The word comes before I can stop it. "Etiquette."

"Really? I wish I could sign up." She lingers for an invite that never comes. What? Does she think I'd allow her in my class? There's no telling what she'd do with such knowledge. It could be a weapon in the wrong farm hands, like giving a pitchfork to a pig. "Is there an opening?" she inquires.

"Like I said, the group is very selective...teens." Turning, I gather this is the best time to exit. I don't want to make the girl cry anymore. I simply don't know if I have the talent to transform someone so tragic.

On the ride home, I tune out, turning up Chopin's Nocturne in E-Flat. The soft piano keys tickle my ear, as outside, the pastel colors of the Art Deco district relax me. I must not sleep, I tell myself. I must stay awake and focus on the music, rather than the men and the noisy mistakes of my past.

Pressing forward, I pet my stomach, taking in a tall building with porthole windows and ship railings.

In the passenger seat, my phone signals with more messages from Hector. I imagine tossing it out the window, watching it explode into a million pieces. No loss. It would be a virtual vacation.

I brake in front of the Savoy.

"How was your day?" Salvador asks, helping me out.

"Busy," I reply. I exit the car with the groceries. Archibald rushes outside, opening the glass entry door "Thank you," I tell him. In the lobby, the reflection on the waxed white tile blinds me. I stumble to the elevator. "Oh Archibald," I call.

He grins. "Yes?"

"You've known me for a long time...."

"Since a young girl, when you'd summer here with your mother."

I hesitate and he approaches – his eyes reading me behind thick spectacles. "I was wondering. When you think of me, you don't think 'mean' do you?"

He considers it, riddled. "No Ms. Lingers, not at all." His voice is jittery but sincere. "I like to see the best in people. Mean is not your best." He smiles, lost in the thought of another place and time. "I remember you as a young girl, so kind."

I smile and the elevator door closes as I take a breath.

Once, there was innocence in my heart – a genuine regard for others. I enjoyed assisting Archibald, keeping an eye on the door, opening it for residents if he were ever in a bind. It was fun being downstairs, away from Bev Dear, who despised the notion of people thinking I was the help. But oh how it delighted me to meet the neighbors, hearing their colorful hellos.

In the elevator I look to the mirrored wall, wondering where is that girl? In my eyes, I still see a sparkle – a remnant of what I was and what I wanted to be – destined for something good, more than the hobby of an indecisive man.

The elevator rises and the awareness of gravity reminds me – I'm stuck. I'm sacrificing my chance at happiness for a man who has no love for me here, now, or ever. Still, I keep him, certain that half of a man is better than no man.

But I can't take it. My body's tired. My mind is too.

"I'll let him go," I say aloud. "I'm better alone."

For a moment I'm empowered – on top of the world – before the weight of the decision crashes down. I have no one in life, nothing but an empty condo with no hope of a man coming to ward off the cold. The isolation ices me and my limbs weaken. Unsteady I drop the grocery bags and grab for the railing, but it's too late. I collapse.

CHAPTER 6

I'M NOT ONE to lie about the past. I've had many dogs in bed but the men I speak of had mainly been potty-trained and invited unlike the holy terror that wakes me up the next morning. Taser, the little devil – I'd split him like a pea if I had the will to pull myself up. Unfortunately, I have a throbbing headache and an upset stomach. Therefore I just moan in discomfort as he barks, running across the bed with his handicap cart.

Tending to my wound, Kitty tells me not to stir. "You need rest," she insists. Applying ointment on my arm she says I cut it on a broken pickle jar during a fainting stint. Apparently she found me blacked out, rolling around with groceries on the elevator floor. She brought me home and bandaged my wound.

However, when she approaches with a thermometer I end the Nightingale routine, directing her to the door. "And take that yappy dog with you."

Arching his head, Taser frowns.

"Awwww. See? He doesn't want to leave." Sitting at my side, she seals the top of her pink nightgown, positioning the thermometer. "Now be a good patient and open up. Doctor's orders."

"What doctor?" I press together my lips, opening them only to speak. "I'm not sick you tart." I push away the thermometer. "I fell."

"Yes. But what caused the fall?"

"Acute intoxication."

"Oh no. Intoxication is never cute."

"Out!" I bark.

She jumps, placing Taser on the floor. He yaps loudly,

jumping to get back on the bed.

"Look. He's protecting you," Kitty exclaims.

"Please. He's out for blood."

"Now, you be nice, Miss Crabby." She places a cold rag on my head. "We'll be gone in two digs of a litter box." From the living room, I hear a meow.

"Is that a cat? Did you bring your cat?" I ask.

She dodges my eyes, filling a bowl with cough drops on the nightstand. "I couldn't leave her at home. She has anxiety. It makes her hair fall out."

I groan, mustering the energy to sit up. I find that I'm still in yesterday's black cat suit. "Please. Fetch my robe."

Kitty grabs it from the doorknob. "You really should stay in bed. You won't get better."

"A glass of wine will fix that."

"Wine?" Kitty wrinkles her face, handing me the robe. "I'm not sure that's a good idea. How about cold milk and cookies?"

"Do I look like I'm barreling down a chimney to you? Like I'm delivering presents?" She looks at me wide-eyed. "I assure you, when I jump it will be from a far greater height. Santa can't hold a candle to me." Wrapping myself, I head to the wet bar. Kitty follows. Near the red chaise I spot a vacuum, its cord in a tangle. The couch pillows are freshly fluffed and the surfaces shine. "Is this your doing?" I ask, pointing to a bottle of glass cleaner.

She hesitates. "Yes."

"That's kind, but I pay a woman for that. She comes Tuesdays." I pour a glass of Pinot.

"I hope you're not upset," she says. I take a drink. "Back home, that's what gals do when a friend has a bad day. We make it better. Whatever it takes. Oh, that reminds me!" She squeals, darting into the kitchen. Moments later she returns, presenting me a plate of almond croissants. "They're from a Parisian cafe. I thought you'd like one seeing that you're French."

I crinkle my lips. "I'm English."

"Oh." She considers it. "But we can pretend, right? Everyone *wants* to be French. I know I do. They're so sophisticated."

It if weren't for her sincerity I'd look for the hidden cameras, assuming I'd been set up. However, God bless her soul – the lady is for real. "Kitty, I'm grateful for the help. But honestly, shouldn't you be job hunting?"

She sighs, setting the croissants on the bar. "I have been. I've gone up and down Lincoln six times. There's all these 'Now Hiring' signs but no one seems to be hiring for real." She sits on a stool and lowers her chin. Golden locks cover her face like mop tassels. "Maybe I'm not Miami Beach material."

I take a drink. "Were you properly dressed?"

"I think so." Sitting up, she tears at a croissant, nibbling the small piece in her hand. "Can you believe one manager asked for my resume? Well, that fried an egg on my head. What happened to the old days of filling out an application?" She chokes down her food. "I just want to be a shop girl."

"That can be tricky in Miami."

Her eyes grow with intrigue. "What do you mean?"

I pour her a glass of wine, handing it over the bar. "Drink." She sighs but reluctantly complies, painfully taking it down and slapping her bar stool, as if she were drinking poison. Taser whines at her feet and she burps, quieting him.

"Excuse me," she says, covering her mouth.

"Look at you. Who's going to hire you? You have no backbone, no style, no finesse."

"I have finesse," she says. Setting down the glass, she fluffs her hair and puckers her lips.

I pay the humble attempt little mind. "Remember your skirt yesterday?"

"The denim one? Yes. It's my favorite."

"Let's use that as an example. I'm sure it's lovely for Arcadia. However, the Backwoods Betty look won't do you any favors in Miami. No fashionista wants the advice of a shop girl who can't dress herself."

She folds inward. "You don't think I can dress myself?"

"I...." Damn it. I can't shoot the poor girl when she's

down. Not after she's been so kind. If only she had one bad bone in her body I could use it for leverage. "I think you dress well for Arcadia. Miami has a much different sense of style. It's about knowing your environment. All you need is a little instruction."

She lights up. "Like the kind you'll be giving in class?"

Oh dear, I view my watch, going on about the time. There's so much to do. I must dress for work and fix breakfast. Trixie needs to be fed. I rush off, knowing that if I leave a second to spare, Kitty will weasel her way into being a student.

"Nice of you to visit," I call out. "Feel free to see yourself to the door."

"I won't make it, will I?" I slow, sensing her distress. "Ma was right. I *can't* do it on my own." Her voice breaks. "I don't know why I'm here. I wouldn't have left home but she was so awful to me. After the operation she made me use plastic utensils at the dinner table. She said she didn't want to catch what I had." I turn to see tears on her face. "She still introduces me to her friends as her...son."

The words weaken my heart. "I...I'm sorry to hear that."

"I'm a girl. I've never felt different. I shouldn't have to defend myself to my mom or a psychiatrist." She wipes her eyes. "I'm being stupid."

"You're not stupid."

She slices her cries with a nervous laugh. "I'm sure you know how difficult mothers can be."

"Yes. Well. Actually, I don't know my real mother." I ponder why I said it. For years, I've kept it hidden. I hadn't even mentioned her to Hector until our last fight. It was always a secret – a detail that made me feel inadequate. "I was adopted."

Kitty sheds an odd smile, seemingly pleased by the fact I shared something sacred. Then she says something so removed from what I associate with adoption that I'm stunned into silence. She says, "So you were a gift."

A gift?

Well, maybe to father, though I'm certain Bev Dear

would disagree. To Bev, I was a rotten apple – never good enough or smart enough to be head of the class. It's why I jumped into three failed marriages before Felix. I admit that I needed a man, any man, to be complete. I was desperate for approval, for love. But I won't say it aloud. Instead, I tell Kitty, "Class begins Saturday. Nine a.m. sharp."

"Oh Dee! Thank you! Thank you!" she sings.

"That's enough. Take your pets and go."

I retreat to my room to take a hot shower and dress. Slipping into a silk dot top and purple pencil skirt, I wonder, why did I give in? The girl can hardly clothe herself, let alone find a job. I must be crazy to think I can teach her etiquette. She can barely hold a conversation. She speaks of silly matters like kissing uncles and divorcing parents. What kind of lady talks divorce when she's never been married? I've been divorced three times and can barely speak of it. It's too close to my heart. Therefore, I only offer clipped versions of what happened.

Take my second husband Ralph. I don't go into specifics of why I married him. I tell people, it's a blur. After all, it happened so fast – our chance meeting in Raleigh where through a friend father helped me secure a job with a textile firm. It had been six months since my first divorce. My life was in upheaval, much like Raleigh, which had been devoured by seven tornadoes just weeks before I arrived. I suppose I was attracted to the safety Ralph could provide. A famed North Carolinian restaurateur, he was tall, thick like Hector but without a weak stomach. At forty, he was older than me, wiser – a successful entrepreneur. We married three months after our first date – a pizza picnic under the stars in Pullen Park. A week later, I came home early from a conference to find him watching *Sesame Street* in an adult diaper. Having wet himself, he stated he had to 'tell me something' then asked if I'd clean him. Have you ever noticed how 'I have to tell you something' is often followed by something you never needed to hear?

Oh, the things teachers fail to teach you in school. For instance, what's a girl to do if she learns her husband's favorite hobby is to act like a baby?

Better yet, what if she finds him in bed with a mannequin?

Does she find another man and try it again?

*****

That Saturday, the first day of class, Mr. Brady sets down the last of three wooden desks, lining them side-by-side in the sitting room of my condo. "Are you sure I can't talk you into dinner?" he asks. "I know a great place for Cuban."

"This is Miami. Every place has great Cuban."

He laughs. "Yes, but this place is great because you'll be with me."

"Thank you," I say, performing some last minute spot cleaning. "But I can't think about food. Class is set to start. I'm much too scattered." I circle the room, picking up one of Taser's chew toys. It's been days and I'm still finding remnants of Kitty's pets. Last night, I found a hairball in my laundry basket that resembled the Mona Lisa. I phoned Kitty about it, and instead of throwing it away she came over to frame it in a scrapbook.

"How about another night, when you're not busy?" he asks, rolling a black chalkboard to the front of the class.

I sigh. "Mr. Brady, I'm flattered. But you don't want to date me. You're too good. And I don't know what I am anymore. Crazy perhaps." I head to the kitchen to finish a batch of chocolate chip pancakes and he follows, removing his straw cowboy hat.

"With all due respect I'm willing to take that risk," he says.

I shake my head and blush, caught off guard by his defined chest – the way it clings to his shirt, sculpted like a Greek statue. What *would* he be like to kiss, to wake up beside in bed? Oh, I shouldn't think like that. The poor man lost his wife to a car accident. He doesn't need another wreck in his life. What do we have in common? Could he carry a conversation about philosophy or the arts? A knock at the door chases the thought, and I walk him out.

"Sorry to badger you," he says. "I'm having a hard time getting back in the game." His voice trails. "You have this person that's your whole life, the reason you wake up, and then one day that person is just gone." He looks to me, his face ridden with grief. "You have friends, family to get you through it. But then you're supposed to go on like it's ok. How do you go on?"

I've think of Felix and my heart skips. "Because it *did* happen. And that's good enough to give you hope it can happen again."

He considers it. "You think it could for me?"

"A smart, handsome man? Certainly if you put yourself on the market." He smiles, and I open the door. "Now go. Take a risk." He takes my hand, squeezing it unexpectedly. I warm from the hardened touch.

What's wrong with me? Could I like him? My heart flutters with the possibility, hitting a cement ceiling when Lisette walks past me with a puss.

"Puta," she mutters.

I point her to the door. "How about we try that twice?"

She coolly shrugs, turning to stroll by a second time. "Puta puta," she says, proudly.

I fold my arms, raising my chin. "How 'bout this? Call me a puta again, and I demonstrate the meaning of the word." I direct her to the door one final time. "I may be a puta. Yes. But remember. I'm a puta with the number to your probation officer. Need I make that call?"

Returning to the door she manages a plastic smile. "Good morning."

"Better."

Entering she tugs the neckline of her black tee, taking in the house as if it was a wax museum and she feared touching the art might make it come alive. She passes, and I breathe in the odor of cigarettes and cough.

She cautiously approaches the dining table.

"That's breakfast, if you're hungry," I say. Before closing the door I notice Cici in the hall.

"When should I pick her up?" he asks. In a striped blue

jersey, he cleans a gold tooth with a pick.

"We finish at two."

He stretches his neck to eyeball behind me. "What are you trying to teach anyway?"

"Etiquette."

"Yeah. See, I already got them mad skills." He takes a bow and removes his baseball cap. The elevator door opens to reveal Jasper. "Damn. You let *him* in? I thought y'all had standards."

Jasper lowers his sunglasses, rolling his eyes. "Oh Cici. Shouldn't you be off saving the planet? Remember. You're only one vasectomy away from making a difference."

"Whatever punk." Cici goes to push him, but I block his arm.

Jasper inspects my tan four-button pantsuit. "Absolutely divine," he says. "I never could stitch a jacket." He runs his fingers along the lapel. "Breakfast?"

I point to the inside. "Freshly prepared."

Pleased, he lifts his chin, sniffs, and follows the scent inside, tugging a black duffel bag like a purse.

"See him," Cici says. "Forget etiquette. That boy needs to learn respect. If it weren't for Lisette I'd...."

"Return to dragging your knuckles on the ground?"

He manages a laugh. "Whatever. You're just cool with him 'cause he likes your style." Lowering his tone he pulls me close. "Listen. So you know. I cleared the air about the other night. I told Lisette, ain't nothing happened between us. I slipped one time so she...."

I gasp for air, refusing to dunk myself in the Bermuda Triangle of teen love. "Anything else?"

"One thing. Don't be feedin' Lisette any of that ma'am stuff. I don't want her thinking she's better than...."

I promptly close the door. I don't require unsolicited advice. I can function on my own if only I could get the students to their seats. However, they seem content, standing up to inhale pancakes at the dining table. One would think they hadn't seen food before. Lisette doesn't use a fork. She eats like a rat, nibbling the pancakes with her short fingers. To her credit, that's a step above Jasper who stuffs one pancake in his mouth for every two he shoves in his duffel bag.

I fight from commenting as Kitty arrives.

"Am I late?" At the door, she extends another Kitty Litter Cake, speaking a mile a minute. "I met the nicest man and forgot about the time. I hope the class is hungry."

I grit my teeth. "Put that away."

She frowns. "Why? Is it the Tootsie Rolls? I can take them off. It can be a clean litter box."

Good heavens. Clearly the art of making a first impression still needs to be fine-tuned into her country-kitchen-cooking mind. One simply does not approach a stranger with an introduction, cradling a pan of cat poop, edible or not. And look at her outfit. Her dress is no bigger than a napkin – a flowery corset attached to a Chinese fan.

I push her into the hall. "We need to discuss aesthetics," I state.

"What does that mean?"

"PUT down the CAKE."

She wrinkles her nose. "Here?"

"Put it down." She doesn't budge, and I lose my cool. "Now!"

"Ok! You don't have to get in a snit." Bending, she delicately sets down the cake, wobbling on her white heels. "What if a roach gets in it?"

"We'll pity him." She flinches, clearly offended. "Get your hair out of those pig tails."

"What? You don't like them?"

"Not unless you plan to milk a cow."

She gasps in horror. "Well. I suppose I just can't please you." Flustered, she quickly removes the black rubber bands that fasten her tails. "Ouch!" she says, tearing a hair.

"Quit being a child." I help tame her wild locks. "I can't have bad grooming associated with those under my instruction." I fluff her bangs and inspect her head-to-toe. "Unfortunately, we haven't time to deal with your outfit. Next time, cover yourself. There are children present."

Steamed, she folds her arms, blowing air out of her nose. "You don't like my cake, my hair, my clothes. Well, fried fish sticks! What's next? Want me to change my name too?"

My eyes sparkle. "Splendid idea. Let's see." I finger tap my chin. "I know. You like the French. How about we grant you the name of a French femme fatale?"

Her eyes blink, blink, blink. "A femme fatale?"

"Yes. We can play it off your true name." I momentarily ponder. "Oh, I got it. Now pay attention. From today forward, you're no longer the cake-baking Kitty Fritter. Instead, you'll be the charismatic Kitay Fittois. Pronounced Fituaaaaa."

She gulps. "Kitay Fituaaaaa?"

"Isn't it so now? So fresh? So French?" I don't allow her to answer. It's part of the plan — a head-spin of sorts. I don't want feedback; I just want her to move. Isn't that how it works? Leaders avoid feedback by providing a million news leads to prevent the general public from having time to question their plans. I'm more than aware of how power works. Confuse them into submission. Now, if only I can apply it to the classroom.

At their desks, Jasper and Lisette finish breakfast as I make introductions. "Class...Kitay Fittois...Kitay Fittois... Jasper and Lisette."

"Nice to meet you," Jasper offers. Seated upright, he wins bonus points by exuding poise. It's perfectly fine, except he has a way to go, particularly in regard to table manners. I take to the board to address the topic, turning to see Lisette observe Kitay with shifty eyes.

"Uh...uh...uh," Lisette stutters, as Kitay sits beside her. "I said I'd take this class. I never agreed to no freaky shit." She puts a hand up to Kitay's face like a stop sign.

"Is it my makeup?" Kitay asks. She pats her powdery face. "I should've gone with another lipstick. It's so red. You'd think I spent the morning sucking a chip from a cherry."

Lisette wrinkles her lips. "Sucking what from a what?"

"She's here to learn, the same as you," I interrupt. "Is that understood, Miss Lisette?" She reluctantly agrees, mumbling under her breath. "I said did you hear me? Lisette?"

She taps buttons on her cell phone. "WHAT?"

"Do you understand what I said?"

"Ugh. Yes."

"Splendid. Put away the phone. I want all eyes on me." I write on the board. "I'm Ms. Lingers," I state, spelling my name. "That's how I'll be addressed. If you have a question you are to raise your hand." I look back to note Kitay and Jasper are being attentive. Lisette stares at her fingers before taking a bite off a mangled nail. "All right. Please open the journal I've supplied on your desk. On page one, write the course title. Etiquette for Ladies."

"Ladies?" Lisette remarks. "What do you mean, ladies?"

I straighten my jacket. "Is your hand raised?"

"Damn." She lifts her arm and a series of gold bracelets fall from her wrist, clicking at her elbow. "What ladies?" she asserts. "I'm the only with a *real* crica."

"A crica?" Kitay questions. "What's that?"

"What do you think? You had one drilled into you."

Perplexed, Kitay shoots me a worried glance, searching for an explanation "I know I should know." She strains, thinking. "Crica, crica."

Lisette groans. "Damn girl. A *vajayjay*."

Kitay's face reddens. "Oh."

I gain my composure. "Now is not the time or place." I take a breath. "But I suppose that's why I'm here, to teach you to be civilized. It's part of the job."

"What's the *other* part?" Lisette asks. "Scaring us straight with your nose?"

I'm aware of what's taking place: a challenge, a test of power. To maintain control, I must rise to the occasion. I can't allow a bully in my class. Still, I must maintain my wits and remain calm even if the slice stings. "Ah Lisette. You're quite right," I say. Walking up to her desk, I cuff my hands behind my back in fear of piercing the dear girl with a nail. Reaching her space, I bend. "You might very well be the only *real* lady in class. But if so, I implore you. Grow bigger balls."

"Oh shiii..." Jasper says, covering his mouth with his hand. I shoot him a wicked glance.

Lisette is confused into silence, fumbling for words. "What'd you say?" she asks. "That doesn't even make no sense."

"Neither does your grammar but you don't see me raising my hand about it."

She cracks her neck, talking herself down. "Hell no. I don't THINK so. You can't talk to me like that." She slams her journal on the desk and stands. "Forget this. See Jazz, I told you she's loco."

"Lisey, stop," he urges.

"I'm not gonna be disrespected."

"Let her leave," I remark, returning to the board. "It's a privilege to be here. Do you know how many students I turned away?" True, it's a little white lie with a wink of pink in it, but sometimes the truth must be stretched, particularly when one chooses to trivialize the extension of a helping hand.

The delinquent should be grateful to gain my knowledge. Does she think it's easy to be a minority of a minority? Foul language and foolish antics will only carry one so far. That's what she doesn't understand. She's expected to fail. She's been ruled out. I should know. I've long been ruled out as well.

"She don't want me here," Lisette tells Jasper. "I'm just a way to make her feel good about herself. She don't want me."

"But I do want you to learn," I explain. "Otherwise, I'd let you get away with speaking the way you do like the other teachers. Is that what you want? To be pushed aside? To be known as the foul-mouthed filly with the faulty temper?" Lisette grimaces. "Enlighten me, how far do you think that girl will go before she's behind bars?"

"Don't talk like you know me," she returns. "You ain't got a clue about who I am."

"Then sit down and teach me."

Lisette's beady brown eyes fill with suspicion. Is it a hoax? Could it be true? Why would a witchy lady like me care? I ask myself the same question as her eyes hopscotch from the board to the faint yellow sunlight streaming through the glass balcony doors. Then her hardened gaze falls upon me, and I gather this is the first time someone has offered her the upper hand rather than waiting for her to steal it.

"Pssst. I ain't no teacher," she says. "I don't even know why I'm here."

"Well. I'm no expert," Kitay says. "But maybe if you stick around you'll find out."

"Yeah?" Lisette says, taking a childish tone. "Well maybe you need to mind your own business."

"Oh, I'm not in any business. I'm unemployed," she explains. "That's why I'm here. So I can be a lady and find a job." She sits up, proudly. "Ms. Lingers is going to help me. She can help you too. I just know it."

"You don't know nothin'. You're crazy like she is."

"Lisey, quit being rude," Jasper says. "There's no one else out there tryin' to help you." He points to her desk. "You need this class. How do you plan to keep Cici if you keep dressing like a boy?" Lisette slaps his shoulder. "You know I say it with love. Sit down."

"Whatever," Lisette says. She scratches the polish off her nails, settling in her chair. "I'll stay but I'm not talking."

"Splendid. I'm sure you won't have any complaints." I clap to gain the attention of the class. "Now. Let's focus on the subject at hand."

With that, the class begins, leading with the topic of table manners. Thank heaven for Emily Post. If I hadn't her experience and instruction as a guide I'd be at a loss about where to start. Keeping it simple I begin with the proper way to chew and carve meat, along with how to butter bread. Then I sketch the outline of an informal table setting on the chalkboard, figuring a diagram would be a good teaching tool. That is until the students continue to have trouble.

How hard is it to understand the concept of utensil placement? Simply set the utensils – starting with the salad fork – in the order in which you intend to use them. For most occasions, remember: forks to the left of the plate, knives and spoons to the right. Is that so difficult? If all else fails, take a breath, find your center, then look to the center of the table; the plate is the focal point – the place where you set a folded napkin. Compliment it with a wine and water glass, just above, slightly to the right. Salad plate? Simple. Left of the forks. Think sequence. One eats a salad before the main dish. Then one eats dessert.

Oh Dee, only a fool wouldn't understand such simplicity.

Listen to Bev Dear.

Solids to the left, liquids to the right.

Is that not easy enough?

Jasper raises his hand. "But which utensil goes with dessert?"

I tap the diagram on the board. "Good question. If one requires a fork, use the one placed horizontally above the dinner plate. But if one is served, let's say, yellow custard, one should use the dessert spoon on the right side of the plate, the one just left of the soup spoon."

Kitay chews her pen. "All these rules are just plain menacing. How are you supposed to enjoy a meal with all that remembering? I'd be happier on the farm eating twigs with the pigs."

"But that wouldn't be civilized," I reply.

"Oh no. Pigs can be very proper."

I sigh. "Is everyone *else* clear on how to create an informal place setting?" Jasper hesitates before nodding. "Splendid. Lisette?" Head down, she scribbles in her journal, refusing to reply. I pay the behavior little heed. Instead, I instruct her to help Jasper clear the breakfast items off the dining table. "Time for a hands-on lesson," I say. "Kitay, follow me to the kitchen to gather clean plates."

Kitay and Jasper comply, but Lisette stalls. When I approach her desk she pops up like a porcupine.

"I heard you!" she snaps. Then following Jasper's lead, she stands to clean the table without another word. When the task is complete, Kitay and I set down a stack of clean plates, along with glasses and utensils. I step back, motioning to the table.

"All right. Begin."

"Begin what?" Jasper asks.

"Prepare an informal table setting."

"Oh. I thought you were gonna feed us lunch."

"Is there no limit to your belly? You just had breakfast." He grins, and I point to the dishes. "Quit thinking about food and get to work." He begins and the others follow, positioning their dinner plates before freezing. They study the table, sprinkled with insecurity. Kitay counts fork tines.

Had they been listening? This is elementary material. During the teaching, I made sure to talk slow, resisting ancillary matters like good Feng Shui and how the plates should match the walls. Do I need bigger diagrams?

"Forks confuse me," Kitay says. "There's not enough difference in size."

"Is it liquids to the left or right?" Jasper asks. He slides a water glass back and forth. "Liquids to the left, that sounds right."

"No, liquids to the right," Kitay says. "Right, Ms. Lingers? The water glass is on the right? Next to the salad plate?"

"Yes, that's ri..." I begin. Then I pause and think, salad plate? No, that isn't right. What a jumbled mess. "Remember, think sequence, left to right. Start with the salad, the main course, and then dessert. Look. Lisette has it." Still, I wonder if she really has it because she keeps looking over her shoulder at the diagram on the board. "Tsk. Tsk. No cheating."

"I ain't cheating," she insists.

"That's right," Jasper agrees. "Lisette don't cheat. That's Cici's job."

Lisette reaches for a butter knife, pointing it at him. "Boy. Don't make me cut you."

He grabs a fork. "Don't make me eat you."

"You wish you could eat me. I taste so good I'd turn you straight."

"That will be ALL," I instruct, snatching the weapons. "If you two would put that much energy into learning we might have this lesson down."

"Sorry Ms. Lingers," Jasper says. "I appreciate what you're doing. I'm just not used to eating at a table."

"Aw. What's the matter?" Lisette says, in a baby voice. "They make you eat on the floor in those foster homes?"

"Shut up."

"Look at your bony butt. I bet they barely feed you at all."

"Sometimes they forget," he mutters, the announcement muddying the mood of the class, turning the rest of the day somber. Even after lunch, consisting of grilled cheese sandwiches, tomato soup and apple cobbler for dessert, I'm hard pressed to keep the class upbeat.

Perhaps, I should've known better than to turn the lesson to table manners. I suppose the proper way to eat isn't intriguing if one can't afford food, even with my arsenal of tips. *Never reach for an item past an arm's length. Don't slouch. Refrain from finger drumming. Never place a used utensil on the table's surface; set it on the edge of the plate.*

If only the class listened they'd be primed to dine with the Queen. But I'm afraid that's not the case. At the chalkboard, I explain the rule regarding elbows (allowable if not eating) on the table, turning to find each of them asleep.

"That's it. Up!" I call. Frazzled, they open their eyes, entering the bemused state between wake and sleep, their happy bellies full of carbs. "Class is over. You can go." I point to the door, admitting to myself that the first day was indeed a flop. "See you next week." I erase the board and Jasper apologizes, heading to the door behind Lisette, who exits without a word. Kitay gathers her journal, giggling to herself.

"Is something funny?" I ask.

"Oh, I apologize," she says, reddening. "I just remembered...." She twirls a lock of hair, biting her lip. She stalls, building the big reveal. "Oh my God. I never thought these words would come out of my mouth. I got a date." She grins madly, clenching her teeth.

I smile, paying the triumph a grand return. "Good for you."

I head to the dining table to clear the lunch remains, and she doesn't move. She simply stands there, relishing the thought. "I wanted to thank you," she says. "Without you, I would have tongue-tapped a toad before asking a man out. But I did it and he said yes." She follows me to the kitchen. "Isn't that exciting?"

"Thrilling," I say, before rethinking it. "He's not related to you, right?"

She chokes a laugh. "Oh dear. I deserve that. But don't you think we're all related?" An ambassador in the realm of arbitrary she's the type of woman who'd get philosophical in Wal-Mart, given one too many choices of Kool-Aid. "C'mon, don't you think we're all related, just a little?" she asks.

I eye her peculiarly. "Not really."

"But if I hadn't met you and you didn't teach this class, then Jim wouldn't have come to this condo, and I wouldn't have a date. That's more than serendipity. It must mean something, right?"

My eyes grow wide as I imagine the bubblegum tumbleweeds in her mind. I appease her to keep her quiet. "I'm certain the universe is working in your favor," I say, piling the dishes in the sink. I turn on the faucet. "Now if you'll excuse me, I have a million things to do, including cleaning up after your pets."

"I'm sorry," she says, picking up a chew toy on the kitchen floor. "Taser has a habit of throwing toys everywhere, but that's how I met Jim," she says, excitedly. "He picked up one of Taser's bouncy balls. That's why we started talking down in the lobby." She hides the toy in her purse. "Well, that and the fact that we both know you."

"Me?"

"Yeah. You know him. He works with you, right?" Her green eyes spark as she says his name. "The man who brought the desks. Jim...Jim Brady."

CHAPTER 7

Trrue, I can't expect every Miami Beach morning to arrive on a crystal blue palette, complete with the cumulus clouds of a Magritte painting. However today, I wish the rainstorm graying the Monday sky could find another shore. That way, I would find a way to wake and work in order to feel alive.

Oh, if only Felix was here. I'd find peace, understanding like Magritte, one must paint life with incongruity, bizarre people, and nonsensical landscapes to be complete. I could look for the surreal to accept the dull; life would seem balanced with more than one moon in the sky.

Last night, that's what I envisioned – three moons. I'm not certain how the second and third arrived, but the tequila on my pillow might provide the answer. Tequila has a fun way of tricking the brain. Suddenly, you're seeing double, triple, then God. Then it's bible-study time at the toilet where you pray for forgiveness, casting the empty promise of never drinking again.

Interesting, how we all find religion at death's door. Perhaps even the most stubborn drop of water secretly yearns to accept its source.

As for me, I'm alive, sleepy but alive, still reflecting on Kitay's revelation.

She's going on a date with Mr. Brady.

How lovely. I'm happy I brought them together.

Cheers!

Oh dear. Who am I kidding? Let's cut the salt from the bread. The idea is more rotten than the last egg in my uterus.

I know. I'm being petty. Territorial. *I don't want him*

but she can't have him either. I can't stand being one of those women, but I haven't slept more than two winks since the words leaked from her mouth. Does that mean I have feelings for him? With all of his persistence, he hasn't posed a threat before. Why be upset if it was my decision to refuse him? Should I have given him a chance? Look where risk-taking has led me in the past.

Even this morning in the midst of a migraine I continue to battle demons of a relationship gone amok. I thought I'd heard the last of Hector, but heavens no. What we once had verbally, or should I say orally, we now have electronically. In sum, I have to rely on text messages to get my daily dose of why I'm an awful person.

I need 2 talk.

U can't answer?

Be a witch.

Text me when u want 2 change.

How did we arrive here? When did it become all right for him to speak like this? Even on this gloomy day, as I dress in a yellow business suit, I recall how animated Hector once was. He'd write poems for me, knowing printed eloquence was the best way to my heart. In one, he likened me to a mermaid – slippery and subtle, the way I floated into his world, quietly in his thoughts before splashing in his sheets. A year before the separation, his life with Anna had evolved into little more than reading an arm's length away in bed. That's why he'd come to me with such passion. The first time reminded me of Pamplona, the Running of the Bulls. No reason to fear. I longed for the prick. If only I'd known how big it'd be.

"Huge! Huge!" Vita says. Breathless, she rushes to greet me outside of the office. Students take cover from the rain, hustling to class. Vita shields her head with a gossip magazine, water dripping off the cover. "I can't talk inside. Isss Principal Rivera. I have huge news," she says.

My heart jumps. "Is he ok?"

She grabs her heart, panting. "No...he...."

"What?" I struggle, fighting the wind under my black umbrella.

"He signed the papers. I saw them. He's getting divorced. For real."

"What?" A fire lights my chest. For years he said it was over, dating back to the first night we made love, but he never pulled the plug, stating he was too busy at work to begin to think about the process. I could tell the thought plagued him. A devout Catholic, he struggled with the fear that he'd be damned for negating his vows. I'd admired that about him enough that I tried not to pressure him, hoping someday he'd fight the same way for me. Is that what made him take action today? Our fight? Is this how he hopes to fix it? The thought consumes me, as Vita grabs my arm, shaking me. Watered-down mascara creates zebra-stripes on her face. "I care for Principal Rivera. He gave me a job when everyone thought I was too old." Lightning divides the sky, and she shudders. "I want him to be happy. He's a good man. I bring him coffee. He won't take it. Isss no good. He always takes it." I look off, sensing she's set to cry. "Please. Talk to him."

"Me? Why?"

"You make him smile like no one else."

I painfully sigh. "I'll think about it. Anything else?"

"We need more chaperones for the fall mixer."

From behind, I hear the splish-splash of feet and turn.

"Ladies," Miss Robb cheerily says. I catch a flash of red hair as she bounces up the office stairs, shielding herself with a black briefcase. She vanishes inside.

"So you chaperone?" Vita asks again.

"Fine. If you quit pressing me."

I follow Miss Robb inside, watching her sneak into Hector's office, only to feel another slice at my heart. Nurse Ferrera waves from the infirmary, tending to a girl with a thermometer in her mouth.

"We're in flu season!" Nurse Ferrera calls. "You better get vaccinated, Dee. It's important as you get old."

As if the sight of the young new hire isn't enough I have the school nurse to rub alcohol on the wound of my imminent fossilization. I nod with a forced smile, swiftly heading to my office where I contemplate why Miss Robb is paying Hector a morning visit. Does she know of the divorce? Is she consoling him? I'm certain Vita has already sent an e-blast regarding the matter, seeing as she's always good for bad news. Lucky me, today she has more. It seems Ms. Harper caught the flu. Setting coffee on my desk, she tells me I'll have to see all of the children until she returns.

"I feel ssso bad for Ms. Harper," she says. "After she hurt her back last year, she's been in so much pain. Now this."

Yes, well I didn't pull my back out on a spiritual journey on a mountaintop in Peru but most days I suffer too. Have you seen my nose, the faulty plumbing? Recall my recent knife fight? I make it to work, not that it goes noticed. In fact, I don't receive a client all morning. My only interruption is a phone call from Jerry.

It seems that money-milking midwife Roberta Smith took a spill during an unauthorized bathroom trip, causing her to be whisked off to a nearby hospital in Valdosta. She is yet to be allowed visitors. Luckily, before the event, Jerry managed to loosen up the old woman with more cash coupled with an array of prohibited food items.

"She loves chicken fingers," he says. His nostrils echo as he sneezes. "Sorry. Caught a cold."

"What does she know of my birth?"

"She said your mother became pregnant with you in high school."

"High school? What high school? Where? Did you get a name?"

"She couldn't remember."

"Not even the city?"

"Nothing."

"I bet a hundred dollar bill could jar her memory." I emit a muffled scream, balling a fist. "The thief!"

"Hey, don't get heated. At least she's talking." I breathe, allowing my heart to settle. How could this woman prevent me from meeting my family? How could she be so cold? "Your grandpa was a holy roller, taught Sunday school. He helped arrange the adoption. She wouldn't give up his name."

"Of course not." My rage grows.

"She did say your mother was the youngest of three sisters. Didn't get on with the other two. Said your mother was different, *special*."

"Special? What's that mean, special?"

"I don't know. Special," he repeats.

"Is she delayed? Missing an eye? Special is never good."

"Baby, you gotta take it down a notch. If we want to solve this you can't get crazy."

That's me – Crazy with a capital C, batty enough to be in a bin if anyone would have me. I scream for him to GET ME NAMES before hanging up. That's all I want – names, locations and other identifying information that may lead me to a family member who may know something about Elise, my dead mother. Is that too much to ask? Oh, perhaps the world would be safer if I were in restraints.

Here, now, I squeeze my palms to my ears, set to hear the soothing sound of the ocean but it doesn't calm me. Instead, it brings turbulent waves, crests of doubt. How could I believe that I could counsel, let alone teach? What makes me an expert on life? Yes, I was hardened at a young age – gnawed upon by mother's biting wit – but does that make me any more skilled than the average woman on the street? I can't even blackmail a student to talk.

"No! Anyone but her! Get someone else!" Lisette yells, led into my office by a security guard. Handcuffed, she drips with rain and fakes a seizure – her entire body shaking when the guard forces her to sit. An hour before the final bell I hear running water, Vita cleaning the coffee maker in the office kitchen.

"This one was vandalizing her boyfriend's scooter," the guard explains.

Lisette kicks my desk, one, two, three times a lady. "He's not my boyfriend anymore." She attempts to stand, but the guard presses on her shoulder, forcing her down. She trembles.

"If you settle down I'll release you," he says. She snaps away her shoulder, uttering something in Spanish before she calms. The guard locates a key when his walkie alerts him of his next problem – a fight by the vending machines. He looks to me. "You got this?"

"Yes."

He frees her hands. "Holler if she gets rowdy again."

I nod, waiting for him to leave.

"So. Tell me. What happened?" I ask. Lisette shrugs, wringing the water out of her red basketball tee. She wipes her runny nose. "Are you having a problem with Cici?" She stares at the ceiling. "I could find you dry clothes. A towel?" She clears her throat and begins humming. "I can wait."

Forty minutes later, I'm still waiting. Thankfully, it's near the end of the day. Otherwise, I don't know how much longer I could remain calm. The trauma on Lisette's face takes a toll. I consider my own relationships, how they shaped me. I think of my first husband, finding him in bed tangled with a mannequin. I breathe the stench of my second husband's diapers. I remember how it is to feel like shit. Leftovers. Used goods. With my third husband I rolled with the punches until a hard jab knocked me in the....

I can't think of IT, not with a client present. But that happens in this line of work. Bev Dear called it human nature; a therapist would define it as transference. We can't resist connecting, comparing experiences to relate. We're just drops in a drip cycle, fated to return to the same pool.

The bell rings and she stands.

"I'll see you here bright and early tomorrow morning," I say. She looks to me in disgust. "Oh, you didn't think the silent treatment would work, did you? No, I'm quite skilled at it, you see. Blame the woman who raised me. She'd go months without talking to me."

The silence lasts for the next three days, before leading us to Friday, where Lisette chews her nails between shooting dirty glances in my direction, going hmm, hmm, hmm. Eventually, I find being shunned beneficial, using the time to sharpen my wit.

So Lisette, how does hating me make you feel? You know, when you don't speak, you seem alarmingly insightful. Are you a practicing Buddhist?

Then all jokes aside, I admit. "You know, I haven't had this much fun with a student in years."

"That's 'cause you haven't had a student come to you in years," Lisette says, finally opening up.

I frown, looking to the hall. Another student bypasses my office in favor of Noni who just returned from sick leave.

"Gosh Dee. Is that a real student in your office?" Noni asks, as I take a trip to the bubbler.

"Yes Noni. It is."

"Wonderful." She artificially smiles, closing her door to tend to her client. "Let me know if you need help. I know you have trouble...relating."

I could clip her ankles. I could. But I'm a lady, so I swallow my distaste for her corkscrew face and fill a cup of water, returning to my office.

Lisette nods in and out of consciousness.

Oh, if the blasted girl hates me why does she keep coming back? Does she think I'll phone her probation officer? Is fear that much of a motivator?

Perhaps. Take the faculty at Horizon Institute – they're no different. I see them shuffling into Hector's office, bearing gifts. Once news of his divorce spread, it's been a campus priority to keep him upbeat. After all, happiness equates to job security. No one wants an unstable man at the top of the chain. The sentiment might trickle down, resulting in job dissatisfaction or worse – job loss.

Still, does Miss Robb need to provide him support? I look up to spot her en route to his office with a plate of food for the second time this week.

A chill fills my heart. No. It couldn't be.

Are they having an affair? No.

Wasn't it last week when he sent me spray roses? What about his texts? Why must I endure poor grammar if another lady is reaping the benefits of sex?

Fine. I've been ignoring him, dodging phone calls, but I'm punishing him for refusing me a teaching position. So what if I wish him dead, that doesn't mean I don't care. I'll talk to him eventually. But that's not enough; he needs everything now. So go. Cry on the shoulder of Miss Robb.

See if I care. See if I come running when I receive a call from Vita on the intercom saying he needs me.

"Tell him I'm busy," I affirm, deep in the midst of an eye-duel with Lisette. She chews a toothpick, seated across from me.

"Please Ms. Lingers," Vita begs. "He wants to talk."

When Ms. Robb leaves the building I pick up the phone. "Wasn't the ear of that little redhead enough? Or did he require her mouth too?"

Vita gasps. "I worry. He won't come out of his office. Not even for lunch."

"His belly will thank me."

"But he looks so skinnnnnny." After a pause, she whispers. "You know, he asks about you. Every day." I take a breath, allowing any hint of intrigue to pass. "This morning, he asked if you and I talked about his...." She can't say the word divorce again. God might see it as a request. "If you cared."

"I...*care*." Shifting in her seat Lisette pauses from texting to take a mental note. "However, right now I'm with a student."

"My apologies." She emits a muffled cry, ending with an exaggerated sigh. "I worry. He's a good man. He cares so much for you. I know you don't like to see him in pain."

I hang up – my heart afire. Must that woman pester me? If only she knew what that man put me through. So what if there's love for him beneath these ribs? I can't divvy the little I've left; he won't return it. I can barely get a dinner invite. What? Am I too old, too hideous? I may be more beast than beauty, but I'm worth more than that. I deserve a man to hold our love up like a banner, post about it on the streets. That's how sacred it is, how happy one should be to find it, even if Bev Dear told me different.

I'm the only one honest enough to tell you love is a lie, a con – frivolous talk to fill fairy tales so females have something to look forward to other than frown lines. Let the lesser girls chase boys on the playground. Don't waste your time until they're old enough to pay the bills.

How old was I when she sang these faulty notes?

Could I have been seven? Is that right? I believe father was on business in Boston the day I found her drunk, babbling in a clawfoot tub after a fight with her masseuse Marcello.

Earlier that day she took me to a movie. She wanted to cheer me up after I told her about a boy at school who had kissed me. I felt pretty for the first time 'til I discovered he did it to see if he'd turn into a toad. My nose had convinced him I was a witch.

"Disappointment is good," she said. "You needn't be weak. We're all merely water. Tomorrow, you'll be strong, with a thicker layer of ice." Still, finding traces of red in the tub, I learned no skin – cold or otherwise was too thick – that even frigid beings had the ability to thaw. "I should've known he'd rather make love to a man. He's prettier than me," she said, lifting a martini glass. The broken stem dripped with blood, matching her red hair, perfect in a Hepburn updo. I noticed her wrist was cut.

I kneeled at the side of the tub. "Mother!"

She laughed, splashing water in my eyes. I was terribly frightened. Should I phone father? 911? I crawled across the slippery white tile to the far side of the room, unrolling paper.

"He said I was part of the job," she spat. "I was never more to him. He was being paid." I attempted to wrap her wrist, but she dodged the paper, laughing and taking the voice of a child. "Don't you see? He never loved me."

"No, father loves you. He does!"

Suddenly, her laughter ceased. "Silly girl. Who said I was speaking of your father?"

For the first time in my life part of my heart died. Bev Dear survived though, the scar on her wrist a faint reminder of that horrible day.

Funny, how fast the fountain of youth can dry. Tell a young girl the truth about her parent's dilapidated marriage, and poof, adulthood finds itself at her front door. That's what mother wanted – to erase my immaturity with a spotty friendship. That way, she could prepare me for life by teaching me things a child should never hear. I was lucky, she said. Most mothers keep the truth from their children.

"To swallow growing old one must acquire a taste for it while young," she professed.

That's where I find the strength, the iciness, to knock on Hector's door. I expect and fully prepare myself for the worst, taking a respite from my session with Lisette to visit him after receiving a text stating he needs to speak to me at once. I wouldn't have responded but I want to know more about his relationship with Miss Robb, why they've become fast friends.

"I didn't think you'd come," he says, allowing me inside.

"I've only a moment. I have a student waiting to ignore me in my office."

He chuckles, returning to his desk, and I close the door, setting my back to it. The chaotic space has the overwhelming scent of spoiled food, his wastebasket overflowing with plates of black beans and rice. I wrinkle my nose.

"People keep bringing food. I can't eat," he explains.

The quiet that follows tightens my throat. I struggle to speak. "I'm sorry to hear about your divorce. I was... disheartened."

"Disheartened?" He dubiously eyes me, his tangled hair forming a pseudo-Mohawk. "I thought you'd revel in the news."

"We're no longer together. Your marriage isn't my concern." He grants me a skeptical look, lowering his chin. I huff. "Fine. I may be a tad pleased."

Satisfied, he smiles. "I know you too well."

"Please. You don't know me. You don't know the first thing about...." I take a breath, chastising myself for being heated, for becoming Lisette. That's what he wants. "Shame on me. I sound like one of the students."

"Maybe you're finally listening to them." He smirks, triggering the wild fire within me to spread. Why am I here? It physically hurts to be close to him – my heart tricked into a ravenous beat, as if being starved for attention has led it to forget what it means to be truly loved.

"Hector, you called on me. What do you want?"

"I need a reason to see you now?" He frowns, as if offended. "What if I just need a friend?"

"A friend?" After the pain he's caused? I'm not sure whether to be insulted or laugh. Wasn't it days ago when he was texting me about love? It's a miracle I'm not crazy. But perhaps I am and that's what causes me to make comments like the one I'm about to make. "Hector, I'm afraid we jumped the 'friend' shark the day you dove head-first into my crotch."

He shakes his head, becoming frustrated. "There you go. You had to start."

"To demonstrate a *point*. We are not friends. Please do not attempt to blur the boundary with me. I'm far too...." Hurt? I can't admit. "Old."

"You're not old." He rises, stepping out from behind his desk. "Sit. I'll clear some space." He removes a stack of paper from a wooden chair.

"I'm not staying."

"Please." He drops the paper to the floor. "It's a mess but —"

I cut him off. "What's going on with you and Miss Robb?"

He pauses with a guilty sigh. "You don't beat around the bush."

"I prefer to burn it. Keeps things biblical."

He nods to the chair. "Sit."

"Not until I hear more about the fabulous Miss Robb, the promising young teacher who came so highly recommended."

He stalls, gathering patience. "Don't."

"Don't what? You want to be friends, right? I'm talking. That's what friends do." He grunts. "Aren't friends honest even if it isn't easy?" His breathing is quick and harsh, like a wolf before the attack. He can try stress-relieving techniques all he wants. Nothing prevents the heat from rising when a woman knows the proper trigger to make a man boil. Often that trigger is called the truth. "So tell me about Miss Robb."

"Ah mena, mena, mena."

"Tell me."

"Jesus Christ." He swats at the papers on his desk, and white sheets fill the air, falling in twirls. "Do you always have to battle me?"

I don't stir. This is what I expect: intimidation prompted by Paleolithic era aggression. It's how his deadbeat dad handled his mother, he once confessed. But that doesn't grant him the right to use the method on me.

"Shall I chatter my teeth?" I delicately ask. "I'm ever so frightened of paper cuts, you see."

"I just FILED for DIVORCE." He alters his voice low-to-high, struggling to contain his rage.

"Congratulations. Were you expecting cake and balloons?"

He eyes me like he'd enjoy picking his teeth with my bones.

"There you go, again with the words," he says.

"You want a word? Here's a word. Prick."

"Say it again, Dee."

"Prick. And here's another. Narcissist."

"Dee."

"One more, best for last. Bastard." He lunges toward me, but I beat him to it, hurling myself into his chest. "Want to hit me? Go ahead. I've been hit before." I see red then darkness, and I shiver, remembering the hospital bed, the coldness of the sheets the morning after. The water hardening. Cubes. "I've lost more than you. I'm not scared of losing myself. I can live with madness if it helps me forget what I've been through." He grips my arms, forcing them down.

"Just stop Dee. I'm not gonna hit you. You know that." He pins me to the wall, pressing into me. He covers my mouth with his hand. "Relax."

I push but I don't want him to go anywhere. I squeeze into a safe space in his arms until the warmth of the world reappears, offering color, light, happiness. Then the hardness returns in the form of his penis stiffening against my leg.

I should resist, but I don't immediately. I like the security that comes with being desired. Regaining control, no matter what amount, is a wonderful feeling. I allow him to kiss me. He punches me with his lips, fast at first, then tender and slow, his tongue overflowing with sweet juice. The kiss muddles my mind, leaving me indecisive. Is this what I want? I know. It's not best, but I like the tingle of his tongue, the taste of spearmint. It reawakens me, empowers me, sending shivers down my spine. Sensing it, he becomes bold with his actions, pinching my breast. Thrusting his pelvis, he hammers into me like he has before. I become possessed, wrapping my legs around his firm ass. He backs me against the wall.

"I'm not a whore. The desk!" I urge. Like it makes a difference.

He grins, carrying me across the room on his torso. Walking backwards he turns, clearing papers before lowering me to his desk. I look up and the room is white again with thin sheets of paper tumbling down.

I hear the loosening of his belt, his pants falling. He lifts my dress, quieting my moans by filling my mouth with a sock. I'd spit it out, but I don't want anyone to hear, to know how foolish I am. How could I allow a man inside me who hides me from the outside? Who needs a teacher now?

I lay back, shielding my head from the desktop computer, welcoming him along with the pain. I look to the monitor, the image of an orange sun half-dipped into the blue sea. We all connect, bobbing up and down like the tide. Hector goes in and out.

What am I doing? I...love...I want to be loved. But this doesn't equate. It's mechanical, animalistic – raw with no grounding underneath. Pain outweighs the ecstasy. It's sex. Not love. It hollows me, draining tears. Hector makes a final thrust and settles.

"Damn babe," he utters, his unbuttoned shirt drenched with sweat.

I sit up and remove the sock, shielding my face when he comes in for a kiss. I look away in shame. "No."

"Hey." He takes my hand away, reaching for my chin. "Are you crying?" He guides me to his eyes. "What is it?"

He doesn't need the truth; he wouldn't care anyway.

"I'm not crying. I had an allergic reaction to the sock." I push his hand away to gather myself.

He mischievously laughs, pulling up his pants. "Not a problem. I'll gag you with something else next time." His confidence irks me.

"There won't be a next time," I affirm.

"What?" He searches my eyes for a speck of insincerity. Perhaps I'm joking. One look at my gaze and his hopes are dashed. "C'mon Dee." He pulls me toward him, wrapping me with his arms. "We have a good time together."

I grow shaky. "I can't do this anymore. It's not healthy for me."

He kisses my forehead. "Look at you. Acting crazy. That's why I love you."

My heart shrinks and he wins. I'm the weaker person – all the rage when I'm spread eagle on his desk, but the minute I display an ounce of vulnerability, a dirty bird.

"Don't say that. You don't love me."

He tries hushing me with a kiss to the lips and I turn away.

"Hey. HEY," he says. "We were having fun."

"Let me go."

He puts his head on my shoulder, his arms locked around me. "No."

"Hector. I want off this desk."

"What if I don't let you?"

"I knee you in the groin."

He lifts his head, smiling with his cheeks puffed out. "Challenge accepted."

So I do it; I drive a hard knee into his balls. What? I gave him fair warning. So if he doubles over in pain and I have no remorse, does that make me a sociopath or a firm believer in following-through?

I pucker my lips and triumphantly hop off the desk. "Before I go. Let's try this again. What's going on with you and Miss Robb?"

He groans, leveraging his hand on the desk to stand. "What do you want me to say?" His desk phone rings.

"The truth."

"She's a kid."

"Who's been in your office numerous times this week. Shady if you ask me. Should I call child services? File an abuse report? I'm a mandatory reporter, you know. "

He stands, gaining in strength and tone. "She's new. She wanted my advice. Is that enough?"

"What kind of advice?"

He grimaces, waving me away. "You know Dee. If I didn't care about you I wouldn't put up with this insanity." He adjusts his penis, letting out a tiny yelp. "You kneed me in the nuts. You don't do that."

"You got off easy," I say, with a sparkle in my eye. "And look at me, I barely got off at all." I smirk, spreading salt on the wound. "Perhaps you shouldn't try so hard next time."

"That's it." He staggers to the door. "I want you out."

"You didn't answer me. What type of advice?"

"That's private. Now, ándale, ándale. OUT." His cell phone rings, playing a festive Latin number. His hand grips the doorknob.

"You'll have to push me through that door," I declare. "Charge over me like a bull. But then again you're accustomed to that. You're so handsome I never see the horns." The flattery lubes his lips.

"She's pregnant, all right?" he blurts out. "I'm not supposed to tell anyone. It's confidential. Is that what you want to hear?"

I allow the moment to pass, calculating the information. I might not be good with numbers but it doesn't compute. "So we have another pregnant girl on campus? Why is that important to you?"

He resignedly looks away. "Mena, mena, mena."

"Hector?"

He tightens his fist, punching the door. Then gathering his might he looks to me and cops to what I wanted to hear since entering his office – the truth. Not because he loves me, but because he *cares* for me. He reveals, "She thinks I'm the father."

CHAPTER 8

66 "T HINKS? THINKS!?"

"Dee, calm down."

"Calm down? Calm down?" Raising my voice I yell something profane and Hector silences me, sealing my mouth with his hand. I breathe in the scent of his palm – the odor of sex. The muskiness encourages me to ponder how many other lovers he has.

Did I think I was the only one? Could I be that naïve?

Nauseous, I put my hand to my mouth and push him away. I see the door. I think exit but can't remember how. Turn. Turn the handle. What's the problem? I grab it – my hand burning as if it were a hot skillet.

She thinks he's the father? Is there a doubt? Have I been sharing my body with both of them, along with the others he or she has brought in the mix? I need a doctor. I need to check my hoo-hoo. What if I have a disease?

Squeamish, I cry out, pushing my way into the hall where staff members pop up their heads from cubicles. Is it Groundhog's Day? Do I see a shadow? Will spring come early? What about death, can I speed that up?

"Ms. Lingers?" Vita says. She approaches with caution. "What happened to you?" She offers tissues, calling for back up when I refuse. "Ms. Harper! Come! Quick!"

Noni opens her door. "What now?"

I turn into my office and close the door. Gathering my purse I smell smoke, looking up to find Lisette lighting a cigarette. Short of breath, I scatter the toxins with my hand, refusing to pay her any mind.

Breathe. Breathe. Breathe.

Kill. Kill. Kill.

Die. Die. Die.

"Yo," Lisette interrupts. Again, she sparks the lighter. My eyes follow the flame. "Want to torch his car?"

I...I...of course I do. Does she think becoming an adult makes a lady any less cagy? That attribute comes ribbon-wrapped for women no matter the age. I mustn't show it though. I must be a role model. That's what the most assiduous teacher would do in the midst of a painful event. Poise, presentation, perfection – that's the mark of a true lady.

Lisette needs to witness it. Learn from it.

So I say, "Thank you, but no."

Then I flee in a flash. Or is it a hot flash?

The truth is I'm tired. So when I say I'm fleeing I'm merely walking out of the office at the pace of an ignored housewife – the kind who creates crop circles in her community to stay in shape for a husband who no longer gives a fuck in the most literal sense.

Outside, Noni catches my arm. *Do you want to harm yourself? Do you have a plan?* I blow her off and she calls two guards whom I reluctantly allow to escort me to my car. *Have you been drinking? Can you drive? Should we call you a cab?*

I ignore them, proceeding through the parking lot where Mr. Brady beeps at me from his golf cart. Braking behind my car, he steps off, clad in an orange safety vest. He tips the bill of his hat. "Howdy ma'am." Tree branches poke out of a can in the cart's rear.

I sigh. "Let me guess. Noni sent you too?"

He removes work gloves, wiping sweat from his face. "No ma'am. I wanted to say hi."

I put on my bumblebee shades. "Well then. Hello."

He eyes the guards. "Hey guys. Do you mind if I take it from here?"

They hesitate.

"I'm a grown woman. I don't need a babysitter," I urge them.

The broader guard nods to Mr. Brady, tapping the walkie on his belt. "Call if you need assistance."

They leave, and I dig for the keys in my purse.

"Hold on," Mr. Brady says. "What's all this ruckus about? Why were they following you?"

Frustrated, I stick with the truth, hoping it will save time. "Because I'm on the verge of a meltdown. I'm crazy. Wouldn't you agree?"

He reacts as if bullet-holed. "Ma'am?"

"That I'm crazy? I'm batshit crazy?"

"No."

Tossing my purse in the car I collapse in the driver's seat. "Please. You find a single woman just as handicapped as them and that rattles you. You need to fix it. That's why you desire us. And if we turn you down, you instinctively turn to the next one because not a day can pass without a woman requiring your aid. Is that it? Is that what happened with Kitay? I said no. You couldn't handle it. So you ran to the next one?"

He struggles to make sense of it. "Whoa. Wait now. Kitay and I—"

"I don't need specifics."

I close the door and he taps the window. "Ms. Lingers, don't go." The glass quiets his voice. "It hurts me to see you like this. Roll down the window."

"No." I turn on the ignition.

"Ma'am. Please. I'm pleading with you here."

I surrender my hands. "Fine! Let's see you fix it!" Lowering the car window, I dig in my purse for mascara to avoid his eye. "How well do you know Kitay?" I ask, before he can speak. I stroke my lashes with a brush. "Did she bother to tell you who she is? Who she really is?"

"You mean the surgery?" He shrugs it off.

Shocked, I lower my jaw. "It doesn't bother you? She didn't just have her tonsils clipped, you know." On the outer rim of the lot, yellow school buses begin to line up, head to toe.

"Ms. Lingers, with all due respect I only care about the woman she is now."

I sigh, plunking the mascara in my purse. How could he be so agreeable to date a woman who'd been a man? How does one make that large of a leap without knowing what waits on the other side? Is it for the same reason I stand pigeon-toed, peering over the balcony on most nights? Is he so alone to risk everything to find heaven?

I place the car in reverse only to discover Mr. Brady's parked golf cart behind me. "Move your cart," I say.

He bends, his eyes warm. "After we talk."

I slap the steering wheel. "Don't test me."

"Just give me a minute."

"Look. I get it. You're a good man, great even, more gentle than I'll ever be. Is that what you want to hear? I should have said yes to you. I only let bad ones in." I cling to my last scrap of pride. "I was raised to mistake kindness for weakness. I'm not good."

"You are good."

"Not like you. Not like Kitay."

"Kitay?" His eyes widen in amazement. "She idolizes you. She looks to you as a mentor."

I laugh him off. "She sleeps in my class. She doesn't care what I have to say. None of them do. I try to teach them the important things in life...."

"Whose life? Yours?" I gasp, and he calms with a smile, setting his hand on my shoulder. "Or theirs?"

What is this? A challenge?

Well, I don't see anyone else sacrificing their Saturdays for a trio of tactless misfits. So I'm a novice. So what? I design the lessons and priority number one is etiquette. I don't require assistance. I was taught by the best. Poise. Presentation. Perfection. Bev Dear had it down to an art.

"Please. Move your cart," I beseech him.

Hesitating, he tells me to teach them something they can use. "Remember, teaching is a gift," he says. It reminds me of Rose, how she'd tell me love comes in all shapes but the package you expect. Is that what I'm to give them? Love? Can I find it in me? Where is it? Where is it?

Poise. Presentation. Perfection.

Poise. Presentation. Perfection.

I think of Hector, the other men who've wronged me. My heart burns.

I try to be good, but it gets thrown in my face. It's easier to return punches than learn from them. I'm weak.

Poise. Presentation. Perfection.

Poise. Presentation. Perfection.

I think of Bev Dear and belt in. Then setting the car in reverse, I offer no warning. I press the pedal, sending the car backwards.

Mr. Brady jumps back, and I scrape his front bumper before pressing the brake.

What am I doing? Have I truly gone mad? I look out to the world to see Mr. Brady, the way sunshine erases his face. I wonder if he's an angel, if men like him are sent to lift the spirits of those ready to take flight from life. My heartbeat soars when he mounts the cart, providing a clearing.

Minutes later, I'm an abstract on a muddled highway – a woman with the idiosyncrasies of a Kooning. My eyes don't correlate; one tenses as one goes wide, allowing light. My breasts are with me but I fear my nipples are erased. I question, are these breasts for me? Or are they fodder for men? A buffer? A buffet? If I give too much what have I left to bargain? My skin feels smudged, finger-painted by men into a portrait of a monster to which I can't relate.

Oh, I can't think of it. Tomorrow I must teach so I stop at the grocery store to replenish food. At the checkout, a screaming baby pointing at my nose startles me. Is that why I wasn't enough? I'm no longer able to provide Hector a child? I like the thought of kids too. I had one once. Then she left, along with my third husband. I never saw the punch coming. Then or now.

At the register I double over from phantom pains forming in my abdomen. How did I make it this far? If I could teach that...if I could....

Wait....

Perhaps that's what I can offer. I can teach...real life... how to make it alone. That's what I decide as the scent of a baby's soiled diaper hits my nose. I convince myself to stand up, listening to the baby's mother complain after being denied purchasing candy on her food stamp card. The baby's cries follow me to the aisle where the toiletries are kept.

I think of real life. What does a lady do if a husband chooses a mannequin over his marriage? I think of Walter Woody then Ralph Lightwine – the man who primed me to clean his diaper. So you're married? Who gives a shit? I do if I have to clean it up!

I storm the aisle, searching, remembering my third husband 'It' and how his fist found my body on four occasions before finding my belly. I think of Felix, his love, his untimely death. I envision Hector as I find the item that brought me here.

Reaching down for a plunger I lift it to the sky.

*****

The next day a plunger awaits each student in class. Jasper's the first to notice. Full of strawberry jam and biscuits he heads to his desk.

"Is this part of today's lesson?"

"Yes," I say.

"Ms. Lingers you have some dark dreams." He lifts the plunger and flicks its cup.

"What's that? A plunger?" Lisette selects a croissant from the dining table and heads to her seat. "That's straight-up nasty. I'm trying to eat here."

"It's clean," I explain, writing 'good morning' on the board.

"Well. FYI. I don't plunge 'cause I don't poo," Jasper says. He takes a seat. "I hold 'til it shines like a diamond. No man wants to date someone who stinks up the bathroom. It's unladylike."

"Pfft. I'm not clogging myself for no man," Lisette says. I'm relieved to see she's speaking in class again. "I go when I have to go." She casts Jasper a haughty look. "And I don't care who smells it."

Jasper stretches the collar on his feathery white tee shirt, pulling it off one shoulder. "Wonderful. Now we know why you don't have a man."

Lisette scrunches her jaw. "What do you call Cici?"

"A dog."

"Whatever." She blocks his face with a hand. "Go kiss another one of your foster daddies. Then talk to me about dogs."

He flashes her a cold look. "I told you. I'm moving home on Monday. Mom finished her case plan. Got a house."

"Yeah? How long's that gonna last?" He grows quiet, turning away. Lisette huffs before relenting and tenderly squeezes his shoulder. "I love ya Jazz but you gotta stop talking crap. You're just gonna get hurt again."

"It's not crap. She's gonna make it work."

Lisette glances my way with a doubtful look, her lungs expanding with air. Then she lets the fight go, perhaps for Jasper, whose demeanor clouds until she laughs, plucking a feather off his tee. "You're so crazy," she says. "You can't tape on feathers and call yourself a designer. You need a sewing machine."

"I hand stitch."

"You crazy glue."

I silence them, answering a soft knock at the door. On the other side, I find Kitay in an ankle length geranium-print dress with a collar that could double as a bib. Pairing it with a cardigan and glasses she looks like a librarian without the charm.

She lifts her hand. "Last week you lectured me, the *old* me, on classroom appearance." I nod as she reaches in a purse, revealing a red apple. "How about we start over with a new look?"

It's an admirable gesture, a delightful change, if only she hadn't taken it to the next level. Yet this seems to be a pattern for Kitay – living life in the extremes. Perhaps that's my task, teaching her how to blend. She smiles, handing me the apple. I offer thanks and wave her inside.

"Wait. I need to tell you something." Her lips curl into a smile. "I want you to be the first to know about my date since you helped me." She blushes, a tooth finding her lip. "I kissed him."

"Who?"

She laughs. "Mr. Brady. That's who."

"Oh." I act as if the revelation is neither here nor there. Though inside, the oven turns on low broil.

"He started it," she whispers. "I just opened my mouth."

My head feels heavy, the blood rushing in. I should be happy for Kitay but I can't shake the idea that I missed out. What if I'd given Mr. Brady a chance? Would it have worked? Oh, I'm being foolish. Here I am, ready to teach that one can make it alone, at least until the love is right. But can I model it?

"I'm happy you had a good time," I say, urging her inside. "Class is starting. You can tell me about your night out later."

She breezes past me, taking a biscuit. "Oh, we didn't go out. I cooked." She waves to the others. "Hey y'all."

I close the door, following behind. "Cooked? On a first date?"

"Mhhhm." She proudly strolls to her desk with her head held high. "I made ma's favorite recipe, Southern Apple Butter Brisket and all the fixins." She sits, reaching for the plunger and waves it like a wand before turning solemn. "He said he liked it, but I don't know. Ma says I don't make a very good cook. She never did like me in the kitchen. Felt that was a woman's place." Reflecting she becomes anxious. "Oh Dee. I have to find a job. Fast. I'm running out of time. You'll help me, right?"

"Girl please," Lisette interjects. "She might need to find herself a job. You should see what she did to the janitor's golf cart at school yesterday." She plays Zorro with her plunger. "Counselor gone wild!"

"Stop that," I insist. "Mr. Brady parked his cart behind me. I bumped into it."

"Bumped?" Lisette smirks. "Try crashed."

Kitay's hand falls to her throat. "He didn't say anything about that on our date."

"My friend Dina said Ms. Lingers tried to run that skinny white man over," Lisette says, leaning into me. "She said you're one crazy puta."

"Well, Dina is a liar."

"No. Dina don't lie. Not to me."

"You really tried to run him over?" Jasper asks.

"Not entirely."

"That was right after she yelled at Principal Rivera. I heard it," Lisette adds. "She hollered like a ho."

"A ho?" Kitay questions.

"Like she was flagging down Hondas in Homestead."

"That's it!" I state. "I will NOT be compared to a...."

"What made you scream?" Jasper asks.

"Tell 'em," Lisette says, sitting there with a wicked grin like she's never lost control. Little does she know momentary lapses of reason arrive more frequently with each passing year, each passing man. I can't just batter my stomach with baked goods each time I'm scorned. I scream because mewling doesn't work. That's why these whimpers turn to wails. So I can be heard.

"I screamed," I begin, standing directly before the class. I stall, thinking of Hector and Miss Robb making love. The thought saturates my head like mucus. I can't erase the thought. So I can't have a baby. What else does he want? My blood? Have it! He's not special. I couldn't have a baby even when I could.

"Are you ok?" Kitay asks.

The pressure builds. I can't stay grounded with my head flying.

I need to move, move!

Noting a plunger leaning against the chalkboard I take a breath and reach for it. It feels powerful in my hand, a scepter to separate the muck from the men. I raise it. "I screamed because I can!" I declare. "Because I'm a woman who's had enough!"

The class sits captivated, Lisette the first to speak.

"Ok. Crazy train done left the station. Can we go now?"

Kitay blinks, fearfully. "Ms. Lingers. Sorry to ask, but are you feeling ok? I can get the thermometer."

"No need. I'm glorious. Perfectly grand." I wave the plunger at the heavens. "Did you hear that world? You can collapse on my face but you can never count me out because I'm a woman. A lady!" I punch the sky and Jasper giggles.

I gaze at him and he shields his mouth. "Do you find this humorous?" I ask. "Aren't you here for the same reason? To succeed?" The class stirs. "Well, you better learn to be vocal, because that's part of it." Lifting the plunger high, I urge them to follow. "Go on. Raise those plungers! Scream!"

"Hell no," Lisette says. "Like mama said. I don't feed crazy 'cause I know it will grow a belly and eat me."

Jasper smacks her arms. "Give her a chance." He lifts his plunger, emitting a squeak.

Kitay follows but her arm goes limp. "I've never been much of a screamer. I laugh like a loon but I can't scream."

"Try!" I urge.

"Aaa...aaa...aah," she strains.

Jasper emits a Minnie Mouse yelp before apologizing.

Lisette crosses her arms. "Y'all need to get laid. That's what this is about."

I relax my plunger. "Oh, this is useless. No wonder why men walk all over us. Good girls don't say peep. Peeps send men packing. Seen but not heard. Isn't that what you're taught?"

"Mr. Brady and I talked on our date," Kitay replies.

"Yes. *After* you cooked him dinner." Plunger to palm, I advance to her desk. "I'm afraid to ask what else you offered."

"Nothing!" I needle her with my eyes 'til the lie bursts. "Fine. I gave him a foot rub. But he works hard."

"Aha!" I clear my throat with a laugh. "So to summarize your first date, you made him dinner *and* rubbed his feet." Jasper covers his mouth in disbelief. "In return, what did he do for you?"

Kitay considers the question, a car alarm interrupting the silence from the street. She puffs her chest. "He complimented my brisket." Satisfied, she removes her glasses to polish the lenses. "And he kissed me."

Jasper gushes. "That's sweet."

I shake my head. "Oh Kitay from Arcadia. You don't get it. You really don't get it. You're going to require hours of catch up." Her face flushes and I return to the board. "As for the rest of you, are you equally challenged on the subject of men?"

Jasper extends his bottom lip sideways. "Um. I've never dated one. At least one that's consented." He fidgets, picking at his shirt. "Pathetic. I know." He stalls. "I've done... other things."

Lisette laughs. "Who are you kidding? You've done *everything*."

He shrugs, biting his finger. "So? I'm marketable."

She furrows her brows. "That doesn't mean you have to offer your body to anyone with money."

"Lisette, how about you?" I ask. "What's your experience with men?"

"I have no problem with them. I know what I like and how to get it. That's all I need to know."

"So you're a scholar? Splendid." An idea forms. I take to the board. "Then you should lead the conversation on how to...." I take a moment to ponder how to frame it. "How to survive womanhood." I write it in large letters and clap. "Ok class. Put away your plungers, open your journals and take this down. Today, I'm teaching a lesson one can't find in an etiquette book."

Writing, Lisette raises her hand. "You mean the womanhood or the woman hood? 'Cause I don't know about survivin' in a white ladies' world, but down here the 'Ricans and the rest, we live in the woman hood. It's the space that separates us."

"Two words?" I question.

"Mhm."

I erase the board, making the correction. "How to survive the woman *hood*. There. That's a good place to start." I clean the chalk from my fingers, wiping my hands together. "Now, we celebrate." To keep from losing momentum, I allow no time for a response. "Everyone up." I briskly head to the bar. "Always be on your toes. That's the first lesson of the day. Are you writing this down?" Glancing back, I see a line has formed, Jasper in front. Taking down a note, Kitay steps on his heel.

"Oops. Sorry." She pats his back.

"That's lesson two!" I exclaim. Leaving the class at the stools I swing behind the bar. "No apologies. Women have engaged in that behavior for centuries. In return we earn seventy-seven cents to every dollar compared to a man. Does that mean we're twenty-three percent less effective in the workplace? Is that right? I've never been good with numbers."

"Twenty-three percent. Correct," Kitay says.

"Thank you." I motion for them to sit.

Lisette twists her stool until her back faces Kitay. "How about the bearded ladies, the she-men like...." She motions to Kitay, wrinkling her lips. "Chicks with cojones. How much do they make?"

"I do NOT have cojones," Kitay protests.

"You did," Lisette returns. "You and your freaky self."

"Lisey, you're the one dressed like a boy," Jasper says, eyeing her baggy tee and jeans combo. Lisette waves him away as if he were little more than a fly.

"I'm transgendered," Kitay affirms.

"You're a freak," Lisette says.

Resting her large hands on the bar top, Kitay maintains her poise. "Well, maybe to you, but I don't see a freak when I look into the mirror. And I only have to answer to myself and...." She braces to resist shaking. "God."

"Why are you talkin' about God? If He wanted you to be a chica, He would have made you one."

"Not if He wanted me to meet you."

Lisette tilts her head, concocting a face that appears unsure whether or not to be offended. "What's that mean?"

"That it's time for a drink," I interrupt. I set a frosted wine glass in Kitay's hand. "We don't have time for this drivel. That's the problem with women. We're always fighting, pulling each other down, focused on labels." I offer Kitay a choice, holding up two wine bottles. "Red or white?"

"Huh?"

"The wine. Red or white?"

"Golly. Isn't it early for that?"

"Not if I have to put up with you. Which is it?"

She caves. "White."

I smile, helping myself to a glass as well.

"Hey, you two can't drink in front of us," Lisette says.

"Yeah. Not fair," Jasper adds.

"Life's not fair," I refute, tapping Jasper's journal. "Back to your notes."

"What are you, some kind of alcoholic?" Lisette asks.

"Hardly. I'm merely modeling that's it all right for an adult to have a drink without it being a sin or an issue. Teens like you need to witness that so you find a more clever way to rebel than turning into lushes."

Lisette's pupils make a diagonal upwards leap to deliberate on the thought. I gift her and Jasper bottles of sparkling water in the hope that it will quiet them. After all, I don't know if I believe what I just said either. It merely sounded like a reasonable enough excuse for a morning cocktail. Cheers!

"As I was saying, we women are often our own worst enemies," I continue. "The question is when will we take ownership and admit that our own behavior is the root of our biggest problem?"

"What problem?" Lisette asks.

"Courtship." She seems puzzled. "You see, when women allow men to treat them in a damaging way the remaining female population is adversely affected as well. So what have we learned? Being easy is contagious." Jasper flushes, chewing the tip of his pen. "You. Star that in your notes."

He giggles, jotting it down. "Easy. Contagious. Done!"

"Good. Let's give an example." I take a sip of wine, as Lisette studies me with newfound interest. "Let's look at the lost college girls, binge drinking themselves into submission for men who want nothing more than a hook up. There's no date, no dinner, no intimacy. There's simply cheap beer and an unflattering bop in the fraternity house later that night."

"That doesn't sound bad. Even better if he's cute," Kitay announces.

I cast her a critical eye and she hushes. "So why do these girls do it?" I ask. "Well, because their friends do it, and the good girls don't want to sit home alone. They deserve fun too. So they drink themselves into stupors where kissing beer-faced behemoths isn't so awful, even if the boys don't respect them enough to buy dinner. So you see, it's not entirely the man's fault. Rather, it's the woman's fault for lowering her standards. Men are crafty. They know if one woman won't agree, six will."

Lisette shrugs. "So girls like to get their groove on. What do you want them to do? Stick a plunger in it? Girls have needs." She gives Jasper a high five.

"Abstinence isn't a realistic option for everyone. I understand that," I state. "But why not save yourself for a man who's willing to work for it?"

"Because we're horny," she says.

"Yes, but what's wrong with being selective? Why not liken your vagina to the Ivy League?"

Disturbed, Lisette shuts her journal. "Are you already drunk? Look around. We're fighting to graduate with GEDs. What do we care about the Ivy League? We don't go to college or drink no fancy water." She swats at her drink. "I can't even afford a tutor. How am I gonna go to college?"

"You can get financial aid," Jasper suggests.

"Yeah, 'cause my grades are so good. I'd sure they'd give me a scholarship." Her face takes a solemn turn, as if she's considered what could be out there if she applied herself, if she had the courage to take the necessary steps. "Who's gonna care for my family while I'm trying to take care of me?" she asks. She cuts me off before I get in a word. "I don't need to sit here and be lectured about men. I know they're runners. I know what they're worth."

"But the question is what are you worth?" I ask. Heading to the chalkboard I locate a plunger. "It's a simple question. What does your presentation say about you? The way you walk, talk and dress." I swing the plunger, slashing the air. "These are the tools a woman has in this world. Whether a lady has pennies or thousands she should always look like she's worth a million bucks." I click my heels. "Now, gather your plungers. We're going on a field trip."

*****

Ten minutes later, I lead the class on a brisk walk along the business fronts on Lincoln Road where the heavy sun brightens the sidewalk, creating room for a crowd of morning joggers and shoppers – a mix of well-tanned locals and tourists speaking all tongues.

"Do we have to carry these hideous things?" Lisette asks, falling behind. She uses the rest of us as human shields.

I proudly lift my plunger, bypassing outside brunch patrons under veils of black umbrellas. They pay little heed, immersed in eating and conversing on their phones. "We carry the plunger as a symbol of strength, to separate the muck from the men," I declare. "Now, raise it with pride!"

"I-don't-know-you," Lisette says, hiding her face. Still, I don't stir from my task of making a classroom out of the world. I charge forward, smiling at a pair of swanky Asian ladies beginning cocktail hour early with mojitos.

Following my lead, Jasper uses his plunger to scissor the sky. "C'mon. It's fun," he says, nudging Lisette. "Catch up."

"You need to stop hitting the crack pipe. It's straight up embarrassing, the way you're acting. Look at everyone lookin' at us."

"Who cares?" He laughs, before reminding her of the payoff. "She's buying us clothes." He performs a little jump. "Plunge away!"

"Look! I applied for a job here," Kitay exclaims, passing a dress boutique. In the window, three pencil thin mannequins, shoulders forward, pose with their hands on their hips. Dressed in teal pencil skirts they appear alien-like with large oval heads. "I never did get a call back, not even after I baked ginger snaps for the manager," Kitay reveals. "Back in Arcadia, no one can resist my award-winning ginger snaps. Even ma likes them and she doesn't like anything I cook. Ooh, I'll be a shop girl yet!"

"A shop girl?" Jasper asks. Two male bicyclists brake for us as we cross an intersection. "I should've known you're a fashionista with your ability to play with style. Where have you worked? Gucci? Prada?"

"Heavens no. Better. Dottie's." Jasper does a double

take, scratching his chin. "Now, I admit. It's just a little clothing company with stores in Arcadia and Palatka, but we could make the entire Brady Bunch shine on less than ten bucks." Eyeing a French shoe boutique with a ballerina mannequin in the window display, Kitay quiets her voice, reflecting. "We don't have emerald slippers. It's just plain, simple clothes for simple folks. Nothing like...."

"This?" I interrupt, motioning to a store with Greek pillars at the entrance. Beyond the windows, blue lights cast an icy sheen on the sparsely draped clothing racks. Lining up to see inside, the class becomes quiet except for Lisette who spits her gum, waking a disheveled man with a guitar. Sitting near the store entrance, guitar case open, he invites donations.

Lisette places her nose on the store window. "I don't know what I'm doing here. These clothes are for rich people," she protests.

"I can't even afford the air in there," Jasper says.

"Never mind that," I assure them. "There's no price tag on self-worth. The way one dresses speaks volumes. Take this street person." Strumming his guitar he cocks an ear. "What does that rainbow tie-dye shirt say about him?"

"He's colorful?" Kitay suggests.

"Color blind?" Jasper surmises.

"He smokes killer weed," Lisette adds.

Tuning his guitar, the man nods in agreement.

"Yes. Well. Ahem." I clear my throat. "Perhaps all of the above. Now look at me. My maxi dress is simple, white, clean. It's modern, yet hints at the '50s due to the flared bottom. It says, yes, I'll be at that high society mixer. I'm elegant and sophisticated. But I'm also fun. Flirty."

"Wow," Kitay marvels. "That dress says a lot."

Lisette smirks. "All I hear it say is ho, ho, ho."

Kitay giggles, playfully poking Lisette. "You think she looks like Santa?"

Lisette ogles her in disbelief – her lips shuddering as if she had the flu. "No boy-girl! That's not what I mean." She groans. "And don't touch me. I don't want people thinking I know you."

"Fine, but I'm not a boy-girl."

"Ok. She-man."

"Enough," I say. "Let's head inside. It's a jump, but be civilized."

"Or?" Lisette challenges.

I aim the plunger at her chin. "Or I plunge the blockage in your brain that causes you to be argumentative when faced with a challenge." Jasper hides a grin. "We can't afford a weak link."

"I ain't weak," she says.

"Ain't? Is that what you said?" I laugh. "I'll have you know, bad grammar is the first sign of weakness. It implies a lack of education, a deficiency in discipline. Is that what you want? To be a dullard? Limiting one's vocabulary lends hand to laziness."

Lisette lifts her chin. "Fine. I'm *not* weak. Is that better?"

"Yes. Now, zip that lip until I school you on proper speech."

"Whatever. I don't know why you're doing all of this," she mutters.

I understand her penchant for mistrust. I ask myself – am I truly helping anyway or am I being selfish, fixing the flaws of others that Bev Dear once found in me? I like to believe I'm better than that, that I can be selfless. I need to know there's still a girl inside me who can save the world or at least a few people in it. Lisette and I are no different, just H2O drops, challenged to keep up our numbers so we don't reduce ourselves to the life of a HO.

Perhaps someday we can help each other swim.

I grasp the glass door handle leading into the boutique and Jasper grabs my arm. "Shouldn't we wait for a man to open it for us?" he asks. "Isn't that what we want? Chivalry?"

"Ah. Trick question," I respond. "The answer is yes, but at what price?"

Scribbling in their journals the students grapple with the question, and we stall in hope that a man will open the door, promoting change. However, change like money is earned with time and five minutes later we're no more than four lame ducks standing in the same place. One would think that of the two male employees inside one would demonstrate the decency to wander to the door and open it, but each appears to be the sleek, young, androgynous sort with no regard for anything beyond a reflection. Even the street musician fails to help, falling back asleep.

"Oh phooey. This is the twenty-first century," Kitay says. "Why wait for a man to do something we can do for ourselves?" Gripping the handle, she jerks open the door, holding it for Jasper and Lisette who shrug and head inside. "You're not mad, are you?" she questions, as I follow in the rear.

"No. I like to see a woman take a risk."

She blushes. "You think I could be a real woman? A lady?"

I grant her a wink. "You're off to a fine start. Though we still have to work on your presentation."

She paws at her purple cardigan. "I was just toning it down. Like you said." Lisette and Jasper scour the store trailed by concerned clerks. "Is it that bad?"

"It's a...work in progress, but every artist begins with one stroke." I help remove her glasses, grinning. "Let's paint you into a portrait of a lady with a job." Snapping my finger, I call over a store clerk.

Minutes later Kitay stands before me in an off-the-shoulder white scoop top and tiger-print skirt looking like fashion gold.

Her fingers dance at her sides, as if being dipped in fire. "So what do you think?"

"Turn around. Show it off."

She chews her lip, circling in front of a mirror with restrained excitement. "I really like it, but maybe we should try something else." Moments earlier in the fitting room she was going on about being a country gal who could feed every pig in Arcadia with the price of this one little pencil skirt. *Do they carry one that doesn't write? Wouldn't that be cheaper?* It's the first hard laugh I've had in some time. Still, I can tell she continues to be plagued by the cost. "There are so many better reasons to spend this type of money. Causes.

Charities."

I stand, approaching her from behind. "Well right now I can't think of a better cause than you. You're so giving. You deserve a little charity too." I pat her back. "You look stunning."

She glows, eyeing me in the mirror. "You think so?"

"I know it."

She blushes. "All right. I'll get it, but I promise I'm going to pay you back real soon, right after I get a job."

"That's not necessary. It's a gift." Suddenly, I spy Jasper from the corner of my eye. Staring into a full-length mirror, he adjusts the collar on a bright blue polo shirt. "Fabulous," I say. "What about shoes? Shoes to fit the shirt, a belt to fit the shoes. I want more color, more vision, more art."

Jasper bounces between two salesmen. Flattering him with attention and praise they offer additional options. "Thank you, but I just need the one," he says. "Grab a few," I call.

"But where am I gonna fit them all? I don't have closet space like you, Ms. Lingers."

"Nonsense," I say. He removes his polo to try on a new shirt, revealing his skinny torso. "Clothes can be placed anywhere. One can even hang special pieces on the wall like a portrait in the name of art." A young salesman with blond surfer bangs hands Jasper a sea green tee. As he dons it, I note a scar under his left arm that wraps around his upper back like a hook. "Jasper, what's that?" I ask. "That thing beneath your arm?"

Perfecting his look he questions the man assisting him. Does the tee come in red? Does the store carry tees with swoop necks or asymmetrical cuts?

"He doesn't like to talk about it," Lisette says. Coming up from behind she keeps a low voice. "That's why he's back in Miami. There was a car wreck when he was trying to run...."

Jasper shakes loose from his helpers. "Lisey, what are you whispering over there?"

She stammers, and I quickly react. "I was asking why she has yet to try on a dress."

He tilts his head and sighs, as if I should know. "Because Cici wants her to look like a boy."

"It's my decision," she snaps. "Fancy clothes get a girl in trouble." She sifts through a rack of red dresses. "I don't want to look like a ho." She nods to Kitay in disgust. "Like she-man over there in her skirt."

"Hey! I don't look like a ho!" Kitay defends. A salesman offers her a pair of silver hoop earrings, holding them up to her ears.

Lisette laughs. "You're right. You ain't got enough booty to be a ho. All you got are crack-baby legs holding up a tomato." Growing anxious, Kitay pats at her rear. "Let me guess. You had your real butt removed too?"

Trembling, Kitay points her finger in protest. "You take that back."

"No."

"Yes."

"I don't take nothing back," Lisette says, approaching Kitay. The salesmen scatter. Nostrils flaring, Lisette is barely the height of Kitay's chest. "I say what I want when I want."

"So you're always a...." Kitay hesitates, holding her ground. "Oh, nevermind."

"No. You had something to say, she-man. Say it."

Frustrated, Kitay takes a languished breath, as if exhausted from having to defend herself over the same matter before. A dash of sadness washes across her face. Another day. Another fight. Clearing her throat, she accepts the challenge. "Why do you poke so much?" she asks. "To make sure no one pokes at you first?" Intrigued, Lisette holds her ground in quiet disbelief. "Well I'll tell you, I've been beaten down by hillbillies, rednecks, and shit kickers twice the size of you. I'm not afraid of your horse crap, missy." Kitay proudly lifts her chin. "I won't be scratchy in my skin because people like you don't approve. If you don't care for the woman I am, don't look. Lesson two. No apologies. Isn't that right, Ms. Lingers?"

I fervently blink, managing a "yes."

Pleased, Kitay ventures closer to Lisette. "What have *you* learned in class?" Tightlipped, Lisette shrugs. "Like I guessed, a whole haystack of nothing." Taking a red dress from the rack Kitay drapes it across Lisette's chest. "Stop fighting. Try it on. Without the approval of a man, try it on because you approve."

Lisette wrinkles her nose, turning to Jasper, who nods in encouragement. "She's right Lisey," he says. "You're beautiful. It's ok to let more people see it than Cici."

She grumbles, snatching the garment and darting into the dressing room. Moments later she emerges, standing before the jury of Kitay, Jasper, and me. A hand to each hip, she blows a strand of hair from her eyes, balancing herself on a pair of heels. Cinched with a ribbon the sparkly dress molds to her tiny frame. "Happy?" she asks.

"Thrilled," I return, with Kitay and Jasper smiling in agreement. "Now we can finally pimp you out. How do you say it? Like a good ho?"

She stomps on one heel. "That's not funny."

Kitay and Jasper double over in laughter.

"Wait. Wait. I need to document this," Jasper says, taking her picture with his phone. "People are going to freak. You're on fire. Like neon hot."

"Jasper!" She clenches her teeth before resigning into a smile.

"You're gonna love it. I have a new app that can smooth out the blemishes on a pizza," he teases.

"Blemishes?" Her eyes light with fire. "Boy, what are you talking about?"

"Stop that. She has beautiful skin," Kitay attests.

Lisette grants her a suspicious glance before conceding with a clipped grin. "Thanks." She shoots me an inquisitive look, suddenly impatient. "So. You got me dressed up. Now what?"

CHAPTER 9

MINUTES LATER WE line up shoulder to shoulder on Lincoln Road set to strut our new fashions together with Miami's international elite. Alongside Scandinavian camera-toting tourists and high-legged models, we add to the pulse of cutting edge fashion, paired with plungers raised high to the sky.

To mark the moment I suggest linking arms. Everyone does but Lisette who yells Spanish obscenities and jerks away her body when Kitay latches onto her elbow. The abrupt gesture breaks the chain, sending Kitay barreling into a tall, elegant woman leaving a luxury pet shop.

Apologizing profusely, Kitay bends to pet the woman's English Shepherd. "What a beautiful animal," she says before the lady tugs the dog away in a snit. Kitay stands, tearing up.

"Oh dear. What now?" I inquire.

"I miss my babies," she shares. "Taser and Tacky."

"They're at the condo. You'll see them in a little bit."

She slightly calms as I glance down the white sidewalk to discover a shade of red – not in a fabric of clothing but in the color of hair. It's Miss Robb in a metallic shift dress. She holds the hand of Hector.

I freeze.

Oh, why does winter set in my heart on the warmest of fall days? One would think I'd be over him, that Hector would've died in my mind after I discovered he might be the father of Miss Robb's baby. How could he have an affair with another woman while sleeping with me? Wasn't I enough? I felt enough. So I never had the talk with him about refraining from sexual acts with others while pearl diving in my privates. Certain things go without saying, like the fact I still have feelings for him. That's an easy enough read, with my heart racing and sweat forming at my temples. I may be too old to carry his baby, but I'm still good. It radiates inside me like a small glimmering orb. I can't let him get the best of me. Flustered, I open the door to the pet store, urging the class inside.

"You want to go in the pet shop?" Kitay questions.

"Of course. I love animals. Dogs. Cats. Rats. They're so playful and...furry." I point to a window poster of a Dalmatian eating a carrot. "Look! Organic food for Taser. A healthy dog is a happy one. Let's go!" I take the lead.

Inside, caged hamsters spin erratically on silver wheels and the scent of minty canine shampoo fills my nose from the grooming section. An Asian female with a buzz cut rings up customers.

Allowing the others time to mill about I remain by the window, pretending to be intrigued by animal art – the cartoon imagery of a Boxer in an Armani suit and a Basset Hound in a black corset. Still, my eye is on the outside.

First, I see Miss Robb's red hair. Then I simply see red. Is that the effect of blood rushing to the eyes? Temporary blindness? Or had I been blind all along? Hector would never consider holding my hand in public.

"Check it out, Ms. Lingers," Jasper calls. At the grooming table, he watches a tall man trim the mane of a Lhasa Apso. I smile, attempting to lighten my sullen mood, but it won't clover the dirt. All I see is Miss Robb taking my lover. I must realign. Who needs love, a family? Do I need it all to be happy, everything I'm programmed to think I need? A husband. Kids. Perhaps a full house isn't in the cards for me. No matter how much I desire it, no matter how much I try to obtain it, the other girls always gets the....

"GUY! No!" a female customer yells. Running with a leash she chases a small, fluffy white dog barking and racing toward a large muzzled Doberman. The bigger dog tugs its male owner away from the register. The white dog nips at the Doberman's leg, causing a stir.

The cashier calls on the man grooming the Lhaso

120

Apso. "We need help!"

Kitay grabs a bone from the doggy snack bar and squats. "No big deal," she says. "They're making introductions." She calmly extends a hand. "Hey little one, like cookies?" The white dog barks then approaches, the treat disappearing in one bite. "See? No worries."

The owner leashes him. "Thank you. He's a master at escaping. He needs a harness."

"Aisle four," the groomer says, approaching. She thanks him, heading in that direction. He helps Kitay to stand. "You hurt?" he asks, examining her body. His accent is foreign, Scottish.

"I wasn't attacked," she explains. "It was just an excitable little dog."

I'm reminded of Taser wrecking my house and mutter, "Little *monster* is more like it."

The two turn, the groomer speaking first. "Excuse me?"

What? Must I explain myself? The man wears jeweled jeans and white wingtips to shampoo dogs so surely he has a sense of humor. So I made a joke. Is that a crime? I smile awkwardly, noting the disparaging looks of nearby shoppers. "I said—"

"You don't like dogs?" he asks.

"What? No! She loves dogs," Kitay gushes – too fast to be credible.

"Right. Love dogs," I agree before whispering, "from a distance."

The dog groomer tilts his head, gazing upon me with intrigue as if to him – a man gifted with no wrinkles but seemingly around my age – a brazen woman is a beguiling challenge. A smile spreads, lifting his handlebar mustache. His teeth shine bright as his waxed head. "Maybe you just haven't met the right one," he says.

I consider it, only to be reminded of my barking cat Flippy, how he'd purr me to sleep, curling his furry black body around my neck. That's more than I can say of Hector who'd take a crack at my toilet then vanish before the crack of dawn.

I turn to see Hector in the pet store window, stopping to peer inside.

I begin to ramble. "I prefer cats, barking. Barking cats."

The groomer, Wes – as indicated on his blue nametag – eyes me peculiarly. I imagine how crazy I must look, holding a plunger and talking of cats that bark. It's Hector's fault. He has me mad. Why would he be peeking into a pet shop? He has no interest in a pet that doesn't come in the form of a woman half his age. He can barely take care of himself; that's why he needed me. But now, he has her. I look again. He's gone. I pull it together, rambling about Flippy, how I'd read him the newspaper. "He liked the arts section, especially theater reviews."

Wes perks up, shifting his footing. "Theater?"

Jasper calls my name. Grateful for the distraction, I turn to view the top of his head by the aquariums. "Come look. They have baby water turtles!" he says.

Kitay brightens. "I love water turtles!"

I wince. "Those are the smelly ones, right?"

She tugs my hand toward them, leading me down an aisle of bubbling fish tanks with bright swimmers.

"You should get them," Jasper tells Lisette. I peer over his shoulder to view two tiny turtles airing their brown shells on a plastic log. The tank is lined with red pebbles. "They need a mom," he says.

"I got enough to feed," Lisette replies. "They're ugly anyway. Look at them, thinking they're hard and shit."

"Noooo! They're sweet," Jasper insists.

"I'd take them," Kitay says. "But Taser and Tacky take up all my time. Baby turtles need lots of attention."

Jasper cranes his neck. "Ms. Lingers?"

"Oh no. We won't have any talk of that."

"Why not? You don't have a family."

Taking the unsuspected hit, the wind leaves me. I grow unsteady, leaning into the tank for a closer view. A family? Me? Once, that came in the form of Bev Dear offering to pay a driver to take me to lunch. Father was on business. I settled for a phone call 'til settling became a habit. Father was the first in a line of men.

But I'll never cheat. I'll never make you change a diaper. I'll never hit you. It was accident. You never wanted a baby anyway.

"But, but," I repeat, staring at the turtles. Still as glass, they seem peaceful, open eyed, ready for the world simply by being together. I angle further, eager to learn their shelled secret, only to bump my head on the glass. Humiliated, I run off.

Oh Dee, think of the bulls, the horns, the pricks. That's what's behind you. Don't look back. But I do, turning to see the troubled expressions of the class, the confusion. Still, what of those who look down from heaven? Daughter, you know I don't believe in apologies but as Kitay would say, this is between us gals. I'm sorry. I should have left him. I believed that having you, a piece of him growing inside of me, would change him, us, for the better. I should have known. I've never been good with kids or numbers. I've made a million mistakes but the one I count is you.

That's why I keep pushing, another day, another step. I hope the crumbs will add up; I'll find a way home. I could have been a good mother. Believe. Even if it seems like I'm always running away I'm merely chasing after you. That's why I scream, so you'll hear me all the way from heaven. I believe in magic. I have to. That outside, beyond the pet shop door you'll be waiting. I've seen your face so many times in the park, in traffic, at night, in the stars. I'm not crazy. You're out there. I know it. That's why I go on when everything inside tells me to....

"Stop!" Kitay says. She grips my shoulder, spinning me like a sun-warped record before I exit. "Where are you going?"

"I'm out of time."

She clutches her plunger to her chest. "For what?"

"A family!" I flush, hiding my face. Damn! Damn! Damn! What is it about this woman that makes it seem safe to spit information others have whetted their lips on, only to use against me later? "Oh, I'm a fool!"

"Don't say that. You can have a family. There's still time."

I dry a tear, ashamed. "You're just being kind. It's your nature. It's all you know to do."

"No. I'm being honest. Anyone can have a family."

"Not me. I'm too old. I don't know where to look, how to begin."

"That's why you have me," she says, taking my hand. Shushing my protests she returns me to the turtles where Lisette and Jasper clear space for me. It's odd to see them quiet, Lisette declining an incoming phone call to hear Kitay speak. "Remember, family is what you make it," Kitay says. "Now, it might not be a nuclear family, but who wants a family that's set to explode? You need something with a little pig in its poop. That way you don't go expecting life to be so clean." She points to a green sticker fixed to the top of the turtle aquarium. Earlier I'd missed it or didn't care to read. *Desperation! Turtles need good home! Must go!* "See?" she says. "Sometimes family chooses you."

"An employee donated them," Wes explains, approaching from behind. "She moved up north to care for her mother. She couldn't take them."

I look north myself, up to the ceiling, taking in the stenciled clouds, dogs and cats wearing halos, playing harps. It's silly but whimsical, better than facing the class whose eyes drip with disillusionment in the aftermath of my weakened state. I can't let them down. I won't. Therefore, I make a bold leap with a simple 'I do.' Heaven knows I've said it to enough men. Why not turtles? Thrilled about the purchase Wes agrees to a free delivery later in the day.

*****

Back in the classroom I ensure it's business as usual, setting a balled up white tube sock on each desk. "Lesson three. Semantics."

Lisette raises her hand. "Why do you have to use such big words?"

I sigh, writing on the board. "In simple terms, I'll no longer accept another ain't, yo or whateva in class." I draw a large X, turning with a grin. "Proper speech is paramount, particularly in the workforce. But it helps with personal relations as well. If we better ourselves we inherently better those around us."

"And if we slip?" Lisette tests, as the others write.

"You eat the sock."

She sticks up her nose. "Ew! I'm not sticking that nasty thing in my mouth. That's not ethical."

"What's unethical about it?"

"It's unsanitary, just like this smelly 'ole thing." She kicks the plunger under her desk.

Jasper smiles. "Relax Lisey. You've gagged on worse." He bobs for the sock on his desk as if it were an apple. "She's just making learning fun. Try it."

Kitay follows, choking. "Aah!" She spits it on the desk. "Is that what a man tastes like?"

Jasper ponders the question. "Kind of. It's sweaty like that, but a tad more salty." He reconsiders it, becoming scientific. "It has a musky taste. It's spicy, you know, like the chili powder at Taco Bell."

Gagging, Lisette covers her mouth. "What kind of men have you been with? If they taste like that you better watch out for an infection."

Kitay casually flaps her wrist, boasting. "Oh, I get UTIs all the time. That's not a big deal. It's part of having a vagina."

Lisette breaks into laughter. "Girl, you're a trip."

"What?"

"I bet you get UTIs just to prove you *have* a vagina, taking yourself to the doctor so he can see it." She fans her face, giggling.

"All right. That's enough. Settle down," I say, sensing the class is too tired to hold a useful conversation. I surrender my arms, erasing the board. "Class is dismissed. See you next week."

The students gather their belongings and I check the text messages on my phone. I have three from Hector.

I know.

Things r not what they seem.

Luv u.

Love me? Love me?

He can't even spell it right I tell myself, staring at the text. Why do I waste time straining to find meaning in the abstract, treating each word as if it's a work of art? That's the thing about texts – they leave a lady a million ways to read into one wily sentiment. It's a blind ball game – no body language, no fair pitch, just a curveball to ensure she loses balance.

"Hey. Got a minute?" Lisette asks.

I take breath, lowering the phone. "Yes. How can I help you?"

She signals Jasper to leave and plunger to the sky he heads out, calling for Kitay who stalls, gathering her books.

Lisette squeezes the sock in her hand. "You know I wrecked Cici's scooter." Her voice trails and she lowers her eyes. "I need a ride home."

"I'll give you one," I smile and agree, satisfied to finally get an admission. Could this be the first sign of progress? Lisette tests a toe while the waters are warm.

"I guess your man did you wrong too?" She eyes my phone and I stiffen. "Principal Rivera?"

"I...." How does she know? It doesn't make sense even though it's nice to have her initiating conversation. Stalling at her desk, Kitay lifts an ear.

"I was there," Lisette says. "At school. That's why you screamed. You were coming out of his office. I know that type of anger. He wronged you."

So she's right. That doesn't mean she needs to know the thick of it. She's a kid, a student – learning of my unfavorable antics would only justify her hostile behavior toward Cici. I tether my tongue to my cheek. "I shouldn't be speaking to you about this," I say. Yet the instant the words leave my mouth they seem to create a distance between us. The damage lies in the manner her lips shift, sealing away her remaining thoughts. Fearing another setback I quickly speak. "He acted in a way which I let him. Like I taught you in class, a man can only take what a woman is willing to give. I allowed too much." I shake her gaze, wondering if I should

126

tell her all of this and if I believe it myself. "That's why I want you to have an education. A man can never take that. No one can."

"But he *can* take you to the symphony," Kitay interrupts, lifting the mood. She'd been so quiet I'd forgotten she was there. She places her belongings in a bag. "That's where Mr. Brady's taking me tonight. Did you know he plays the violin?"

I forfeit a smile. "No."

"Oh yes. He's quite the magician, full of tricks."

"Remind me of that when he slices you in two."

She chuckles. "Now you stop. The only thing he'll be slicing is some old-fashioned Kitty Litter Cake." She holds her heart, glowing. "That is, after he takes me to the Gusman Center. He got us tickets to the Miami Symphony Orchestra. Can you believe it? The closest thing I've come to a symphony is that Bugs Bunny cartoon, that one where he tries to kill the fly but kills the orchestra people instead." She laughs, caging it when she realizes no one's following. "Ms. Lingers, you've been to the symphony. Is it like the cartoon?"

The cartoon? Is this woman for real? Better yet, is Hector when he tells me he loves me but has never demonstrated an ounce of it? Well, I'd love to immerse myself in this bout of idiotic banter but first I must realign my spine to deal with the stress.

"Ms. Lingers, you're not talking," Kitay notes. "Is it about Mr. Brady? Did I say something wrong?"

I shake my head, wondering when the table turned. How is it she's going to the symphony like bloody Bugs Bunny and I can barely get some lesser version of a man to hop in my bed, let alone spend the night? I'm supposed to be a swinging single, screwing like a hare. Now, I'm waiting on two turtles? Wait. Am I jealous? Oh what rubbish. I don't have feelings for Mr. Brady. I barely have feelings at all. "I'm...thinking is all," I say.

"You approve of Mr. Brady, right?" She closes the bag containing her new clothes, tucking a plunger under her arm. "You don't think I'm making a really big mistake?"

"Heavens no." I dodge her eyes. I can't sabotage her

chance at happiness. Bells and whistles sound in my head telling me not to be that woman. I can be better, more than the bitter soul that mother molded me to be. I can be a friend if I rid myself of negative thoughts.

Still, on the street I hear a crash, a bender, and it becomes crushingly clear: I can foil Kitay's entire affair with a single sweep. I can say, go Kitay, go where Mr. Brady wants even if you don't have a clue what you want. That way he'll lead you. Coffee, tea, the symphony – the sky's the limit for a woman with a limited mind. I'd say this, but I can't because I've grown to like her too much. So much that I know she's better off than to have a friend like me.

So go.

Leave.

I have...Hector.

Busying myself, I dig in my purse searching for my cell. It's a mistake, my need to reread the same texts over and over. The writing is on the wall. Hector doesn't want me. He lies. Even my Lichtenstein knows. I look to it, the dotted cartoon image of a blonde woman wiping a tear. Why have I allowed such a portrait to hang in my home?

We all connect. We're all rain – transparent paint drops on a canvas called life. Better make each mistake a masterpiece, each stroke count even if the picture doesn't add up.

I look in the mirror. Who is this monster that even I would avoid in the street? What happened to the girl who wanted to better the world, or at least find love in it? I sense a tear, only to deny it. Mustn't be weak. Hector would like that. Shake me with a fastball. Strike me out. Attach ambiguity to a text and be ready for a homerun. *I know. Things r not what they seem. Luv u.* I read text one, text two, text three. Then, when I'm ready to scream I see a text from another man. I must have missed it earlier. I place a hand on my heart, releasing a faint cry.

"Ms. Lingers? What is it?" Kitay asks. "Are you all right?"

"It's Jerry!" I declare. "I hired him to find my family, my real family." My hand trembles. I raise the phone, revealing the message. "He found someone. An aunt. He has a name."

CHAPTER 10

A NAME. WHAT'S IN a name?

Names change. Evolve.

Bev Dear wasn't always Bev Dear. She was Beverly Thompson then Beverly Finch after her first marriage to a young American soldier who fancied her accent during a chance meeting at a pub in Finsbury Park. They resided in Virginia where his family earned wealth and affluence as tobacco merchants. For Beverly, life was spirited, sprinkled with society benefits and plantation parties. That is, until the night she returned from a routine visit overseas to find her house had burned down. Her husband had fallen asleep in bed with a lit cigarette, leaving behind a will that had no mention of her name. The estate had been on loan from his parents.

At the funeral reception – with no place to turn – Bev sought the financial advice of her husband's childhood friend St. Clair Lingers. Previously, the two had met at a gala in Richmond where any evidence of attraction was quieted. The unexpected death of her husband changed that, leading to a series of phone calls and letters that prompted an intimate affair. A year later, she changed her name to Lingers, becoming the wife of a coal tycoon with a low sperm count. He wanted children. They adopted a baby girl. Me.

I was never told my history. What I've come to know I've picked up like paper scraps along a highway, leading me on a chase. Today, a bit closer, I drive Lisette home, taking in the colors of a street mural depicting devils and angels embraced in a holy war. Somehow an image so magnificent pales to the fact that somewhere out there I have an aunt.

Passing a set of orange-roofed shops in Little Havana

I call Jerry for more information but he doesn't answer. Lisette directs the car to turn right then left, texting at an accelerated rate. She leads us into the parking lot of a convenience store, the Latin equivalent of 7-11. Pocketing her phone she warily eyes two teen boys smoking cigars in the stairwell leading up to the apartments above the store.

"Damn," she says.

"What?"

"Just thugs packing heat."

I take a closer look, discovering the shorter boy has a neck tattoo of a red dragon. The other wears a blue bandana as a headband. Baggy white tees hang over their olive skin, the same shade as Lisette. Passing a phone between them they eyeball the car as I park.

"Heat?" I ask. "You mean those two are hot for you?"

"I mean guns," she moans. "Damn, Ms. Lingers. You've been living in the condo clouds too long. Don't they teach you these things at counselor training school?"

"We learn about different cultures, yes."

She sighs, pointing to her chest. "I'm Puerto Rican." She directs my eyes to the boys. "Those are Mexican gang bangers."

"Enough," I snap. "I'm not ignorant. I can see."

"Then look." She stares out the window with one closed pirate's eye. "The guns hang right...about...where their dicks are."

"Lisette!" I say, covering my ears. One boy flicks a cigar to the ground and the other stretches, exposing his tattooed belly. "Don't be so foul. It's unladylike. Call them penises or pee-pees."

"Pee-pees?" Her head jolts as if repelling the words. "I don't say that unless it's on a baby in a diaper."

"You would if you married a man in a diaper."

She grimaces, inflating her bottom lip. "Damn girl. What kind of freaky shit you into?" She shivers, keeping a vigilant eye on me. Digging in her bag of clothes, she pulls out what she had on before our field trip. "Be cool, ok?" She motions to the boys. "Those two. That's why I don't wear dresses."

"I thought it was because of Cici."

She throws on an extra large black tee, wipes the lipstick from her lips and musses her hair. "I don't have time to be in the middle."

"The middle of what?"

"Boys."

"That's part of life. You're a pretty girl." She blinks, taking the compliment with a squirm. Had I gone too far? I recall our first encounter in the restroom, being wrestled to the ground. It doesn't seem long ago. How had we arrived here? Early this week I couldn't get her to open up. Now, she's allowed me in her head, asked me to drive her home. What changed? Was it something in me? "I just think you should be able to wear a dress if you like. That's all," I say.

She eyes me suspiciously. "Yeah, well, it's best for thugs to think I like girls, ok?" Sliding on jeans, she trades heels for sneakers. "Look, I gotta go. They won't bother me. I got a weapon, right?" She waves the plunger with a laugh, as a short Hispanic girl exits the convenience store, sparking a cigarette. "That's Eva. She's got my back." Opening the door, she stalls. "Hey, I was thinking about what you said, about bettering ourselves." She places gum in her mouth, waving for Eva to wait. "I need to pass the GED test so I can go to cosmetology school. You know algebra?"

"Not well enough."

"Oh." She looks away, the wind taken from her sail. "That's cool. I was just thinking."

"Kitay's good with numbers."

"Yeah?" She mulls it over before shaking the thought.

"It's Kitay. She'd help a flea to fur," I remind her.

"Yeah, but that flea doesn't think she's a freak."

"You really think she's different from you or me?"

"Be real, Ms. Lingers." She steps out, tapping the car roof with the plunger. "When you look at Kitay, what do *you* see?"

Without thinking I say, "A friend." The ghastliest of thoughts I know, but I can't conjure another way to answer the question. Have I grown soft? On the way home I attempt to think of something mean or biting – anything to divide the two of us but I can't think of a single reason to dislike her aside from her sense of style. Even that, I find myself defending. *She's from a place where window treatments are inspired. Why not double the pattern for a dress?*

It's like how I'd angle for father when Bev Dear would start with the cracks. Sure, he had a frog's way of clearing his throat and his breath smelled of smoky cigars, but that never deflated my heart when I'd see his Bentley turn up our stone drive in Richmond. I had an impossible way of greeting him, rushing into his arms before he had time to exit. He'd set me on his lap, holding me, sheltering me from Bev Dear's cold words, sharp as icicles when she drank. *She's lonely. I'm on the road too much. I want you to blame me.* Even years after her death he couldn't surrender the excuses. He should've spent time by her side, traveled less, worked from home. I learned not to ask questions. It was better to live in the clouds until I wanted to jump. That idea began to seed days after father's death. When Felix died my brain was branching with it. I had no connection, no hope, no family left. Until now.

I get the update from Jerry over the phone, curled up with my back against the shower door.

Roberta made good on her word. It took a combination of fifty-dollar bills, chicken fingers and vanilla shakes, but stomach happy, she disclosed the name of my aunt: Heather Pratt. Roberta wasn't sure if she was alive or deceased. Since then Jerry has been searching on the Internet – a difficult feat due to the name's popularity.

"Pratt is pretty common," he explains.

"Yes, but couldn't Roberta give you a birthplace, a school she attended?"

"Not until I bring more money and pork and beans. You know, for a sick old lady, she can...."

"What of my mother Elise?" I interrupt. "Did she talk about her? Perhaps the two share the last name."

"There you go jumping the gun," he laughs. "C'mon baby. Don't you think I thought of that?"

I slap the tile floor. "Don't call me baby. I'm your employer."

"Testy. Testy."

I take a breath. "Jerry, I've been waiting on this information for some time. I don't know how much longer I can hang on."

"I'm getting there. I'm getting there. Geez lady, you need to lighten up." He sighs, clearing his throat. "Pratt is your aunt's taken name."

"And her maiden name?"

"Roberta can't remember it."

"Rubbish! Perhaps a sandwich, a BLT can jar her memory."

"Hey. She's going senile. You have to cut the old lady some slack. She's going wacky, tellin' nurses she's Amelia Earhart."

"Splendid. Then they won't search for bones when she disappears."

"Ms. Lingers, with all respect, you should be grateful she's helped us come this far," he says, his voice full of concern. I think of a happy place, the classroom. Students take notes, listening. I must be a role model. "You're this close to all the answers," he says. "Can't you smell it?"

I take a whiff, breathing in nothing but the trace of a French vanilla candle burning from the dining room. I hang up the phone to rest my eyes and an hour later the turtles arrive. I grant Archibald permission to buzz up the deliveryman. I touch up my lipstick and lap down a Tic-Tac. I pour a glass of wine, gulp it, and pour another. Bloody hell. Why do I fuss?

I open the door to find Wes and the turtle tank. His smile is a mile wide, lifting his mustache curls. He nods courteously. "Ms. Lingers."

I eye him with suspicion, crossing my arms. "I wasn't told you'd be making the delivery. It seems that puzzle piece was left out of the equation."

His grin grows. "I figured you'd demand the best service. I didn't want to let you down."

"Is that right?" I study the freckles at the base of his eyes, the smoothness of his lips. He recently groomed. I take in the lasting fumes – the scent of a clean shave that adds shine to his head. He nods at the tank. "May I come in? It's pretty heavy."

I direct him to place it on the bar and he crosses the room. Disturbed, the turtles paddle in the water as if needing food, attention. Can I be a proper parent? Is it too late to learn? I fill with anxiety, considering the demands of caring for another life. How did I become involved? I drink more wine.

Wes hands me a yellow cylinder from his pocket. "They eat these tiny pellets and leafy greens." He rattles off a list of other instructions. *The water must remain seventy to seventy-five degrees. The tank should be cleaned at least three times a week. The turtles need light to prevent shell rot. Take them out now and again for a walk.*

I gulp. "Sounds easy enough."

"Oh, and I put in a filter, free of charge." Flexing his bicep he aims a thumb at the bubbles. Another bulge. Another man to save the day. I'm not impressed. "So what do you think?"

On guard, I keep ample distance from him. "It's adequate."

"Adequate?" He itches the back of his head. "Well, that doesn't sound like a satisfied customer. What can I do to improve the service?"

I bunch my lips – a kiss to the wind. "You could leave."

He cocks his head, studying me with a smirk. "Is there a problem?"

Please. Am I supposed to melt at the sight of his heroics? *I put in a filter free of charge.* Well la-di-da. I know what he's up to with his muscled arms and his Scottish accent. I'm certain the routine worked on a thousand women before but it won't work on me.

"I don't have a problem," I say, sipping my drink. "I'm a satisfied swinging single. I don't know what *you're* trying to swing."

"Whoa." He surrenders his arms, backing up. "Did I miss something?"

"Oh please." I take another drink. "I know what you're all about. You come in here with your mustache and mouth from across the pond, passing yourself off as some kind of savior. I bet most ladies lap up every word."

He doesn't fight. Instead, he eyes me like I'm on a ledge, lifting one leg. And what if I am? I look at him and see another Hector. I want to scream that I'm worth a public stroll. I deserve the same amount of affection as a woman half my age. I've made it twice as far. Shouldn't I receive double? The numbers seem off.

That's why I keep firing at the mouth, the words are meant for more than Wes. They're meant for the man who wronged me before him and the one before that. And so forth. Unfortunately, Wes is in range of a direct hit.

"I don't buy it," I tell him. "The brawn. The brain. The accent doesn't work either. So, you see, it is you who has the problem." I raise my glass. "Hope it's not a teeny weenie problem though." I laugh. "Tell me Wes. Is that the reason for the muscles? Do you have a teeny weenie?" His eyes flash to my glass and he lifts his chin, knowingly.

"Is this what you do?" he asks. "Push people?"

I clam up in fear he'll react with anger like Hector. Is that who I'm talking to? No, Hector wouldn't be with me in the daylight. I'm best left for the dark. Not like Miss Robb.

"Are you going to answer?" he persists.

"I don't push people. I don't have people. I have drinks." I shake his gaze, becoming white, barren like the condo walls. I turn my cheek, looking to the only piece of visible art – the Lichtenstein painting capturing the image of a distraught woman. Her eyes fill with tears that seem to be applauded by her face. Is that like me? Do I push to pull through? So I drink. So I say things I shouldn't say. Is it abuse if I welcome it? I motion to the turtles. "All right. You've done your job. You dumped them on me. You're free to go."

"No," he challenges. "You bought them. I didn't twist your arm."

I choke on the bullet, watching the turtles claw the glass as if reaching out to me. I fear holding them, dropping them, another fall. I panic, taking a drink as Wes continues to smile in support. What does he see in me that I don't?

What if I make a mistake, another one dies?

"Fine. I'll be a good parent," I say. "Is that what you want?"

He nods. "That's a start. But I'd rather hear it when you're sober."

I'm taken aback. How could he talk like that? I'm a customer. I deserve the courtesy of respect even if I am in the wrong. It's best to send his sort packing. If only I could stop my mouth from leaking. I place the empty wine glass on the bar, harder than I should.

"There. Sober!" I announce. "Happy now?" I go over to the turtles, bending to observe them. Wonderful. I have a family – positively slippery and somewhat slimy. But then again, aren't they all?

"You're a piece of work. You know that?" he asks.

"Art...a piece of art," I correct, nodding to the woman in the Lichtenstein. He turns his neck to view the painting, and the sun creates a pale yellow halo over his head, the rays coming in from the patio glass. Is it a sign?

"You read theater reviews to your cat," he says, remembering my words at the pet store. He smiles, his mustache tips forming twin crescent moons.

"Yes. And?"

"I like theater too," he states. A light flickers in his eye. I can tell where this is headed and I panic, rushing to the kitchen. He follows, failing to take the hint. I search the cupboard for ingredients to prepare a recipe I don't plan to cook. Let's see – corn kernels and leftover catnip, thanks to Kitay. Tasty. "Uh. Hi. What just happened?" he asks.

"I...I'm hungry. I need to eat."

"Catnip?" He stalls with a smile that lasts long enough to make me wonder what he's thinking. Why do I care? I'm purposefully leaving the worst impression. I don't like him. I want him to leave. Yes. Please. Go away and never come back. "So what's with the desks in the other room?" he asks.

"I teach."

"In the house?"

"You ask too many questions," I say. Then locating the leftover Kitty Litter Cake on the counter, I hand it to him, hoping he'll take it as a parting gift. "You'll like it. That's not real poop. Those are Tootsie Rolls."

He's taken aback, studying it. "You're giving this to me?"

"Why not? I didn't make it. Kitay did. The woman you met at the store."

"Your friend."

"Yes."

He nods and I escort him to the door, where he taps the pocket of his jeans, producing a card. "Call me. You know. If you have a problem with the turtles." I take it and read his full name: Wesley McKay.

"That's generous of you."

"Or I could call you." I stiffen, even though my heart tingles. I'm not ready for another man. I've yet to heal from the last one; the stitches are still intact. I look off uncomfortably. "You're right. I shouldn't mix business with pleasure. It's not professional. I didn't mean to—"

I put up a hand, quieting him. "Perhaps if you didn't come on so strong."

He laughs. "How would you like me to come on? I talk and you run. What else should I do? Come on weak? Yeah. Now, that's a turn-on." He cleverly smiles and nods to the hall. "Walk me to the elevator."

I emit a heavy sigh. "If it means you'll leave." I briskly take the lead and he catches up, explaining himself.

"When I saw you in the store with the kids and the plungers I thought you were part of a theater troupe. You don't see that in South Beach. People cutting up. It was a nice change." I press the elevator button, producing a green arrow. I stall, avoiding his eyes. What does he see in me? I'm no beauty, nothing special. I hit the button again, losing patience. "What's the rush?" he says. "I wanted to ask—"

The truth slips. "I'm not ready."

"It's ok. I'm not looking for —"

"Sex?"

He smiles through it, taking a more serious tone. "Can I ask you something without being cut off?"

I cross my arms. "Fine."

"Join me for the theater? One night. No commitment."

"No."

He shields his heart with the cake. "Why not?"

I take a breath, catching a whiff of his pinecone cologne. For a moment, I envision him shirtless in a Carolina forest, splitting firewood with his hands. So I find him handsome – a polished barbarian doll. He doesn't need to know. "I'm picky," I explain.

Then why can't I pick him? He's charismatic, kind, owns a shop. Perhaps a certain principle or principal still stands in the way.

"So I like musicals," he defends. "I'm man enough to admit it. Is that so bad?" He sticks one leg in the elevator, holding the door ajar. "I see you with a plunger and I think there's a fun lady. She doesn't care what people think. I bet I can tell her anything. Wouldn't that be great?"

I blush. "It's an illusion. I care all too well about appearances. I assure you, I have a belly full of problems."

"At our age, who doesn't?" Catching himself he circles his head in a mental rewind. "Not that we're old." He stops himself, briefly sealing his lips. "Look. I'm not here to fix your problems. I just." He helplessly sighs. "I think you're pretty and I could use a night out."

My heart lifts. Pretty? Is he being honest?

I try to separate his face from the others, the liars of my past. He seems innocent enough, clinging to the Kitty Litter Cake like he's actually going to eat it. How can I not find him endearing? The thought lasts until my cell phone buzzes with a new text message. I hadn't realized I was holding it. It's Hector.

Still mad?

The interruption weighs me down.

"How about a rain check?" I ask Wes. Dashing his gaze, I look to the phone. "It's not you. I've unresolved issues I must address before I can consider someone else."

He scratches his brow as if uncomfortable with the thought of competition, the possibility of another man. Good. It's best to keep him restless, make things a little difficult. It's human to disregard things that can be easily had.

"Do me a favor. Work fast," he says, a grin rivaling his hard tone. "There's a new musical opening next week. I have orchestra seats. I plan to tell my buddies that you're dragging me. Think about it?"

I agree, telling him to run along so I can tend to the turtles and start being a parent.

Moments later, I prepare a Swiss cheese omelet and make my way to the sofa, keeping a watchful eye on the slimy buggers who stand motionless on a log. I ponder their purpose, their reason for being. They appear equally baffled by the sight of me. A parent? Ha! The merciless way in which they gaze indicates they know better. Am I that obvious of a novice? What should I do, talk fine art? Read theater reviews? For babies they seem too perceptive, studying my every move. I don't like it. Therefore, I tell them it's bedtime before napping on the couch.

An hour later, I wake to the sound of a heavy wind striking the glass slider and take to the patio to find purple clouds a few miles offshore. With a long breath I fill my nose with the salt of the beach before sensing an oncoming headache, likely due to dehydration.

Heading inside, I take an aspirin with water before uncorking a bottle of Pinot Grigio. I finish two glasses before a third erases the thought of Hector. My memory grows dark 'til I look to my phone to find more of his texts. What does he want? What does he need from me if he has Miss Robb? She can bleed, deliver a baby. I can only hemorrhage from the heart. It aches now. Thankfully, the Pinot slows the bleeding. That's why I drain the bottle, capping it with a glass of Chablis.

Twiddling my fingers atop the aquarium, I pour a pellet, no two, no three, tapping the bottom of the turtle food container.

Look at me, being a mother. I would have been good at it. It was my dream. If only I had protected my baby girl before it was too late. I blame myself. Could I have acted faster, blocked the blow? I had little time to react. He hit below the ribs and then came the pain. I hung up on the cable man. I wasn't flirting. The tele was on the fritz.

I can't think of it. Shouldn't think of it.

It's the small things that haunt me, the dirty grout between the tiles on the floor that day. That's what I recall of the fall, that and the blood. I froze, unprepared, like Bev Dear, who wouldn't sit to witness it when I first bled at age twelve. It was another sign she was an aging mother and no money or drinkable gold could stop it.

That's when she enrolled me overseas at the Royal School in Hampstead where I sought a mother in another. In England, there was Patricia, the nurturing headmistress. In America, during the summer, there was Rose.

I recall the morning Rose woke me on my sixteenth birthday. It was the day I truly became an adult.

"You're rising but you're not shining," she sang, sitting softly on my bed. I sat up and wiped my eyes, hearing the ocean and the sea birds calling the sun to shore. She held a plate of croissants and red grapes. "Your mother said I could take you wherever you want."

"Is she coming too?"

She hesitated, making light of it. "She has plans. You'll see her tonight."

I kicked off the covers, rushing to Bev Dear's bedroom. I found the bed was made. The scent of coconut oil remained in the air.

"Let's go to the beach," I told Rose.

"But you don't like beach. How about the museum?"

I stood firm and she sighed, knowing I was too old, too clever to be fooled. We both knew Bev Dear was nestled somewhere down there in the sand. And we were right, later discovering her in the arms of a dark foreign man. His long limbs wrapped her like an octopus, the lovers snuggling up on a bamboo mat. Her bikini was no more than an inkblot.

Spotting them, Rose wanted to turn back, saying she felt naked with her shins exposed. Her scalp was burning, but I wouldn't budge. I needed to see the man who was more important than my birthday. His boisterous demeanor when he fondled Bev Dear made me despise him, but I was strong. I only cried when I got too close, finding her drunk on his lap. She never saw me. I never spoke of it. I just lived to grow up, having my own struggles with men, alcohol, divorcing one, two, three times until Felix. I miss him, his lust for life and art, and the safety I felt waking next to someone who truly wanted to be there. Our time was cut too short. I grieve the loss 'til this day.

I hover over the aquarium, wondering why the turtles aren't moving. Had I fed them too much? Are they even alive? I'm sloshed, too dizzy to tell. I can't phone Wes. He'd take it as a cue to return and save the day. I go to the next best source: Kitay. She knows plenty about animals.

I stumble to the elevator, dipping to the fourth floor where palm fronds decorate the wallpaper, creating a dark interior jungle. Kitay's home is behind the second door. I knock with an unsteady feeling in my feet. I fight a case of sea legs. The floor bobs.

We all connect.

We're all but rain returning to the ocean.

I place my palms to my ears to drown everything out. Then I knock once more, nearly collapsing when the door opens.

Have I the right condo? It all seems hazy. This fuzzy person can't be Kitay. She hasn't a stitch of makeup and her hair is tucked under a white Marlins cap. What's happening? Wait. Is it a man?

"For heaven's sake. Who keeps knocking on the door?" a gravelly voice calls from inside.

"Dee?" the person at the door says. I make a hearty effort to focus. "It's me, Kitay."

I strain my eyes, recognizing her nose. "Kitay," I utter, my voice cracking. "It's rushing in. I...I wanted to be a mother. I was for a moment. She rained down before it was time. I lost her."

"Oh Dee." She reaches for my hand and pulls it to her lips, kissing it.

"Charlie?" a voice calls from inside. "What kind of person shows up at your door at this late hour?"

"Ma, please. Hold on."

"Who's Charlie?" I ask.

Kitay shakes her head, flustered.

"I...I...." Losing balance, I speak incoherently before falling into her arms.

We're all raindrops bound for earth, only to be smashed into a million bits. Some nights, it's good to be small, seemingly insignificant. It lessens the impact. Like tonight, I wake up feeling small as a bug, no pain in my shell. I look up and the couch seems large, uneven. I gain focus to realize I'm slouched on the tall end of a red Victorian fainting couch, freshly upholstered with a walnut trim.

I pull myself up, wiping my lips. The room spins.

"Where am I?" I ask the old woman sitting on a loveseat across from me. "Who are you? What did you do to me?"

"Oh geez Louise," she says, lowering her smudged glasses to get a better view. Wide as a pancake, she wears a blue blazer and a beige skirt, crossing her legs at the ankles. Her perm is a bowl of Cheerios. "The better question is what did you do to yourself." She has the country tongue of Kitay but crisper. She takes a sip from a white mug. "You made yourself sick on that devil juice. Any fool can see that. I had Charlie bring you water." She points to the glass on the coffee table. Tacky sniffs the rim with her pink cat nose. Taser licks my ankle. "Get! Go on you two!" the woman hollers. She slaps her knee and the animals flee. "Mangy beasts! They have no respect!"

"You don't need to yell," Kitay calls, out of sight. "They listen the same."

"Baloney and Swiss. They need discipline or those fur balls will ruin this house like you tried to ruin mine."

Kitay crinkles a plastic bag. "Special snacks for special children," she says. The pets race to the sound of her voice.

"Quit catering to them and find me that resume. I'm not going to have this night ruined. You're wasting time on everything but what's important." She clears her throat, returning her gaze to me. She forces a smile. "How impolite. I haven't introduced myself. I'm Charlie's mother, Gladys."

"Charlie?" I inquire.

She nods. "Yes Charlie. My son."

I gasp, and Kitay sits down at my side. Her troubled

green eyes peek out from a baseball cap, pleading for me to remain quiet. I honor her by not saying peep. Looking across from Gladys I note the bareness of the sitting room. Shouldn't it be full of knick-knacks? Isn't that what country people do, clog rooms with tchotchkes and taxidermy? My eyes search for a scrapbook before I realize there's not much to the room at all – just two couches and a coffee table with pinecones in a bowl.

A tele is mounted to the wall and a flickering pumpkin candle sits atop a stack of hardcover books near the sliding glass patio doors. Four cardboard boxes clutter one corner of the room. The closest box overflows with teddy bears. It's as if she's barely moved in.

"You look tired," Kitay observes, patting my knee. "Let me help you back to your condo." I try to stand but plop back down, breathing in heavy waves. Kitay and Gladys argue over what to do. Gladys suggests phoning 911. Kitay disagrees, stating I'll be fine once I'm home.

"You never listen to me," Gladys says, upset. "You've always been obstinate, ever since you were a boy."

"Stop. Stop calling me that," Kitay utters.

I cover my mouth, overwhelmed with nausea, as Gladys tells me to forgive the confusion. I focus on her face, the way her powdery white makeup shifts with her expression. "Sometimes Charlie pretends he's other things," Glady says. "Reason his father fell ill."

Kitay tenses. "That's not true. Stop saying that."

"It's why you lost your job at the plant. Isn't it?"

Kitay attempts to lift me, causing the couch to slide. "Ma. Please."

"What? She won't remember anything I say in the morning. She's clearly a drunk." Gladys sighs, shaking her head. "Go fetch your resume."

"Really ma? Right now?" She struggles, lifting me up with a bear hug. "I'm kind of busy."

"I'm only trying to help."

"I told you. I'm tweaking it."

"Why do you need to do that? You had no problem obtaining a job with it in Arcadia. You loved your job at the plant."

Kitay boosts me to a stance when a polite burp escapes me. The wine burns my throat, and I see double when Kitay slowly assists me to the door. "I'm trying something new," she explains to Gladys.

"New? What do you mean, new?"

"Retail," I slur. "Your child has an eye for fashion."

"Fashion?" Gladys becomes irritated, hurrying past us to block the door. I do a double take, trying to determine which of her two heads is real. I raise my arm to erase each face with my palm but neither one disappears. She fires from the mouth, "Is that why you had those dresses pinned to the wall?" Kitay lowers her head. Gladys points to the tele. Her two mouths address me. "He had one up there and one near the fridge. He had them hanging like paintings." She flings her hands in the air. "Am I the crazy one?" She stalls, calming herself to make sense of it. "Was that your plan before I made you take them down? A career in fashion?" Kitay doesn't respond and Gladys stomps her foot, nodding to the tele. "I told you that thing would put thoughts in your head. Now you have shameful ideas. Remember when you applied at Dottie's? Tell your girlfriend how that ended."

Kitay begins to cry, her throat vibrating. Taser approaches, whining at her feet. "Ma, please. Just go to bed. We'll talk about it in the morning."

"I'm just trying to help. Don't you understand? Fashion has no place for a man."

"Ha!" I say, igniting my heartburn. My voice has the rasp of a dragon. "Tell that to Gucci. Versace. Yves Saint Laurent."

Kitay squeezes my arm. "Dee. It's all right."

Gladys narrows her eyes. "Missy, I don't know who you think you are...."

"I'm your daughter Kitay's best friend," I assert. Gladys leans back, stunned to silence. "And I don't appreciate you coming to my town and ripping down her art or her soul." I begin to say more but the wine rises in my throat, pouring out like a fountain. Kitay holds back my hair and I lean forward, splashing liquid on Gladys' clunky beige shoes. She screams in disgust, jumping out of the way.

Is this the kind of friend you keep? What would your father say? This is what I warned you about. This is what you find in the city. Drunks! Hell-seekers!

"Ma, stop!" Kitay pleads. With a gentle tug she lifts my head, whispering in my ear. "Don't listen." She opens the door. "Remember. What *they* say doesn't matter."

"It's a miracle your father's alive," Gladys says, following us into the hall. "Charlie! Charlie! Come back!"

"What they say doesn't matter," Kitay repeats, leaving Gladys behind. I say it too, clinging to Kitay in the elevator. Her body is warm, comforting. She smiles, pressing the button to my floor. I let go of her body, pressing my palms to my ears. I squeeze, listening for the sea, the call of a conch shell, all the while surrounded by the girl they once called Conch. Quite a beautiful shell, I always believed. Now I believe it more.

"I shouldn't have come without calling," I admit. Kitay helps me to bed. "I needed your help with the turtles. I'm not good at caring for a family."

She leaves, returning with a wet washcloth. Through the window the moon make her skin glow a light shade of blue as she leans in to clean my lips. I wonder if she's truly human. I've never known one to be so kind. "I'll check on the turtles when you fall asleep," she says. She cracks the window. Outside, waves fall on the shore, the sound settling me.

"The turtles weren't moving. I became scared, unsure if they were alive." I reach for her hand. "I can't bear to lose anyone else. You understand." I moan, a dull pain in my head.

"You need rest." She sets another cold washcloth on my forehead. "Close your eyes."

I do, drifting in and out until entering a dream where I hear a downtempo beat accompanied by the harrowing sounds of a jungle. Standing barefoot, I find myself in a red-walled museum with Baroque paintings of angels and saints. Dressed in a black suit Hector stands by me, enraged because I won't allow him a dance. I don't want to. It's not right, not here. I'm focused on the mountain lions circling the art. I should fear them, but I don't. I fear Hector who grabs my hand when I try to leave. "The next room is no different," he states.

"But what if I'm different?"

I go to the next room where I find a painting of St. Michael raising a mighty sword. A lion roars, charging toward me. I don't budge. He stops before pouncing. He bows.

I wake with a heavy breath, the heat of another warming the bed. A Paris runway show is on the tele. Cameras flash.

"Bad dream?" Kitay asks. At my side, she cradles a plunger. "You've been shaking." I recall her helping me home, cleaning me up. My heart settles, hearing her voice. "I hope you don't mind me spending the night."

"No. Not at all," I say, checking the clock. It's three a.m.

She wipes her nose with a tissue, tucking her knees under her chin. Having removed the baseball cap, her blonde hair falls in tangles along her face. "I lied to you." Her tears reflect in the tele. "I'm tired of lying, of not liking myself, thinking how I got here, why I ended up in this...this shell."

I sit upright, muting the tele. "Where's this coming from?"

"I shouldn't want to be a female. It's not natural."

"That's not true."

"When ma came, I spit at myself, right in the mirror. I made my father sick. How could I do that? I spit and spit and spit." Her body trembles.

"And where did that get you?"

"Nowhere." Frustrated, she slaps the bed with the plunger. "I'm so stupid. I'm not a real woman. You even said that. That day at the market."

Oh dear. Yes. That's me, forever with a foot in my mouth. But I can take it out. Take it back. "I was wrong," I confess.

Burying her head in her arms, she sobs, leaving me to ponder what to do. I'd offer her a drink, but she'd likely start talking about her uncle again. I don't want that to start.

How do sober people handle grief? There must be some way to cope without altering reality, though I don't know how to do it.

I pat her back.

Kitay lifts her head, sniffling. "If only I knew why I was born like this...with these thoughts."

"Why not?" I reply. "We all face a challenge, each of us. Why should you be spared?"

Kitay considers it. "Ma won't see me as anything but Charlie." She turns to me. "Dee," she says, lightly. "Tell me the truth. When you look at me, what do you see?"

I gaze at her tenderly. "A lady."

"I wasn't born one."

"Nobody is," I declare. "We all have a choice, how to transform." Dabbing her nose, Kitay calms her cries. "Now stop feeling sorry for yourself. That's never done a lady a bit of good." I raise the volume on the tele, viewing a young woman with a long neck slinking down a Parisian runway. Her white dress billows around her chest, forming an open flower. The sound of the ocean provides the soundtrack. I think of Rose. "Do you know what an friend once told me?" I smile. "That God sends His most precious gifts with a little extra packaging. Ever hear that?"

"No. What's it mean?"

"It means some have to shed more skin than others. That's all."

Nodding, Kitay pulls herself together. "I never worked at Dottie's."

"It doesn't matter."

"I would go there to shop and tell other ladies how wonderful they looked trying on dresses. It made me come alive, helping them pick out things that made them happy." She drifts, lost in thought. "I filled out an application seven times." She squeezes her eyes shut, the memory fresh in her mind. "They'd never give me a job, because they said some of the customers were afraid of me." She shrugs, her eyes opening to the tele. "So I hid away at the sewage plant, separating the muck from the men." She feebly waves the plunger. "It was boring, reading meters and adding chemicals all day. And the smell? Oh God. In the summer, you can't imagine how bad it was." Her eyes lock on the tele where a baby-faced model poses at the end of the runway, staring into the flashing cameras. "She doesn't look happy about her job either."

"She isn't paid to be happy. She's paid to make other girls feel unhappy in comparison. That way, they buy the clothes."

"Is that why you buy them?"

"No. I buy them because I view beautiful clothing as art."

She lowers the plunger, trying to make sense of it. "Why would you buy art that makes you unhappy?"

I shift in the bed, looking off. "It's easier to be unhappy. You don't expect as much."

"But you should. You should expect the best in people."

"I used to." I think back to father, Felix, and Rose. "But I don't have many people left in my life to remind me of that." I glance at her with uncertainty. "Well, until you."

She smiles, lifting my heart, until I hear a knock at the front door.

Before I can say 'boo' Kitay bounds from the bed, pleading with me to help her hide. "It's ma. I can't go home," she says, rushing into the closet.

"How could it be your mother? She doesn't know where I live."

"Oh, she's very resourceful. She can find out anything," she says, her voice weakening behind the closet door. "I know her. She doesn't drive in the dark. She won't leave 'til morning."

I gather my robe as the knocking growing louder. "Just stay here," I instruct. "I can't have this racket keeping me awake all night." In the dimly lit living room I call out. "Who is it?" There's no response except more knocking. "This better be good," I say, unlocking the deadbolt. I open the door to find Hector with bloodshot eyes.

"You don't return my texts?" he asks. No hello or apology – it always starts with a question, leading to a fight, leading to sex. I can't do it. I swiftly shut the door, leaning into it, my hand to my heart. He speaks through the barrier. "C'mon Dee. Don't shut me out."

I bite a finger to remain quiet. Why must he be so insistent? He can't know his fragile, heroic voice is enough to make me second-guess myself. I know why he's here: sex. He's lonely, horny, searching for the comfort of something familiar. He knocks repeatedly 'til I speak.

"How did you get in? I didn't buzz you up."

"What does it matter? You can't hide from me, Dee. I'm a part of your life. Open up."

I release a small cry, cupping my mouth. "Hector. Please. Just go."

He turns the door handle, pushing the door open a crack before I realize I hadn't locked it. "I made a mistake. I'll own it. I want to make it right." He waits quietly as I push against the door. "Please Dee. Give me a minute."

"I've given you enough. I don't have anything left."

"Please," he begs. Though the crack his breathing warms my neck. I smell beer, smoke from the bar. I flash back to the taste of his skin, the last time in the office, his hands gripping me, taking control. My heart melts, so capricious. I move, allowing him inside. I'm a fool. I know. "Thank you." He enters, loosening the red tie around his neck.

I don't budge, blocking him from coming in any further than the entryway. I don't trust myself. I've made enough mistakes to know that all bets are off after midnight. Add a pinch of loneliness and nothing is a long shot.

"What do you want?" I ask him.

He runs his hand through his ruffled hair, the alcohol in his belly slowing his movements. "I miss you Dee. Isn't that enough?" He plays like he's hurt – the perfect first card. "Why do I always have to want something?"

I tighten my robe. If only it came equipped with a deadbolt. "Because you always do."

"That's not true."

"So you're not here to sleep with me?"

He grins, as if talking dirty is part of the plan. That's how it works. He lays the bait. I get angry. He laughs. Then playing it cute he pretends a belly of beer is enough to make it ok. At least 'til he gets what he wants. Then he leaves and I'm left alone, having been denied what I want. Something more. "Sleep with you?" he says, like it's the last thing on his mind. "Is that what you think?" He chuckles, shaking his head like I'm one of his buddies beating him to the punch line.

"I no longer find it funny," I tell him.

"Aw. C'mon. Why don't you want to play anymore?" He leans in to caress my cheek. "What'd I do that's so bad?"

I jerk my head away. "In which chapter shall I begin?"

"You're right. I screwed up." He tilts his head, his watery eyes urging me to let him off the hook. "You can't hold it over my head forever. I won't let you. I'll quit breathing if you stay mad at me." He deeply inhales, puffing his cheeks, as if my decision dictates when he can let go. I fold my arms, waiting 'til he turns beet- red. He grins madly, urging me with his hands to say something, anything.

"Pig," I utter.

He lets out a breath, relieved. "Whoo." His childish smile sends me reeling. I'm reminded of the truth – he's having a baby. And he's a baby himself.

I throw down my arms, screaming in a whisper. "How could you sleep with me...be inside me without telling me you were inside her too? You didn't even use a condom."

"So? You can't get pregnant."

I muffle a scream. "You could have given me a disease!"

"You think I'd sleep with someone like that?"

I see red. "I want you out. Out!" I turn, covering a cry with my hand, but he doesn't leave. His eyes burn my back, melting me. Each passing second the flame grows brighter. I hate the burn, but I'm drawn to the sting. I've learned that about myself. I must change it.

"Dee. I'm not ready to be a dad," he says, sadly.

I swallow my lips. There are so many hurtful things I can say, things that seem to naturally slip from a scorned woman's tongue. I have to rise above it – be the adult even if it feels like I'm giving up. My words white knuckle the roof of my mouth before I find the courage to release. "How far along is she?"

He stalls. "Nine weeks."

Nine weeks? Is that why he's been distant, why he can no longer do whatever it is we're doing? Flames fill my heart but I rise up like a phoenix. "I don't know what to say. What you want to hear."

"You counsel people. I thought...."

I turn to him, my arm providing a boundary. "No! I'm not your counselor. That is not what we had." How could he say that, think it? My heart has a spasm. He inches in. "Stay back. I'm not playing this game. I'm too tired. It's hot. It's cold. It's boiling. My mind is fried!"

"You and I have a good time together."

The words spill in slow motion. "Stop saying that! You...ch-cheated on me. You think that's a good time? That I'm made of stone?"

His phone buzzes, but he doesn't look at it. He knows better, that I'm in no place to deal with another distraction, another woman who wants to screw him in the middle of the night. How many are out there? The thought stabs at my chest.

"Will you stop getting yourself so upset?" He lowers my hand.

I struggle. "No. No. I don't want this." I push him away.

He snaps. "Well, what do you want?"

"More!"

"Amena mena mena mena." He paces, sealing his lips each time he's about to talk. Then he says, "You've been married four times." He holds up four fingers. "Four times, Dee. You know how it ends."

"Yes. The man leaves." I point to the door. "Out!"

He sighs. "You want more? Is that it? I'll stay the night. Will that make you happy? I'll wake up next to you. Hold you. Hell, I'll even make breakfast."

I can't listen anymore. His voice pricks me like pins. I rush to the door, opening it.

He doesn't budge. I head into the hall.

"I called the police," a neighbor says, cracking her door. Her eyes peek out, big like an owl.

"Thank you," I reply. "Invite friends too. I'll make

lemonade."

As she closes her door Hector uses the distraction to back me into the wall. Without warning he kisses me hard and deep. I slap his chest and limbo under his arm, back into the house. He follows, grabbing my arm to spin me, to kiss me again.

Why do I give in? Why? Why? Why?

Why does my heart drink up the attention even if it's polluted?

Luckily, this time I can taste the difference. He thinks this is what I want – a fight for the sake of making up. It doesn't sit right on my tongue. My mind goes to Kitay. She waited a lifetime to meet Mr. Brady. How can I readily offer my lips to someone unworthy?

I tear myself from him. "It's best you leave."

He tickles my lips with his thumb, silencing me. I look over to the darkness in the sitting room, the only sign of life stemming from a ghostly branch in a vase. He makes a hushing sound, saying we'll be fine. His voice calms me, weighing the branch with colorful leaves. Can he be more? There's kindness to him. I've seen it in his smile, his pep talks to the kids. He can be good, perhaps just not to me.

"Let me stay," he says.

My eyes motion to the door. "Please."

Discouraged, he backs down. "I know you're mad. You have every right to be," he offers. "But honestly, if you wanted more, you would have picked someone else." My throat tightens. "What happened to that girl who could have fun, keep it light?"

I lift my chin. "She left the building. Jumped."

"Dee?" Kitay calls from the bedroom. Her voice is gruffer than usual. "Are you ok?"

Hector loses his breath, his face rushing with anger. "Jumped huh? In bed with who?" Disgusted, he heads off.

"Wait. It's just a friend." I follow him into the hall. He won't turn, advising me to go home. Why do I care? I was ready for him to leave. I wanted him to go.

He heads to the elevator. "You know Dee. I never knew you had it in you," he calls, holding his head high. His voice is triumphant, as if he just cornered me in the perfect checkmate. The perfect win. "I never knew you could be that much of a whore."

And that's it – that's all it takes – one word, one wily word and I take the plunge, landing on his back. He twirls me, blurring the truth, fading the hall light to a dull red. Then he knocks me into a wall and I see black. Still, I kick. I scream, roping my hands around his neck. I don't sense I'm choking him until a neighbor comes out, yelling for help.

But...but I need help too.

I've lost everything. It took one jump. Ledge, no ledge, I allowed him to get the best of me, stripping away my dignity and composure. Still, I can't stop myself from fighting him. I try but it takes two uniformed officers rushing from the elevator to intervene, ceasing the attack.

CHAPTER 11

I F ONLY I could move like the ocean – ebb, flow, rise, fall, accepting that in life one is bound to veer off course. If only I could stand on the shore, the saltwater at my toes, without fear of getting stuck. Then I'd see that by lifting one foot I could make a change, find solid ground and walk again.

Perhaps then I wouldn't end it. I wouldn't be straddling the patio banister, looking to the ground, watching the officers return to their patrol car. Minutes before, they departed without a report. I'd assured them that my lack of judgment was an imprudent response to too much alcohol and an ex-boyfriend who wouldn't leave. Kitay served them ginger snaps and coffee.

From the patio I hear her cleaning the dishes as my robe rides the wind. My eyes follow the blue lights, the police car speeding off to help another victim.

I don't want to die, but the water calls me. A gold fountain majestically lights the street below. It's so bright, full of life, angelic, it reminds of a period of time after my daughter's death when I thought I could tap into heaven simply by turning on the shower. The water soothing my scalp overflowed with a young girl's cries. I could hear it. It was as if God could tell I needed to know there was more to life than what I could see.

Tonight that thought should be enough to lift me but I look down to the street, heeding the calls of Jasper and Lisette. They shout, "Ms. Lingers! Come! Swim!"

Is it real? Is it them?

Their faces appear in the fountain, floating to the surface. They transform green, yellow, red. Then others form, shifting colors too. The rainbow of people is so beautiful I want to dive in it. Drown.

I let one hand loose, dangling by the other and the faces disappear.

Is it a trick?

Gravity tugs and I swallow a breath, listening for the pacifying sigh of the ocean. The night of my sixteenth birthday crashes down like a wave.

Bev Dear knocks on my door, asking me to join her for cake.

I refuse, stating I'd rather die.

Sloshed, she pokes fun.

That's fine dear. Don't make it bloody though. I'd rather my daughter die with dignity, without too much of a mess.

She laughs, unaware that I'm broken, having witnessed her tryst with that man on the beach. Would she care if she knew the truth anyway?

What of father? What was I to tell him? What of cotillion, when he planned to present me to polite society? Does politeness equate to burying one's face in the sand, only to feign ignorance?

In the kitchen, Rose instructs Bev Dear to let me rest. "Desi's not well. She spent too much time in the sun."

Bev Dear snaps. "I told you. Quit calling her Desi. It'll only confuse matters. Her name is Dee." She loudly sings "Happy Birthday to You" on repeat 'til I crack the door.

"You're not funny," I say.

"You're right. Funny is Rose."

So Rose made up ridiculous rhymes for bad words. So what? Mother made it sound like a crime. I'd always found Rose to be more insightful than humorous anyway. I tried to be like Rose. Honest.

"I saw you on the beach today," I tell Bev Dear. "With that man."

She fails to blink, setting a cigarette ablaze. "What else is a lady to do when her husband no longer lights her fire?"

I begin to cry and she closes the door, stating we'll eat the cake when I'm ready to grow up. I fall asleep only to have her return later, tucking me in for the first time. But is it Bev Dear pulling the covers up?

Pulling me up?

Back in the present, I wake in the morning to question it. I remain in bed all day, stirring only to use the loo. Then it's back under the covers where I consider the night before. What happened? How'd I come off the ledge? Did I fall? The thought makes me shiver until Monday, when late to work, I rush to shower, dress, and prep an egg and cheese biscuit for Trixie.

In the lobby, Archibald uses a white handkerchief to clean fingerprints off the glass entry doors.

"Morning Ms. Lingers." He opens the door to a sunny day, the minty scent of Eucalyptus filling the air. "Ms. Fritter just left to escort her mother to breakfast. You blinked and missed her."

Outside I blink again, the splashing water in the gold fountain triggering me to recall Hector's surprise visit along with its aftermath.

I remember dangling from the banister when Kitay found me. With a fast swoop, she pulled me up and held me in her arms. She tucked me in bed.

"If you jump, *they* win," she explained. How could she be so kind after I made a fool of myself in front of her mother, playing the town drunk?

Waiting for Salvador to retrieve my car I see Trixie in Kitay's black corset and crinoline skirt. She proudly struts up, reaching for her breakfast. "Hey, not so fast," I say, holding it hostage. "You never wear anything I give you. What makes Kitay special?"

She spits, lifting her chin. "She's French."

"Hm." I grant her the food. "I thought you only liked me."

She digs the biscuit from the bag, taking a bite. "I like people who are kind like you, the kind who give and don't expect something in return." She wipes crumbs from her lips. "I heard you have a class. Is that what your teachin' her up there?"

I take a breath and smile. "She's teaching me."

At school, students take notice.

"I was told to find Ms. Lingers," a short, fidgety girl says, sliding her fingers in the pockets of her lime-green jeans. I sit at my computer while Noni assists her in the hall.

"Are you sure?" Noni asks. The girl confirms with a nod. "Well. I...I...."

My heart soars and I stand. This must be some sort of mistake. How long has it been since a student asked for me?

"I'm Ms. Lingers," I call, welcoming in the pretty, dark-skinned girl.

"I'm Dina." Her eyes fall to the ground. "Lisette said you'd be cool."

Beside herself, Noni triple-guesses the referral. "Are you sure she said Ms. Lingers?" Vita lifts her head from her keyboard, listening to every word. "I know Lisette. We've spoken once or twice. She wants to graduate and become a...."

I fill in the blank. "A cosmetologist."

Noni shoots me a sharp look. "Excuse me?"

"Lisette. She plans to learn cosmetology."

"And how would *you* know that?"

"I listen."

Aghast, Noni feverishly exhales as my heart warms, spreading fire to each limb. Could Hector be right? Is that what it means to be a teacher? To affect a student, does one have to look beyond the classroom to find a place to start? All of my students face obstacles in real-life and their everyday interactions. I never realized those difficulties would lead to learning blocks in the classroom. I never considered it 'til I gave up power, allowing them to lead the way.

Dina says Lisette told her about the *woman hood*. With a space. Then she opens up to me about her boy troubles and issues at home. She speaks so fast it's hard to take it all in. I catch up when she pauses for a breath, telling me she has a hard time with trust.

"We all do," I say. "But eventually you'll meet someone worth earning it."

"Lisette trusts you," Dina says. "Says you're hard."

That seems to be quite the compliment, at least to

Dina and the other girls who date the thuggish sort. *Thugs need love* too, Dina tells me. She thinks I can relate because it looks like I've taken a few hits to the nose.

It appears that Lisette's been in more than Dina's ear though. Soon, she has the majority of females on campus convinced that I know the truth about men, including how to handle them when they act like complete buffoons. I don't know the extent of what she shared, but I'm afraid it has something to do with my scraping Mr. Brady's golf cart. The mishap has quickly become legendary on campus.

With my newfound popularity I book three sessions with three girls the next morning. The names change but the stories stay the same. *He said I was different, that if I loved him I wouldn't want to wait. He didn't want me lookin' at other guys. I felt alone so I did it. It hurt when he left. Now he's doing it to other girls.*

On Tuesday afternoon I walk the campus to clear my mind when I see Cici by the juice vending machine. He shades his head inside a black hoodie.

"Lingers!" Breaking off from his boys he catches up to me with a jog. "Look. I don't mean no disrespect." He keeps his distance, talking dramatically with his hands. "I just gotta say, I don't know if I like what you're doing to Lisette."

"What is it I'm doing?"

He checks his back, keeping his voice low. Nearby, Mr. Brady empties a trash can, one eye on me.

"You know, teaching her things," Cici says. "Now she expects me to take her to dinner. I don't got no money for that."

"Work longer hours."

Distressed, he goes on. "She doesn't want me making fun of her anymore. She says it's disrespectful."

"Well, isn't she right?" He shrugs. "How do you expect anyone to respect your relationship if you have no respect for it?"

"Yeah but look. She wants me to dress up to see a movie, a freaking movie?" He gestures wildly. "I don't have time for that. You know what I mean? She wasn't like that before you."

The thought delights me. "Perhaps she's learned something."

A chuckle amplifies his irritation. "Yeah, but I don't know if I like what she's learning. Now she's always busy, studying with that Kitay chick."

I stop walking. "She is?"

"Yeah. I don't see her anymore, and she's my girlfriend. Mine." He thunder slaps his chest. "What about me?" He waits for a response.

"She's bettering herself. Isn't that what you want?" He shifts his eyes. "Ah. I see. You're scared. She'll obtain a degree and move on. She won't need you."

He mulls it over. "Nah. That ain't it."

From across the courtyard Lisette approaches in a purple dress, carrying an armful of books. Her hair floats at her shoulders. "Pretty when she allows herself to be," I remark. "Don't you agree?"

Catching her eye he shrugs. "She's all right."

"She's beautiful."

He nods. "Yeah. So what's she see in me?"

I tap his chest. "The thing that kept me from jumping. Your heart."

He eyes me peculiarly then laughs. "You're crazy."

"Sometimes. Now quit whining and take her to dinner," I suggest. "That's all she wants, a little respect." With a nudge, I send him along. "Go on."

Taking heed, he huffs but listens, pocketing his hands in an approach that says he's unsure of himself, of what the future will bring. Still he goes on, greeting Lisette with a smile. He takes her hand.

I return to the office and run into Hector. He handles me with kid gloves, offering a muted hello and a perfunctory bow before walking past me. Our limited awkward interactions have been the same all week. After the fight I can't blame him. I was volatile. I shouldn't have lashed out even if it felt cathartic. I'd like to talk to him about it but know it's best to keep away. It's not easy. The highs and lows are thrilling – pure entertainment. I'm ashamed to admit it. I miss the rush. There's a part of me that misses him, that even though my head screams no my heart roller coasters over it, performing loopty-loops. If only it would flip for others.

Earlier, Wes texted to see if I'd join him for a sunset trip on his boat. I find him attractive and kind. Why do I resist? I never have weekend plans anyway.

"Remember, the mixer is Saturday night," Vita later reminds me in line at the copy machine. "You agreed to chaperone. Noni will be there too."

Walking by, Noni perks up. "Oh, you don't have to burden Dee," she says. "She must be bushed after seeing all of those clients this week. I can handle it." She cuts me with her eyes, juggling her hands. "I'm used to managing everything myself."

The words feed on my spine.

"I'll be there," I state. Then at my desk, I take the rest of the afternoon to perform computer work, searching the Internet for Heather Pratt. It's become quite the obsession since Jerry revealed her identity. And he's right. The name is common, resulting in one dead end query after another. Each disappointment seems more painful than the last. I could do without the embarrassment and confusion that occurs each time I message my life story to a stranger. Some take it as a scam. Others sparkle with curiosity, requesting more details. Most ask to be left alone.

Can't they see that's why I'm doing this, that the fear of solitude drives me to these sites? I sit here for hours, searching for a sign of commonality – a picture that bears resemblance. A beak. But all I find is confusion – nine Heather Pratts living in nine different states. I can't tell if any of them are a connection. An hour after the final bell I give up, blinking at the screen.

"You can waste a lifetime on that," Mr. Brady says, knocking on my door. I jump in my seat. I thought the office was empty. "Sorry. I didn't mean to spook you. I was trimming and saw your car." He reddens when I fail to speak, unsure of what to say. "You'd be surprised at how many people miss out on life, spending too much time on computers." He enters, removing his cap. "With all this new technology I think people forget the best way to say hi is by talking." I take a breath, reminded of my disorderly conduct. The last time we spoke I intentionally scraped his golf cart with my car. Was it due to my disgust with Hector or was I jealous of his budding relationship with Kitay? Either way I was wrong. I'm so ashamed I can hardly look at him. "Eh, who knows?" he says. "Maybe I just found someone to remind me I like hearing a voice. Kitay loves to talk." He removes his work gloves, dusting a blade a grass from his sideburn. "How 'bout you? You miss it?"

"Miss what?"

"Talking." I nod, offering a grin before returning to the computer. He stalls. "Listen, I know you don't approve of me dating Kitay."

I silence him with a hand. "Please." My heart floods with guilt. "It's not my place. Kitay is an adult. She can date whomever she chooses."

"Even me?"

I hesitate, holding a breath. I shouldn't be upset; I passed him up. He had the right to move forward, even if it was onto my friend. Kitay deserves a nice man. So I tell him I'm happy. Even if it isn't true, I say it because I have to place her needs first. I know that's what she would do for me. "Is that the only reason you're here? To receive my blessing?" I ask.

"No ma'am." He scratches his neck. "I thought you should see something. I don't know if it's my place, but I thought you might help. It's about Jasper."

His serious tone causes my heart to jolt.

A minute later, I follow Mr. Brady down a seashell pathway to the janitor's quarters. The trail ends at a tin-roofed shed where the school's riding lawnmower and landscaping tools are kept. Leading us inside, Mr. Brady clicks on a flashlight. I smell the scent of gasoline and grass clippings in the thick air.

"Watch your step," he says, reducing his pace in the darkness. "The electric is out. The wire's been cut," he explains. Rakes, shovels, and garden tools line the wall. Under my feet, leaves crinkle. I squeeze past a row of green trash cans, turning my body sideways. We arrive at a steel door.

"What is this?" I ask.

He turns to hush me, a finger to his lips.

I hear a thud, the sound of movement on the other side of the door. Goosebumps ride my neck.

Mr. Brady jiggles the knob. "Open up," he says. There's no response. "Did you hear me? No one's going to get you in trouble." We remain still until the door opens.

I peer inside. The space is no bigger than a large closet. A few floor candles splash light on the walls, papered with high fashion advertisements.

Mr. Brady shines the flashlight on the floor, spotlighting Jasper on a floral bedspread, sewing what appears to be a maid uniform, colored yellow and blue. A pile of neatly stacked clothes, his backpack, and a few water bottles surround him. Shirtless, he hunches over his project, his scar wrapping around his back.

"What's going on?" I ask. Jasper looks away, ashamed. "Jasper, answer me. Is this where you live?"

"Yes," he says.

I can hardly contain myself. "What? How did this—"

"The Ritz was booked."

"That's not funny young man." I look to Mr. Brady. "You've known about this?"

"Only for a few days."

"You said you wouldn't tell her," Jasper gripes. Glancing up, he shields his eyes from the flashlight. "Great. Now she's upset."

"It's barely the size of a cupboard," I observe. I see a roach on the wall and fan my face to keep from overheating. "There are bugs and no air."

"But it's safe. And I...."

I cut him off. "I want everything packed in one minute. Mr. Brady will help you to my car."

Leaving no room for an argument, I turn on my heel, heading to the office where I gather my purse. En route to my car the sky is clear and blue, my mind clouding with insecurities. I must be mad. What am I doing? I don't have a plan. Should I take him home? Is that legal? Ethical? I just can't leave him under these horrendous living conditions. How would I sleep at night?

The voice of Bev Dear haunts me on the ride home. *Oh Dee, how can you save a boy when you can't save a marriage?* I tune her out. Turning up the radio, the strings of a symphony pacify me. Jasper remains quiet, as I silently question his mother. How could she let this happen? Is she looking for him? Does she care? Where does that leave me? Do I fill in the blanks?

Oh dear.

How can I be a mother to him when I can barely keep the turtles alive?

At home I struggle. *Are you hungry? Thirsty? Do you like the tele, movies that make you cry?*

We talk house rules, keeping it simple. No drugs, no skipping school, and we eat dinner at the table. Oh, and no houseguests. The basics. Then we order a pizza and after a quiet meal Jasper heads to bed in one of the two guest rooms.

I retreat to my room, wondering if I'm going about this wrong. How long will he stay? We haven't had time to discuss the big picture. Perhaps I should've avoided giving him a rash of restrictions right away. I can't tell if he even wants to be here. At dinner he didn't share much other than he needs new panties. Maybe he would have opened up to me about what happened to living with his mother if I didn't peck at him.

Late that night he taps on my bedroom door as I watch a talk show with an iced cocktail. "You up?"

Sealing my nightgown, I set aside the drink and mute the tele. "Yes, I'm a bit of a night owl."

He wipes at his eyes. "I keep waking up. Mind if I watch TV with you?"

I hesitate, in fear of what the scenario would look like to a spectator with a judging eye. "You have school in the morning. You should try to sleep." I lead him back to his room where I flick on the light. His sewing kit is open on the bed beside the brightly colored maid uniform. "Get some rest. You can watch the tele tomorrow," I tell him.

He takes a pillow and drops it on the floor. "The bed's too soft. It's like sleeping on a marshmallow," he says. "I had a dream that it was eating me." I smile and turn to leave. He calls out, "Just so you know I won't go back to foster care." His voice is firm. I nod, stalling to see if he has more to say. "I'll run. I want you to know that in case you plan to call anyone."

"Do you think I would?"

"Isn't that what you're supposed to do?"

"I don't know the rules."

"They'll put me in a shelter, another home." He speaks from a place of anger rather than fear.

"Fine. I won't call anyone for now," I say. He scans my face for a reason to distrust me. His eyes question why I'd help. What have I to gain? Will I be another adult to let him down? "In time, perhaps you'll let me phone your mother to let her know you're here." He sighs, positioning his pillow to rest his head.

"She has a new man. Bernard. It's his house." He takes the blanket from the bed, covering his legs. "He's old school Creole, says I have a demon. That's why I like boys. He told her I had to leave." He says it unemotionally, lying back and closing his eyes. "I don't like him anyway. He eats turtles and snails. I'm not cool with that. I can make it on my own." He sighs. "You can turn off the light now."

I hesitate. "But your mother? Doesn't she care where you are?"

"Yeah," he says. "But she's fighting to survive. I'd rather her have a home than risk being on the street for me."

I struggle to understand. "Isn't that a mother's job? To put her child first?" He groans, motioning for me to turn off the light.

"I'm tired," he says.

"All right." I hit the switch and the room goes dark. "Jasper?"

"Yeah?"

"I'd fight for you."

I'm halfway down the hall when he speaks, his voice

brightening. "I won't be here long. I plan to hit up L.A., do the fashion school thing. I almost made it last time. I would have if it weren't for the car wreck."

I clear my throat. "You'll get there *after* you graduate." I tighten my robe, heading off. "I'll see you at breakfast."

He says goodnight. Before I close my door, he calls, "Ms. Lingers?"

"Yes?"

"It's ok if you tell me to go. I'll understand."

Then two days pass and he remains.

I begin to see a change in myself. I wonder if each word that waterfalls from my mouth will leave the right impression. I question the small things. Should I have that second glass of wine? Should I spend more time with him or offer space?

Each day I learn something new. An empty milk container does not always equate to a discarded one. And men *can* take longer than women to get ready in the morning. In fact, I'm late to work twice before realizing it's best for Jasper to apply makeup on the drive to school. He's less likely to dawdle and experiment, like the morning I found him substituting my purple lipstick for eyeliner to obtain a 'smoky' look. I couldn't bring myself to object, seeing as he had limited product of his own. In time, I buy him the necessities and also manage to pick up a sewing machine along the way. If he's determined to be in design he'll need to master it. I gift it to him on Saturday before class.

Hand to mouth, he covers his excitement. "For me?"

"Under one condition. For now, our living arrangement remains secret." If word got out that I was housing a student I'd be labeled a predatory cougar. The faculty would be outraged, though I'm certain Noni would be pleased. She's been searching for a weak spot, particularly since the students have begun favoring my services. "Don't even share it with the class," I caution him.

He agrees, and I ready the day's lesson: The Art of the Interview.

I write the basics on the board. *Maintain eye contact. Sit straight up. Nod at appropriate intervals. No chewing gum. Research the company. Read the job description ahead of time. Ask questions. If you get the job, don't squeal.*

I add the squealing bit upon hearing Kitay scream when Jasper presents her with the maid uniform. I hadn't known it was a gift.

"It's French, but with a twist," he says.

She drapes it over her body. "Wow! I'm goo goo over it! I'll wear it tonight to the Fall Mixer." Mr. Brady gave her an invitation. Good thing she mentioned it. With the new houseguest I'd forgotten that I agreed to chaperone.

Kitay kisses Jasper on each cheek in the European style. "What made you do this?" she asks.

He grabs a baguette off the dining table. "Does everything need a reason?"

She buries her face in the uniform, inhaling as if it were a bed of roses then lifts her head in delight. "I guess not. But good lordy, I hope everything happens for a reason, because even the bad things seem worth it if they've led me to all of you." She dabs her eyes.

"Don't," I plead.

"What?"

"Start that, that sappiness." I flutter my fingers, signaling her to take a seat, but it's too late. I sense a tickle in my throat and loosen my Hermes scarf, looking to my notes.

Get it together. Eyes on the prize.

Consider tedious things like the chores that need to be done. Jasper must clean his bathroom. The panties he left on the floor are bound to attract bugs.

Still it's nice to have him, hearing him sing in the shower. He's filled with such a zest for life. Yesterday he even joined me on a short outing with the turtles on the boardwalk.

"They need fresh air too, sun on their shells," I informed him.

But the truth is I needed air too. Jerry phoned. With no luck locating the real Heather Pratt he had to devise a new plan, taking to the streets to knock on doors. This morning, Lisette walks through mine with a special guest.

"A baby!" Kitay exclaims.

Pushing a pink stroller, Lisette pauses a few steps inside, dodging my eyes. "I don't have a sitter," she says. In a teal bubble dress she bends to hand the baby a bottle. "Her name's Amelia."

I try to say hello but my head goes dizzy. She has a baby? I blink to focus.

"Is it ok?" she asks.

"Yes. Of course, of course."

She wheels the baby to her desk. My heart rate rises.

"So that's Amelia," Kitay says. "Glad to finally meet you."

Finally? She knew?

Kitay reaches over her desk to tickle Amelia's foot. "Look at her cute pudgy face. What a beauty!"

"Just like her mother," Jasper says, beaming with pride. "We were worried she might take after Cici. But she only looks like him in the face when she has to poop." He revels in laughter. "Hey, isn't Cici supposed to be on baby duty?"

"He's on an interview for the manager position at his job," Lisette informs him. Rocking the stroller, she turns it to face me. I catch my breath and quickly turn my attention to the lesson, instructing the students to take out their journals. I must focus I think, beginning with a test to match one's personality to a career. Then I dive into interview etiquette, reviewing the points on the board.

But my form is off. Each word yields another bead of sweat and an ache in my heart. I begin to talk in circles about the implications of blinking in an interview.

Too many blinks: a simpleton.

No blinks: a candidate for the crisis unit.

Kitay raises her hand. "Fast fact. I'm not saying it works. I mean, I'm still unemployed." She slaps her knee, laughing. "But I got my first job in high school after offering a plate of chicken and waffles to a supermarket manager."

I crinkle my nose. "Hm. I'm not sure food is a good idea."

"It is back home. Unless we're talking about my infamous prune pie." She fans her nose. "Gives folks the runs."

Jasper plugs his nose. "Phew. Did you give some to Amelia? She just made a Cici face." He circulates the air with his hand.

Amelia begins to cry. I ignore it until a pain lights up my belly. I tell myself to calm down. My daughter is in heaven. She's safe, smiling upon me.

"I never can relax in interviews," Kitay continues. Lisette places Amelia on the floor for a diaper change. "It seems phony. How can someone know the real me in an hour? That makes my head spin."

I look to Amelia and mine spins too, like wheels on a gurney.

I see the brightest of lights, recalling that night in the hospital – the angels hovering above. That's why the sight was blinding. I convinced myself that angels had arrived to help. They're simply transportation, that's all – winged warriors to carry my precious daughter to the afterlife. Then in a blink they were gone.

I cried and cried.

Would you believe the man who hit me was the one left holding my hand? Would you believe he asked if we could try again?

I was so medicated, I replied, "When?"

"Counting yesterday, I've been on six, wait, seven interviews this month," Kitay informs the class. Lisette reaches in her pink padded baby bag, pulling out a box of wipes. "I'm beginning to lose faith. I just wish they would judge me on more than appearance," Kitay says.

"What's wrong with your appearance?" Jasper asks. "You're pretty. They're being stupid."

"Stupid or not, they won't give me job. I can't stay if I can't afford to live."

"Don't say that," Jasper grumbles.

"I'm being honest," she says, growing upset. "I'm not happy about it either. I've made so many friends, people who are nice to me."

"Oh, quit your worrying," Lisette says. "You won me over with your freaky self. You'll find a job." Kitay blushes with a smile. "You want to work? Come down here and hold Amelia while I toss out her diaper." Kitay stalls with apprehension. "What? It's no harder than that math you taught me." Kitay rises from her desk, cautiously taking Amelia in her arms. "See? It's easy. Right Ms. Lingers? You've held a baby."

Tongue-tied, I nod. If only I could admit the truth, that I choke every time I come in contact with a baby. I'd admit that even with Felix the idea of a baby never felt right, not after the incident. When he begged, I'd explain my difficulty with math, how I'd come to find safety in the smallest of numbers. Just let it be the two of us.

Jasper snaps his fingers. "Ms. Lingers, are you ok?"

I smell burning coal, the thought of interrupting father's board meeting to inform him he wasn't to be a grandfather. "I lost my baby girl," I cried over the phone. An hour later he was on a red-eye flight although his doctor advised otherwise. He had a cancerous secret but failed to reveal the extent of it. *Forgive me. I work too much. I'm too stubborn to stop. Too scared it will give me time to think. If only your mother was here.* His body was pale and thin. His arms seemed brittle. *Have you called Rose?*

Then a week later I lost him too. I don't like to think of it. I simply pretend he's in another city, too busy with work to see me.

In the here and now, the memory is heavy.

I fail to hear a knock at the door.

"It's a gift!" Jasper says, returning with a purple orchid. Reading the card, he grins. "From Wes."

Kitay swoons. "Ooh! Pet store Wes?"

Jasper hops up and down. "The guy with the accent? I bet he wears a kilt. Panties underneath."

Lisette grimaces. "Panties?"

He giggles. "Totally. He's too masculine *not* to have a secret." He hands me the flowers and I think of my father's funeral, the purple blooms surrounding his casket. We all connect. When one raindrop goes missing we each feel the splash. I ride the waves like the best of them but can't help thinking it might be easier to let go, sink. I'm tired. I don't want to live with this pain. God, please take me to my baby girl. If you don't, I'll drink 'til I drown. Then I can leave, hurt others before they hurt me. I'll escape first.

Panicked, I excuse myself to the bathroom. Sitting on the floor, my head is so heavy I rest it on the toilet. Closing my eyes, my heart besieges me with a beat, the will to go on. I wake up to find Kitay dabbing my head with a wet washcloth. I lift my chin.

"Vodka," I utter.

Her eyes grow wide with concern. "That won't help."

"Vodka," I urge.

Agitated, she pulls back. "You scared the sawdust out of us. Do you realize that?"

I stand but lose balance. Kitay catches me, leveraging my body on the wall.

I push her away. "I don't like to be touched."

"Too bad." She returns, flippantly poking my arm. "Touch. Touch."

I'm staggered into silence. What is this? When did she develop a backbone?

Perhaps she picked up a thing or two from Lisette during their study sessions that she forgot to mention. It must have slipped her mind along with the tiny fact that Lisette has a baby.

Kitay continues to poke. "You can't keep running from your problems."

"Don't test me," I warn.

"Or what?"

"I'll kick you."

"Baloney," she says.

"Yes I will. I have very good aim. I'll kick you right between the legs."

She smirks. "I don't have balls. Remember? It's honky-tonk hush hush, but the doctor fried 'em up like hushpuppies."

"You're sick."

She jiggles her hips. "Goes great with seafood."

"You're a foul, foul woman."

"Oh stop. It's funny." She playfully nudges me with her

foot.

Losing my cool, I kick her in the shin.

She yelps. "That's it. You've done it!" She throws the washcloth. "If that's how you want to be, I'm not helping you!"

I support myself on the wall until I secure a seat on the toilet. "Well, I told you not to touch me."

She bends, her blonde hair madly sweeping across her face. "Don't you get it? I'm the only one who cares enough to touch you. You've pushed everyone else away." On the verge of tears she stands, unraveling a large amount of toilet paper. "Lordy, I don't know how much longer I can do this."

"Do what?"

She wipes her nose. "What do you think? Look at you!"

I bite my lip, my eyes burning. "What? What's wrong with me? Tell me." I turn to the mirror, the tension flushing my face. "So I shut people out. It's easier. You don't understand. I've lost the people I love. I can't take the pain again."

"I had to pull you off the balcony the other night. Do you know how scary that was for me?" I don't reply and she grips my arm, spinning me around. "I said do you know how scary that was?" Her arm trembles, still gripping me. Her body is electrified, her eyes twitching in their sockets. "I thought I was going to lose you."

I shake her gaze, closing my eyes. I see flashes of light from the other night. I recall cars down below drifting along the street with such calmness. I wanted a lift so I hung by one arm, hoping the wind would carry me down, gently like a dream. "I thought I could kill the pain," I admit.

"By spreading it to everyone else?" Frustrated, she crumples up the tissue, throwing it away. "Move," she says. I step aside and she goes to the sink, turning on the faucet to wet her face. Drying off with a towel, she talks to herself. I've never seen her so upset, not even the other night over her mother. She folds the towel and leans on the sink, craning her neck to face me. "You have two kids in that room who think the world of you. What do I tell them when the city is hosing your chicken guts off the road? That it gets better?

That they should go on and deal with life's crap after you gave up?"

"They're street smart. They'd make it," I defend. "I hardly believe they'd have time to care."

"They would care. They would." She slaps the sink. "And I would too." She rushes to me, taking both of my hands. She squeezes. "Don't you see? You taught us to love the very thing that so many others taught us to hate?"

"And what would that be?"

"Ourselves."

But...but...but that wasn't on the curriculum. It's neither fair nor beneficial to introduce sentimental rubbish into the equation. I might be flawed at math but even I can add that up.

What next? Shall we all become blood sisters, crossing the Everglades to sing campfire songs to the alligators?

Oh, if only I could be mad. But how could I be with Kitay and her big eyes and big heart? Her kindness has a way of taming the tide in me. I relax because of it. I feel safe to admit things I don't want to say. "I lost my baby. I didn't protect her." The truth bristles my tongue. "I let him hit me. I should have left. I lost my girl."

She caresses my hands. "I know."

"You do?"

"You told me. The night you came to my house."

It's foggy but I remember. "When I'm drunk I let myself talk about it." She nods and I try to explain my behavior, even if it seems unreasonable and irrational. "I think if I jump and end it, I'll get a fresh start. Another chance."

She smiles. "But you're doing that through the class. Don't you see? You brought us together. You're starting over again, helping each of us." Looking over her shoulder, she calls out to Lisette and Jasper. "Isn't that right, you two?"

"Totally," Jasper says, from behind the door.

"Yeah. She helps in her own militant way," Lisette agrees.

It seems the two had been listening all along. I should've known.

"Hey Queen Lingers, are you going to be on the throne

all day or are you going to teach us something?" Jasper asks.

Kitay laughs and cheers. "See? You're a force to them. Just think. Jasper is creating amazing new designs and Lisette is taking the test to obtain her GED in three weeks. She's been studying every night. She's going to graduate."

Lisette cracks the door, entering with Amelia. "Don't throw the party yet. I need money to sign up for the test. It's expensive and I'm broke."

Jasper follows, checking his lipstick in the mirror. "I know. Sell your body to the night," he suggests. "But this time find a man with money, honey. The only fortune your Chinese food delivery boy has is inside a cookie." He giggles. "Go on. Bang. Bang."

"You jerk. I'll bang you in the head," she says, making a fist. In her other arm, Amelia begins to cry.

"All right. Out! All of you!" I say, dusting my eyes. Compliments of Kitay, the truth is clear, the class needs a leader, not a weeping widow spinning a dead thread. I must stay strong. "Kitay, please fetch my purse."

I look in the mirror and consider what Kitay said, how I've become a force to the children. How did that happen when I've been cold and aloof, wrapped up in a relationship with a man who doesn't deserve me? I've had so many walls, living life like a Hopper painting – isolated among others with no visible door.

I must change, if not for me for the class. I need to believe I can do it even if I don't believe it, even if I must say it in the mirror a million times.

Believe. Believe. Believe.

I have a life waiting for me. It's out there.

Beyond the loo, there are turtles to feed, people to teach, orchids to spritz, and a new man in the midst. Oh Wes. He won't give up, but can I weather another attempt at love? By the toilet, I look to the plunger and wonder if I can restore my faith in others, namely men. Maybe it's good, this watery body. If I sprinkle it with positivity will the seeds grow?

"Will fifty dollars cover the test?" I ask Lisette.

At her desk, she bounces Amelia in her arms, lifting

her in the air to make her laugh. "I'm not looking for a handout," she says.

Jasper pokes at the remaining baguettes on the dining table.

I take my purse from Kitay. "Please, let me help," I say. I reach in my wallet but find it empty. Odd. I don't recall making any purchases. I always keep at least a one hundred dollar bill. I made that promise to father, that in case of an emergency I could always rely on myself. "My money's gone," I say, surveying the room. The trio stares blankly back at me and I slowly connect the dots until the walls, the pop art, the purple orchid, everything spins. Lisette is in the eye of the storm.

"Don't look at me. I didn't take it," she says.

I search her face. "Are you sure?"

She grows agitated. "Yes."

"I would understand."

Her anger builds. "Understand what? I said I didn't do it."

"O...K. Let's all breathe," Kitay advises.

"Forget that," Lisette says. "I'm not gonna be accused of something I didn't do." Bottle feeding Amelia, she struggles to remain calm. I fold my arms, holding my stance. "I don't believe this. You're gonna call me out like I'm the only one in the room?"

Kitay raises her arms in innocence. Biting into a baguette, Jasper follows suit.

"It was here this morning," I explain.

"So?" Lisette returns.

"So it disappears?" She crosses the room to gather her belongings. "I'm not accusing you, but you have a history."

She pauses, stuffing diapers in her bag. "Yeah? You and I have a history too. Maybe I was wrong to trust you."

My heart empties faster than the room.

With no goodbye, Lisette and Amelia clear out first, followed by Kitay who bids me a dispirited farewell, stating she hopes to see me at the dance. When she leaves, Jasper retreats to his room. Alone, I stare at the blue horizon beyond the glass patio doors. How could I be so thoughtless to make a hasty conclusion? Yes, I'm missing cash but perhaps it was my mistake. Had I spent it?

No. It was there yesterday. I just know it. But does it matter? I've caused a rift in my relationship with Lisette, halting the progress I've made. What did I do? Can I fix it? Should I wait? I go to Jasper's room to talk it over but he's taking a nap, likely exhausted from my antics too.

Bored and perplexed, I spend the afternoon nibbling at a cheese and grape plate and reading the news. I shift from the couch to the bed until sunset when darkness overcomes me with fear. Have I wiped the slate clean with one bad move? This class is all I have, the reason for me to wake. I can't lose them. I just can't.

I head to the wet bar and down a vodka and soda to get my fizz back. Then I have another. Kitay's right. It won't help. It's a Band-Aid but where else do I turn when I've turned everyone I love away?

I shower and dress in preparation for the dance. Placing my foot in a heel, my heart weakens and I lean back on the bed, crawling into a ball.

I can't keep going like this. I want to better my mistakes but who is left to listen?

I press a number on my cell phone, then another. I can't believe what I'm doing. I don't favor my behavior. I simply need to hear a voice, someone familiar, no matter how vile. So I dial the number and wait. Still, Hector won't answer. He lets the phone do it – the sterile recording reminding me that I'm best kept far, far away.

CHAPTER 12

O NE AFTERNOON ON a South Beach road trip, Rose took a turn away from the ocean, leading us to a desolate taco bar in Little Havana. In the dead of summer we sipped virgin strawberry daiquiris and feasted on spicy black bean burritos so hot the waitress made sure to keep our water glasses filled, running back and forth from a table where her two young sons ate lunch and colored on placemats.

Why the day stands out, I can't tell. It was nothing unordinary. Perhaps it was the waitress, the exactness in her movement, the manner in which she taught the boys to cut their food using fast, precise steps. I couldn't help but stare at her fingers, finding magic in her hands, the way she seemed to create a moment even when she didn't have one. In between serving food and clearing tables she danced around time, seamlessly finding the seconds she needed.

Rose had that ability too, to make the impossible appear possible, to make life appear sweet even if my heart was heavy with the sourest notes. After spotting Bev Dear on the beach, I confided in Rose that I'd allowed my anger to control me. I'd spend hours thinking of the wittiest, meanest things to say – devising the best way to get under Bev Dear's skin, like she had mine. I'd stay awake, planning and plotting, the anger bubbling in my bones. Then I'd pounce before she'd bounce out the door. Another rendezvous. Another man.

"It sounds to me like a plea to be noticed," Rose observed.

No. That couldn't be it. I didn't need Bev Dear. I didn't need anyone.

I pushed aside my dish, the half-eaten burrito oozing with beans and rice. "I'm fine. I've learned to survive on my own."

"Oh, I don't believe that," she said. I took a sip of water, observing the boys coloring. I was ever so jealous. "Every child needs a mother."

"So what if I do? She wouldn't care," I protested.

"Well, that's something I've learned about your mother," Rose explained. "You may not see it, but you know that saying about giving someone the shirt off your back?" I nodded. "If you were cold your mother wouldn't offer you her shirt. She'd buy you one. That's the way she shows love. But you'd better tell her you're cold because she won't see you shivering."

Now, lying on the bed dressed for the dance, I think of her words. Why is it hard to admit what I want, how I feel, without being under the influence?

I hold the phone to my ear and for the second time tonight Hector won't answer. So I drive to the dance with silent regret. He'll be there. He'll know that I called. I caved. He won.

If I had the sense I'd turn back but I told Vita I'd chaperone. I must honor that commitment. I owe Vita that much. I tap the string of pink crystals around my neck and pull into the school parking lot where I sit and think. I wish Jasper had come. Then I wouldn't have this vodka bottle. I wouldn't be uncorking it to gain the courage to venture outside. He wanted to stay with the turtles. He said they needed pellets and asked me to stop at the store on the way home. His presence made me feel stronger, that I could keep calm and carry on.

What happened? Staring beyond the windshield, I wonder can I do this alone? I take a sip then another 'til I don't care about the answer. It's just me. I must smile, be happy. That way Hector can see I don't need him to pick up the phone. I can pick up the pieces and move on. Even if I'm tipsy I'm here. I made it in my green mermaid dress without him or another man. Are you listening Bev Dear? I made it.

I approach the dance, noting the blanket of white lights

providing a ceiling to the grassy floor under the oaks. I see no sign of Hector, just scattered faculty members and broad-shouldered guards monitoring the students. On a makeshift wooden stage a DJ creates an electronic beat on his laptop. Green lasers dance on the brim of his white baseball cap. I see Lisette and Cici. Dancing low he pulls her to his chest. She gifts him a kiss. I grin, taking in her brilliant red dress when I hear Vita's voice.

"Ms. Lingers! You're here!" She approaches, releasing an exhausted breath. "Thank you." She inhales, taking a hand to her forehead to gauge her temperature. "We need more water!" she says, urgently. Momentarily I lose balance, my ankle bending before I regain focus. She pulls back. Her eyes widen. "Oh Ms. Lingers, have you been drinking?" With an uneasy grin she shakes her head. "Say no," she pleads.

I dodge her eyes, noting a henna artist offering free tattoos to students at a nearby table. A girl giggles as the young man with dreadlocks draws on her arm. Vita looks at me with concern.

"Fine. I had *one* drink," I say. "Earlier."

"But I smell." She fans her face then performs the sign of the cross.

"Don't be silly. You can't smell vodka."

"Isss no good. The children will know."

"Know what?" I grow dizzy, the scent of sulfur water in my nose, kicked up by dancing students. Vita's eyes light up like a jack o' lantern. I sense doom. It's written on her face, in her twitchy smile. I think of Hector, pondering if he could be in the crowd. Is he dancing with Miss Robb? Will he go public, proud to be her date? Will he acknowledge me? I seal my lips to keep them from quivering.

Vita tugs my hand. "Come. The children can't see you like this. I have a key. I take you." Her voice is soothing, like a mother to a child. It warms me but I resist, determined to fulfill my role as chaperone, to ensure Hector doesn't think he has the best of me. I can make it alone.

"I'm not going anywhere," I state. "I have to see him. He needs to see I'll be fine."

Vita nods knowingly. I don't need to say his name.

I silently thank her with a smile. "Isss only going to hurt you," she says as the scent of pork roasting on a grill sweeps along my nose. Shadows of students eat and chat. I think of Hector. The thought of him making love to someone else cuts my chest like a crafty blade.

I'm good. I'm good inside. I can be beautiful. Can't he see that?

"What do you know? You made it," Noni says, approaching in her black sunflower dress. In one hand she holds a paper plate of chocolate cake. Her other hand supports her lower back. She nods to Vita. "I was about to start taking bets." In high spirits, she forfeits a smile and turns to me. "You'll forgive me if my wager wasn't in your favor."

Vita tugs my hand. "Dee was about to help me. The students need bottled water. We're running low."

"I can help," Noni offers.

"Oh no. Not with your back," Vita replies. "Ms. Lingers. Come."

"But who will watch the children?" I question. The sight of Noni, coupled by the thought of Hector somewhere nearby has me in an altered state. The alcohol must be catching up. "Perhaps I should stay behind."

"Heavens no," Noni says with an impish grin. "We can manage without you. We do most days."

Most days? Most days she's sick and I pick up the slack. What's this about? Is she still upset about a few students preferring me?

I can't bite my tongue any longer.

"Noni, is there a problem?" I inquire.

Vita steps in. "Ladies, not here." The song stops and the students erupt in applause. The DJ thanks the school for allowing him to spin. "There are students present."

I'm too heated to stop. "I merely want to know if Noni has something she'd like to say."

Noni edges toward me. "Actually I do." She smiles wildly, pathologically. I ponder if the pain meds for her lower back are stealing the oxygen from her brain. "Before you...." She exaggerates with a pause to clear her throat.

"Before the students started coming to you we had a grasp on them. We steered them in the right direction. Now we have girls performing oral sex in the restroom because you tell them it's natural when they confide in you." She mimics me with an aristocratic tone. "*It's normal to have urges as an adolescent. It's biological.*"

My chest burns. "And how would you know what they confide in me?"

"The walls are *thin*," she explains, her delivery hot enough to boil the most willful potato.

She's been snooping?

The nerve.

My sessions should be private even if I've nothing to hide. So what if the students want to talk about sex. It's my job to listen.

"The walls *are* thin," I concur. "But so is the air when you're standing ten feet tall looking down on everyone else." I hiccup and my voice soars. "You're too heavenly to do any earthly good. The students are young but they're people like you and me. Why judge them in their search for love?" I lose balance, wobbling on my heels. "You don't agree with my approach. I know. Everyone knows. But if you'd get off my back and get on your own perhaps you'd have a reason to talk about sex too. Tell me, Noni, when was the last time someone made love to you?"

She gasps. "How dare you talk to me like that, you... you...."

"Time to go!" Vita calls. Taking my hand she seamlessly tugs me through the crowd of dancing students. I never considered her strength. Her arm guides me with ease 'til my stomach no longer agrees with the vodka. I bend to be sick.

The students fill with concern. *Is that Ms. Lingers? Oh my God. Is she ok? Should I call for help?* Only then do I consider the repercussions of my behavior. The students look up to me. What have I done?

I attempt to stand and the world spins, the lasers blinding me. I grab for Vita and the crowd divides, allowing us to pass. Cici leads the way, instructing me to hold on.

With one hand he nudges students away. One hand clings to his baggy pants.

I ponder how I arrived here. Had I driven? I flash to a fast chat with Jasper. Before I left home he thought I looked tired, asked if I needed a cab. The question reminded me of Felix, the sense that someone was thinking of me. Felix couldn't sleep without me in the bed. He never said it but I'd return from travelling to find Valerian root in the cupboards and blankets on every couch. It was wonderful to feel needed yet frightening as well. I'd ask myself, what would happen if Felix no longer had me?

What would happen to Jasper?

Guilt fills me as Vita and I separate from Cici and the crowd, reaching the administrative office. Out front, under the crescent moon, Mr. Brady tangles with Kitay in a slow dance. In Jasper's signature yellow and blue dress, Kitay clings to him like a grapevine, resting her head on his shoulder. She lifts her face for a kiss. I hiccup, causing them to part.

"Our apologies," Vita says. "We'll look away. Please. Continue. Kiss, kiss," she urges, leading me toward the office stairs. I cover my face.

"Dee, is that you?" Kitay asks. She rushes up. Pulling away my hand, she gulps. "Oh Lordy. How much have you had to drink?" I try to speak but nothing comes out. Vita wheezes, lifting me step by step. Kitay assists. "Please. How can I help?" she asks. "She lives in my building. She's a friend."

Vita remains cautious. "Friend?"

"Yes. I've warned her about drinking."

Vita sighs, taking a breath. "You can take her home? Isss good?"

"Yes it's good. Of course," Kitay says. "Jim can take us in his truck." I turn my head to find Mr. Brady. He nods, his face full of concern.

Vita unlocks the office door. "No stopping. Straight home," she instructs.

"Yes ma'am," Kitay says. Mr. Brady echoes it.

"Bueno. Wait here. I'll take her inside and clean the

mess off her dress," Vita says. In the office she flicks on the light and I close my eyes, fast-forwarding time. Later, I wake alone in my office chair, facing the Frida Kahlo painting. She seems more disappointed in me than usual. I look down to see globs of food clinging to my dress. I drown in the shame and loss, wondering if Kahlo could relate. I once read a bus accident had left her with a pierced uterus resulting in a miscarriage. If only Frida was here to talk. Perhaps she could explain where my baby's gone, if she heard a goodbye when her baby became a spirit. I listened but I never heard a thing.

Sometimes I think about things like that.

When Bev Dear died, father said he heard an electrical surge in the house. When he found her body he figured it had been her soul escaping.

"Mother couldn't get to heaven fast enough," he told me. "She traveled the speed of light. She had wonderful news to share." He attempted to smile, his eyes full of tears. "About our family, about you, our daughter."

We all connect, all energy waiting to inevitably take on a new form. We're so quick, so fast to need heaven it sets the fire of hell at our heels.

So here I sit with limbs afire, praying the dynamite in my heart will ignite. No match in sight though, just a flare up in the next room where Vita argues with her husband on the phone. She hadn't forgotten dinner. There are enchiladas in the fridge. Can't he do anything for himself? She was hoping he'd come out with her one night.

"But you never take me dancing," she tells him. "So I take myself. What do you want?"

She laughs at his response, telling him she hasn't time for nonsense. There are students are waiting, a coworker in need. She whispers something I'm certain is about me, but I'm more intrigued with *another* voice in the office – the husky tone of a man. I try to disregard it but know it too well. *Quiet. Quiet.* The man sounds distressed so I stand, my shaky legs leading me to Hector's office where I hear him talking through the door.

I shouldn't open it. I should know better.

On the phone, Vita instructs her husband how to turn on the oven.

I turn the knob, discovering the door is unlocked.

I open the door, and oh, oh, OH.

A sizeable hole ruptures my heart.

I find Hector in mid-spasm, naked below the waist, artfully attached to Miss Robb. Hunched over the desk with a sock in her mouth she emits a gasp, her red dress ruffled up her back. The two freeze and the only movement in the room is her fiery hair, stirred by the fan. She spits the sock, turning her head away in shame.

I flinch but can't look away. I need to see it, need my brain to understand why I need to move on. Are you watching this, brain? Are you feeling this, heart? I'm tired of being led the wrong way.

I flash back to my junior year at Vassar, the night I telephoned Rose to voice my excitement over meeting Walter, my first love, at a dance. He said he was interested in challenges. I looked like the biggest one in the room.

He was right. I looked to my toes when a boy came within five feet of me. Could he tell I'd never been asked to dance before? It was utterly childish to yearn for something that small. But to me, it felt as if the world.

"He's courting you," Rose said.

"Oh. Stop. You make it sound like I'm a princess or a queen."

"No. Just a lady."

"A lady?"

"Well, that's what your mother taught you to be," she said, matter-of-factly. "I'm sure she'd agree."

"Really?" My heart skipped before finding its footing. "You think I'd pass her test?"

"I think...." She hesitated. "Desi, funny you should mention tests." For an upbeat woman, she took a heavy breath. "Oh, it's silly. I don't want to ruin your night. You have so much to celebrate." She strained a laugh. "There's no cause for alarm, really. The doctors have been running tests, a few. They found a lump."

Six months later she passed.

The time went fast.

That's when I decided that I must be faster than cancer. Think death can beat me? Not if I start the race early. I began the assault on my liver long ago. One drink became two. Two became four. Four became eight. Foolish perhaps, but it's more clever than waiting around like a helpless bystander. It isn't good to be vulnerable. Why right now, if I were frail, I'd be putty on the floor. But no, I'm headstrong, hell bent on finding the exit. I've learned it's best not to scream. Still, Vita hears my heels. How could she not? I tread like a bull.

"No! No! Isss no good. Sit!" she says. Crossing my path, she blocks me with her bosom.

"Vita, I adore you. I know much you care about me, but please move." Her eyes resist, begging me for a valid reason. "He's here. I have to rid myself of him. I can't keep doing this. Why do I return to be beaten?" Her eyes water, her hand caressing my right cheek. Without warning she slaps me twice.

"There's your beating. Happy?" I stand still, breathing shallow. With a wet cloth she cleans my lips, my dress. She hands me a glass of water. I drink it. "Now go. You've punished yourself enough," she says. "Stop looking for a man to hurt you. Look for a man to love you."

I nod and break off, the humid air hitting me like a fist on the outside.

I start slowly down the sidewalk then build in momentum. In the darkness, my eyes float to a yellow lamppost, guiding me. I think of Bev Dear looking down upon me in judgment. *Never good enough. Not quite smart enough.* I think of Hector. *Not pretty enough to take in public.* I tap the hook of my nose. The ugliness spreads, icing my heart. It chills me.

In the distance I hear music from the dance – a church bell chiming over an overindulgent bass line. The bass, it pounds and pounds, vibrating my bones. My head throbs. I blink, losing balance, looking down to find a heart carved in the sidewalk. A set of initials lies beneath it. What came of the lovers after the cement set? Was the love strong enough to harden? Why do we plaster ourselves with the belief that love is enough to fill in the cracks? For me, Felix set the bar high, loving me so well that I'd forgotten I needed to love myself. It's hard to do. I want to. I want to.

I send out a cry, plunging forth in the darkness until I see Mr. Brady.

He waves, and I fall into his arms.

"Whoa," he says, catching me.

Dazed, I look to his kind face, doubled like identical twins. The vodka is playing tricks. He smiles and his teeth brightly sparkle.

Hector calls my name from behind. "Dee!" His voice is a mixture of anger and concern. He's coming to find me, save the day – make it better. I won't go to him. Not like before.

"Where am I?" I inquire to Mr. Brady. He holds me to his chest.

"At the school dance," he says. "Kitay is bringing around the car. She asked me to wait for you."

I struggle to focus, staring into his eyes. "You're a good man. Isn't that right, Mr. Brady?" He stalls with a sigh that seems to pity me. "What? You don't agree? Should I tell people different? I haven't met a good man as of late. I'm losing faith in the myth."

"Ma'am, she'll be right here," he says in a shaky voice. I grin, breathing in the scent of spearmint on his mouth. He tilts his head back. "Why don't you close your eyes?"

"I'm not tired," I say, his face turning fuzzier. "You're good. I believe that. You'll do whatever it takes to make Kitay happy." Anchoring my hands on his shoulders I smell French vanilla on his skin – a remnant of dancing with Kitay, the way she needs everything to be French. "I taught her that," I tell him. "How to convince a man to give a lady what she needs."

"Dee, where are you?" Hector calls, nearing.

"Does she know the final act though?" I ask, tugging his shirt. "That it all comes to an end? The heart is weak. It took my Felix."

"I'm sorry," he says, sadly. "I know what it is to lose. I miss my wife. I think of her everyday." He smiles through it. "It's ok to love again. She would've wanted me to go on."

"I want to go on too," I tell him. "I look for love on the streets but don't see it, just people treating each other unkindly. I all but lose hope. Then I see a man like you." I draw close to his face and he pulls away. Still I persist. It's a magnet, the goodness radiating from his core. I want to taste it, just a sample, to remind myself what it feels like be loved by someone kind. Maybe then I'll let the hurt go. "It only takes one good man to make a woman believe in the goodness of all men again."

I lean in, my lips nearly touching his before he pulls away.

Kitay screams. "NOOOOOOOOOO!" It rattles the darkness, quickening the pace of people approaching from both directions. Mr. Brady pushes me away and I stumble back, taking a fall. It startles me, the hard cement catching my tail. I roll to my knees and stare ahead. The sidewalk rises, changing its angle. It curves upward and I grab the ground, clinging for life. Should I let go?

Oh dear, what have I done? What was I trying to do? How could I hurt my closest friend? I'm no friend, no teacher – I'm rotten to the apple's core.

I look up to see Hector and Vita, falling in and out of focus, harvesting the moment.

Kitay falls to her knees. "How could you?" she says, weakly. "He's with me. You could have anyone, but you try to kiss him? Why?"

I'm speechless, overcome with guilt as Lisette springs from the shadows to assist. Cici follows.

Lifting her dress, Lisette bends to cradle Kitay in her arms. She kisses her forehead. Amidst the chaos, the sight warms me. I recall a day not long ago when Lisette would barely speak to Kitay unless to bark. Love what they taught you to hate to learn who you are. That's all she needed to reach within and transform.

If only I could practice what I preach.

But I was a good teacher, right?

Right?

Now, more than anything, I'd like to believe I helped

others change for the better, beyond what one learns in the books.

Lisette looks to me. "Is this what you meant?" she snarls. Stroking Kitay's back, she shakes with rage. "About women being our own worst enemies?" I don't answer and she grows louder. "Is it? Is it?" I remain silent, feeling nauseous again. "If it is then I don't want to be a woman or a lady or whatever you call it. You can have it!"

Cici bends, grabbing Lisette's shoulder. "Babe, relax." She shakes her head and he shifts his gaze to me as if in need of guidance. "Ms. Lingers?" He cocks his head to the side like an inquisitive dog, his eyes full of sincerity and light.

I can't face him, not after what I've done. There's simply no excuse. I can't blame the alcohol. I'm to blame. Just me.

So I stand and dust off, then steady myself and run away before anyone can catch me. In the parking lot, I become sick before I find my car. Inside, I start the ignition, my skin perspiring. The cold air hits my face, soothing me, and I rest my head back, feeling drained and guilty. Dear God, what was that? What's come over me? I don't like this person. Oh, whom am I kidding? Person? I'm a detestable beast! Have I sprouted fangs? Bloodsucker does blend nicely with batshit crazy. Perhaps I'm not a far cry from the names the students call me. What causes me to act in such a way? How could I betray those I've come to love the most? I thought I'd made improvements, placing the needs of others first. This shadow of myself frightens me.

Exhausted, I think, breathe, breathe.

I can be better. Good. I just know it, I tell myself – the world growing fuzzy until I close my eyes and drift off.

An hour later I hear car horns and laughter, the sound of students leaving the dance. I wake barely refreshed to stretch my neck and gather my wits, placing the car in reverse.

At the parking lot exit, I fall behind a line of cars. I turn up the radio and take a sip of bottled water. Just ahead, the red taillights on a Jeep blink on and off as if a warning.

Careful to stay awake, I lower the windows and a hot

wind blows through my hair as I head home on Southwest First Street. In Little Havana, I stop for coffee then drive by bright fast food signs and billboards saying no to crime. It's a wonder I'm not stopped. I weave like a water snake when there's no car to guide me. Stuck at a red light behind a Metrobus, the radio plays a Mahler symphony. I look to my right and discover Noni in a sun-bleached blue hatchback.

Oh dear!

I gasp and redirect my eyes as if unaware of the strange, miserable woman beside me. Over on the curb, I notice a drunken gray-haired man fraught with the task of mounting the banana seat on his bicycle. Suddenly, I'm assaulted by Noni's car horn.

Honk. Honk.

I twist to meet her menacing eyes, her face ridden with tension. She nods, keeping her lips sealed as if baking profanities in her mouth. Who knows what's burning her up? Perhaps it's my face or perhaps she's still upset that certain students prefer me. A slut. A drunk. So here she is, away from the school, ready to scold me. But what does she plan to do?

In suspense, I accept her stare-off. She has no idea this game is child's play compared to the damage a gaze from Bev Dear could do. Our eyes remain locked until the light turns green. Only then does she shift her attention, mnemonically mouthing 'go' as if she'd been preparing for the moment since birth. Then boom, her foot hits the gas and she screeches off.

Is it a challenge? I watch her taillights fade, and I press the gas, slow and steady. I know better than to race. I'm in no state for it. I'm not interested in a duel until I catch a glimpse of her arm slip out of the window. She extends her middle finger, and it's ON.

Tracing her tracks, I build in speed; storefronts blur like brilliant watercolors. I think of Bev Dear. She wouldn't settle for second. *What would people think?*

Accelerating, I turn up the radio. The symphony swells as I edge up to her car. She blasts the horn, her ponytail blowing in the wind. She screams out of her window, her mouth opening wide as a sinkhole. She's stuck on one word – whore or bore – something with an o.

Side by side, I build in speed, anticipating the sweetness of victory when she guns it. Just ahead, the three-lane road abruptly turns to two. She must not see the construction, the barricades and flashing lights. Failing to brake, she takes out a line of orange barrels. In the mirror I see sparks – a meteor shower of metal. Noni's car rolls twice, landing upright, facing opposing traffic.

I pull off the road and exit the car to see a cloud of smoke. The street seems gauzy and surreal with headlights backing up behind the wreck.

I run to Noni's car, dialing 911. The smell of burnt rubber overwhelms me. The dispatcher picks up. "There's been an accident!" I call. "What do I do?"

"What is the location of the emergency?" she asks.

People flood from their cars and I get close enough to see Noni passed out in the driver's seat, her face streaked with blood.

"No! No! God! Please," I cry out.

An hour later I sit alone in a chilly waiting room at Jackson Memorial. On the tele a newsman reports on a Homestead shooting. I listen for coverage about the car accident but it never comes. Passing time, I purchase Noni a vase of sunflowers on my phone. Then I purchase her a cactus too, something bound to survive.

The next morning, I visit Noni and notice they are the only two gifts in her room. The nurse tells me she hasn't received a phone call or any visitors since being admitted. I know she isn't married but she must have a parent or a sibling. Someone.

As Noni sleeps, I phone Nurse Ferrera and Vita. They each promise to visit within the hour. While I wait, I astutely listen for Noni's breath, thanking God for each one. Eventually a male nurse in blue scrubs enters to check her vitals.

"How is she?" I inquire. It's the first time I've been brave enough to ask.

"She's lucky," he says. Reading the monitor, he writes

down a note. "Just a minor concussion, some scrapes and bruising. She's still pretty sedated but she'll be fine with rest."

Ten minutes later he returns to check her IV and she wakes with a subtle moan. "Good morning sunshine," he says. She grunts, kicking her feet out of the blanket. "Aw. You can do better than that. The ER doctor says you were talking last night, couldn't get you to stop." He cautions her as she tries to lift her legs. "Watch it. Your body needs to heal." He taps her shoulder. "Look. You have a visitor. She's been here all morning. I wish I had someone who cared about me that much." Noni shifts her neck to view me and emits a muffled cry. Sitting up, she scratches a bandage above her right eye. "Try not to do that," the nurse instructs. "I know it's itchy but you'll pull out the stitches." Noni tightens her lips, lowering her arm to he side. Her eyes brim with anger.

"He's the expert," I advise Noni. "He assures me you'll be better soon." Her mouth opens but fails to release a word. "I'll help 'til then. So will the others from school. I'll make certain of it."

Noni purses her lips, closing her eyes. After the nurse leaves I watch trivia on the tele, rattling off answers about New York Fashion Week until Noni tells me to be quiet. For once her voice brings a smile to my face.

"You're enjoying this," she says.

"No. I'll enjoy it when you return to work." She attempts to move her neck, crying out. I stand to fix her pillow and she relaxes, resting her head. "Better?" Her mouth remains neutral but she nods. "Good."

I sit and Vita sweeps into the room, digging in her purse. Her blonde hair is pulled in a bun, a few strands standing up. She casts Noni a worrisome glance then looks to me. "Is she talking? I pray. I pray all the way here." Clutching her rosary beads, she tosses her purse on a chair and approaches the bed, making the sign of the cross. Noni begins to snore. "I say God. I say take me instead. I'm old."

I stand to pat Vita's back. "Oh, He has enough old people lying around heaven. You should try bribing Him with something else."

"What? What do you mean? Is she going to be ok?"

I peer over her shoulder to see Noni sleeping blissfully. "She'll live."

"Oh." She breathes a sigh of relief, closing her eyes to whisper a Hail Mary. I respectfully bow my head before gathering my purse to depart.

"I'll be back," I say. "Fluff her pillow and make sure her feet can breathe. She seems to like that." I make it to the door before returning to the bed. I bend to whisper in Noni's ear. "I'm not perfect. I admit it. I can be childish." She opens her watery eyes, tilting her head toward me. "Oh, I'm a fool. I don't know what to say. It's been a long night and a longer morning." I shake my head. "I know we may never be friends, but perhaps, if you would allow it, we could be better enemies." I touch her hand, and for a moment she squeezes it. Then her eyes fill with pain and she pulls away. I wonder, could it be we're granny apple alike? Is that why we fight? Is she preparing to be alone like me, to be ready when she ends up there? If so, I don't want to be that person. I'm done practicing for a life of solitude just because it might ease the process at the end. Hiding hasn't helped. The class has shown me that. I've grown accustomed to their spats and their poor table manners. I cherish their cheery, if sickly sweet facial expressions when they learn something new. I can't fathom life without them. How do I get them back?

At home, the turtles are active and Jasper's nowhere in sight. Realizing I forgot to buy pellets, I sprinkle the aquarium with lettuce then head to the loo to wash my face. I haven't slept a wink but I'm not tired. My heart is heavy. I know what I must do.

Without a moment spared, I avoid the elevator and take the stairs to the fourth floor. Remaining quiet, I announce myself at Kitay's door with a knock. I'm hoping to catch her off guard so she hasn't time to tie together a million reasons to shut me out. I'm well aware that I made a grand booboo and betrayed her friendship, but I can make things right again.

I continue to knock, only to hear Taser's bark.

"Kitay? I understand that you're upset." I press an ear

to the door, hearing Taser scratch on the other side. I wait until he stops before I speak again. "I know I hurt you." I grip the doorknob; the cold hard surface sends a chill up my spine. "I'm trying to make sense of it, why I act like I do, if that counts." I have to let my guard down. She deserves the truth, at least the bits I can piece together. "I want you to know I think there's some good left in me. I haven't seen it much since Felix, but I can sense it growing since I met you." I think of her denim skirt and grin. "Perhaps I needed you to remind me that I can be kind and that kindness exists in others. Since I met you, I believe it does." With no response, I whisper, "Please Kitay, I don't want to be alone."

Seconds later I give up, walking off. Then hearing the doorknob turn I spin around. "Kit..." I begin.

"No," Jasper says. He picks a wedge out of his red pajama shorts and Taser dashes out, pulling his cart. "Kitay's not home." He squats to Taser's level. "Let's go mister. Get your snooty booty back in this house."

Taser begins licking my leg. "I need to talk to Kitay. Where is she?"

He hesitates, casting me a cautious stare. She must have told him what I've done. I can't blame him for being upset. What kind of role model have I been? I'm equally disappointed in myself. I raise my chin, accepting my penance.

"Her father died," he says.

My heart sinks. I can barely speak. "What?"

Inside the condo the microwave beeps. "C'mon, Taser. Time to eat." Taser heads inside, and I follow them to the kitchen.

"I'm sorry to hear the news," I offer, as he removes a bowl of soft dog food and vegetables from the microwave. He sets it on the tile and Taser eats, wagging his tail. "Is Kitay ok?"

"She'll be all right. She's pretty strong, you know."

"Yes." My throat closes and I clear it with a cough.

In a flash, I think of Kitay returning to her mother Gladys and being called Charlie. It slices my heart, fogging my eyes. I look away.

"She asked me to care for the pets," Jasper says.

"Wait. Did you tell her you were living with me?"

He avoids the question; his evasiveness suggests he had. "Taser likes his food warm. I cut the broccoli into really small pieces so he doesn't choke." I turn my head to watch Taser eat and fill with despair, wondering when Kitay would come back or if she'd come back at all. She has no job, no money. She sought my help. What could I've done differently? "Did you buy food for the turtles?" he asks.

"I forgot. But I fed them lettuce."

"They can't live on lettuce."

"I'll get food tomorrow."

He runs a hand down his face, rubbing away his disbelief. "Don't you get it? You can't just wing it. They depend on you. There's more important things in life than designer dresses and getting drunk."

"Where is this coming from?" He waves me off, picking up the empty dog bowl and rinsing it in the sink. "Jasper? What's wrong?" He places the bowl in the dishwasher and says goodbye to Taser before exiting the front door.

I take the elevator up, finding him on his bed, reading. He stops me before I speak.

"I need to finish this," he says, holding me off with his hand. "It's for an assignment."

I take a breath. "Well, I'm glad you're working on your studies, but I would like to...."

"Not now," he snaps. I fold my arms, refusing to budge until he addresses me in a proper tone. Bothered, he references the book. "What your problem? It's *The Sun Also Rises*."

"Lovely. However, if *you'd* like to see the sun rise again I suggest you put it away."

He rolls his eyes. Closing the book, he sits up. "What?"

"I'd like to speak to you about the way you spoke to me earlier. I don't like it."

"Fine. We won't speak." He looks down, casually flipping through his book.

"Excuse me?" I inhale to refrain from losing my cool. "Is that sarcasm part of being a teen? Are you on a roll?" He starts reading. "Shall I go to the fridge and find you some butter for it?"

"You could if there was some butter left. There's no food. You need to go shopping."

"Enough!" I say.

Oh, how did this start? It seems like one fight merely morphs into another. Perhaps I'm going about this wrong. It's not fair for me to quiet him just because I don't like hearing what he has to say. I messed up, made a mistake, forgot that I needed more food in the house. I can't get every action right.

"I didn't realize we were so low on groceries," I state.

He looks up, his blue eyes piercing me. "You wouldn't know because you don't eat. You just drink. All the time." Upset, he stands to leave. I block him at the door, grabbing his arm.

"What's going on?"

The vein in his neck pulsates, his blue eyes turning pale. "Nothing. It's fine. I've gone without food before."

"Is that it? You don't think I'll feed you? That's not —"

"Don't you get it?" he interrupts. "You left here drunk. You drove drunk. I was scared when you didn't come home. You didn't call. You didn't answer your phone." In a fit, he breaks free and flees to the kitchen where I find him leaning over the counter with his back turned to me. I don't know what to say. The perfect response would come out wrong because everything he said is right. Luckily, he speaks first. "You're the only chance of a real mother I have."

Then it hits me. For Jasper, this is more than a temporary arrangement. He's counting on me. If only I'd relayed my struggles with math, numbers, adding things up. Perhaps he would have built a home with someone else. He would have had a chance at success. He wouldn't equate me to a mother. Oh, I said it. Mother. Is that what I've become? I never thought it could be achieved this way.

"When you moved in, I didn't expect to be a...mother. I never thought I'd live to see that day."

He turns to me. "Well, I never thought I'd be a foster kid but life happens. Sometimes it sucks, but you meet certain people, and it's like, they're cool. Maybe they can sew up the holes."

My heart is heavy with worry. "I wouldn't be good at being a mother. I'm a miserable person."

"No you're not. You're just saying that to get out of it. You're scared and you're being lazy."

"You think I'm lazy?"

"It's easier to be miserable than to wonder up a better way."

"Perhaps," I admit. The weight of my failures is enough to flatten my heels, plunging me underground. But what if I were to view each letdown as a lesson on how to become a better person, the one standing here now? I shift my footing and eye him with sincerity. "I made a mess of things. I pushed away Kitay and Lisette. I don't know if I'll get them back. I probably don't deserve to. I push. It's what I do."

His voice lightens. "If it makes it any better, I pushed you."

Without another word, he escapes to care for the turtles. I find him, one hand in the aquarium, scooping out lettuce. "If you put too much in the tank it gets dirty," he explains. He takes the turtles out, setting them on the bar. They keep their heads hidden. I stroke one, running my fingers along its shell. "You pet it like a cat," he observes.

"I had a cat once. Flippy. He was special. He barked, you see."

He grants me a curious look, wrinkling his brow. "That's weird."

"A little."

"We'll have to name them sometime, the turtles," he says.

"We will. But for now, can we talk about you?" He remains silent, feeding the turtles when they reveal their heads. "You said you pushed me? What did you mean?" He doesn't respond. "Jasper?"

"Do we have to?"

"I'd like to know."

He emits a reluctant breath, providing the turtles a barrier with his hands so they don't fall off the bar. "It's nothing. Kitay said I should be honest if I want this to work with you." I search his eyes. "I...you see, that money you're missing from your purse." He stiffens his body. "I stole it."

"What?" I step back in disbelief. "What would make you do that?"

"I don't know." Flustered, he places the turtles back in the aquarium.

"Jasper. Tell me."

"Because I've been hurt before. All right?"

"So you hurt me in return?"

"Isn't that what you do?"

Yes, but I gave you a home, the basic necessities. Shelter. Water. Granted, I've been slipping in the food department. I'll never be perfect.

Brewing with emotion, he remains strong. "Are you going to kick me out?"

"Whoa, hold on." I circle my hands, erasing his words. "Who said anything about that?"

"That's what happens when I mess up. I do something wrong and I'm out. So I messed up. Go ahead. Kick me out."

"Jasper, I'm not kicking you out."

"That's what they all say but here I am." He smiles faintly then returns to his room.

Should I follow him? Do I give him time alone? The decision overwhelms me, my heart tugging me to the bar. With a few drinks I'd be numb. I wouldn't have to process the pain of what I'd just heard. I can be like Bev Dear who put off parenting with a cocktail. Oh dear. Is that the kind of person I am now? I race to the mirror and see her face in the cracks, in every wrinkle, every imperfection. The voice in my head ridicules my hooked nose and the crow's feet around my eyes. It screams I need polishing: how to walk, talk, down to how to breathe.

Love what they taught you to hate to learn who you are. Love what they taught you to hate to learn who you are.

I repeat this over and over and spin to view the dining table. I see a purple orchid – a present from Wes. It's another sign. I resist love, even if a seedling of it may grow given the proper soil. I can't keep pushing people away. I don't want to end up like Bev Dear.

I go to Jasper's room and swoop in to tell him I won't let him go. I want to put my heart on the line. Then I say something else before I lose the nerve.

"I love you," I tell him.

On his bed, he cautiously sits up.

My body tingles and I place a hand to my heart, releasing a cry. "Oh dear. It's been a long time since I've said that. I didn't know it'd be so hard."

"It's not," he says. "You just say it. Like everything else."

"But...but it means more than everything else." I allow myself a moment to settle and he laughs, as if finding me silly.

"Seriously. Are you ok?"

The trembling subsides. "Yes."

He smiles, shaking his head. "It's a word. It's no big deal."

"Good, because I plan to say it often." He mulls it over, his face reddening. "That way, you know I want you here. I'd like to do that, if you'd let me."

He grins. "That's fine, but don't get weird about it. Then it won't be a big deal, you know, if I say it too. Someday."

"Oh. Right." I play it cool, but his words hit me like a gust a wind. My heart quickens. I don't know what to say so I exit, breathless, but with a fresh breeze in my heart.

The gusts continue the next day, sailing me through an ordinary Monday morning where Jasper remains quiet as we glide over the waterway to school.

In Little Havana I stop to pick him up a bagel, and once fed, he talks about starting a blog for his fashion line. His plan is to work in orange and gold fabrics, creating clothes for fellow eccentrics of the world. The thought puts a smile on my face as I settle at my desk.

"I prayed all night," Vita says, arriving with coffee. Her eyes fill with gloom. "I prayed you'd be heavy in the Spirit."

"How considerate. But I've been on a diet."

"The whole school is talking. They say you did it. You

caused the accident."

My chest tightens. "Who said that?"

"Noni."

"Rubbish," I state.

"I only repeat what I hear."

"Yes. And how many times did you repeat it today? To how many people?" She looks down in shame. "You shouldn't have driven. You were supposed to go with Mr. Brady and that woman. You know I worry."

"Thank you. I'm fine."

With a sniffle, she lifts her head. "I know you think I'm a chatterbox, but I like to talk. That's all. You're too busy for that. Everyone's always busy." She goes to leave and I call her back. So she's a snoop. So? She's one of the few who seems to care about my life at all. I know I make it hard.

"Thank you for coming to the hospital," I say. She timidly nods as if expecting something severe to follow. "I'm certain it meant a lot to Noni."

"She doesn't have many people in her life. I tell my husband, I think she's a lonely woman."

"I'm afraid I have to agree."

She remains quiet for a moment, contemplating. "I should sort through my email. It's building up." She smiles, taking a step to leave.

"Vita," I call.

She turns. "Yes?"

"Would you like to get a drink out this week? Coffee?"

Her neck jolts. "No alcohol?"

"Coffee."

She considers it, replying with a grin. "I would like that."

"Good. I'll figure out a day and time."

She sets off with a spark in her step and I stand to close the door, heading to the filing cabinet where I locate the remains of my vodka stash. I quietly bury it in the trash. I don't plan to stop drinking but I do plan to end intoxicated public appearances. I can't be a role model to Jasper and the other students if I'm under the influence. I have to think about more than just me now.

Still, the thought of sobriety frightens me, especially with Hector's voice permeating the walls. Later that morning he's in a mad stitch about fresh bullet holes in the juice vending machine. Within seconds, the school goes on lockdown and we're directed to remain in the office while the police deal with the issue.

I only open my office door to console Vita.

The flame of a prayer candle flickers at her desk. "Our students are good," she says. "They wouldn't hurt anybody. It's only juice. All that sugar isss no good for the children anyway." I pat her back, admiring her ability to always support the students.

Followed by two police officers, Hector scurries through the office. My heart drops when his eyes find mine. "Are you ok?" he asks.

My heart swells. "Yes," I manage. "Never better."

Oh dear. Is it too early for a relapse? I picture him naked, hovering above Miss Robb and the discarded vodka calls me. Even if I convince myself I'm ready to move on, I can't scratch the image of him making love to another woman. The thought blinds me, burning my pupils as he dashes out to assist with the investigation.

An hour later I can focus enough to complete my therapy notes when he reappears, poking his head inside. "Can I come in?"

I tap away at the computer as if all is right in the world. "Of course."

He closes the door, standing across from my desk. "Busy day."

"Sounds like it. Is everyone safe?"

He artificially laughs. "Yes, no harm done. Just some damage to a few cans of V8." I smile, continuing to type until the silence takes an uncomfortable turn. "I thought you'd like to know I sent flowers to Noni."

I turn to him, straining to be professional. "That's good." I clench my teeth. It's all I can do not to scream. *He's no good for you! He'll only hurt you!* If I know this, why does my heart root for him? How do I convince it otherwise? I must be the one to teach it – change it. So I do. I tell it, "I'm worth more."

"What?"

I stop typing to close my eyes and exhale, setting my palms flatly on the desk. "I'm worth more." I stretch my spine, sitting upright in my seat. I think to myself, I have the ability to love, to be loved. I've been in a funk, that's all. Loneliness clouded my judgment so I took the abuse and abused him in return. I had so much anger, stored rage. How could God take my one love, my Felix, from me? Hadn't I suffered enough? That's why I gave up on romantic sunsets to court a death wish. I wanted a bumpy ride that would rival those old wooden roller coasters. With Hector I valued each bruise. Even if it wasn't the best way to heal it felt right, solidifying what I'd been taught.

Never good enough. Never smart enough.

I believed it.

But why? Had I forgotten Felix taught me otherwise? What of Rose, who never wavered seeing the goodness in me? I'm still the passenger riding at her side, still the little girl with enough heart to share with the world. But when will I take the wheel?

Is it too much to ask him to attach his name to the flowers he sends? Is it too needy to desire his hand in public?

I say it even if I have to spit it out. "Hector." I clear my throat to ensure my voice is crisp and clear. Slow and steady, I lock my eyes on him. "I'm worth more than you can give me." I take a breath and my heart balloons in my throat. God, this is difficult.

"What is this?" Hector asks.

And I say it again and again, building 'til I believe it. "I'm worth more. I'm worth more. I'M WORTH MORE."

"Stop it Dee." He quiets me with his hands. "I hear you."

"Really Hector?"

Ridden with regret, his face deflates. He looks down upon me as if he knew someday it had to come to this. "Amena mena mena mena." He shakes his head. "I'm sorry." He lowers his eyes, weighed by sadness. After a moment of silence he speaks again. "Can we talk? Like normal people?

That's all I want. Can we do that?"

I hesitate, visualizing a million witty and wonderfully wicked things to say, but where would it lead, back in bed with him? That's what he wants – the fight, the passion – hot air to fill his ego. I can't do it. I'm out of breath. "It's over," I tell him. "We've both acted poorly. I don't need you to clear the air."

"Maybe I need it for me." His anger builds and he slaps his chest. "Are you listening? Do you even care about what I need?" He pauses. "I know the harm I've done. I live with the guilt. I see it every time I look at you." His words weigh on my heart. I frown, the tension cascading down my chest. He wipes his lips to calm himself. The love, the lust, whatever this is, I know I must let it go but it clings to me like a child, like I brought it into this world therefore I must care for it.

Avoiding his dejected eyes, I turn to my keyboard and type. It pains me to see him distraught. I have no idea what to write but I make it seem important. It's the only thing keeping me sane. He knows it. The right look, the right word – I'll cave.

"Look at me," he pleads. "Is this what I get for coming here to apologize?" I shrug and he mutters to himself, pacing erratically. He takes a breath to admit the truth. "Miss Robb left, ok? She quit. You got what you want. Are you happy?" I stop typing to face him. Stay calm, I think. His eyes blink as the pressure builds. I've never seen him so adrift. "She can't take the humiliation of the other night. She's looking at a position at a military school in Homestead."

I simply say, "All right."

"You won't have to see her anymore," he explains. "We're still together, but, you know, she has trouble letting things roll off. She's not you."

A compliment? My mind wanders 'til I net it. When feelings are involved, a bit of praise can become a butterfly in seconds. I can't let my heart fly away.

"She could've said no," I suggest. "She didn't have to do whatever you were doing on your desk."

"She can't put up a fight like you."

"I didn't always put up a fight."

Damn. I'm doing it. I'm giving in. Stop. Stop. Stop.

His lips hint at a smile. "I can't say I don't miss it, the fun we had." I shake my head. He's devious. Even at his deepest low he's always ready to leap. So why does my heart still turn to syrup for him? I chastise it for not recalling there are better men. I think of Felix and it settles. "Remember the good times we had?"

I smile. "Yes, but that's in the past."

With a sly smile, he thumbs through a psychology book on my desk. "And you're sure we can't try it again?"

My eyes narrow. "Hector, stop."

"Ah." He grows frustrated, more so with himself. "Why do we have to stop? I don't want to stop."

"We can't do this."

"Do what? What are we doing?"

I throw up my hands. "This!" I point a finger to him then turn it on myself, waving it back and forth.

My heart quickens. Mixed messages and subtle innuendos are how the cycle starts – no gas required. Our relationship IS the gas. It's become a running joke that's no longer fun even if it sporadically fuels the furnace of a lonely heart.

I recall long, listless nights on the couch, waiting for him to call or show up. How I wished for a way out.

I can't be afraid of what being alone might bring.

I stand. "Goodbye Hector."

"Dee," he utters. "Don't."

I shake, telling myself, be brave. To begin again I must end this. To flower, I must free these petals from the dirt. "You have a girlfriend. Go. Be decent. For me. Please Hector. Be good so I can believe there's a chance I can find a man like that too." The words chew my throat. "She's having your baby."

His eyes drift downward. "Dee."

"What? What do you want from me?"

His eyes rise. "To teach."

Wait.

What? Did I hear right?

I'm at a loss.

"I'm offering you a job," he says.

The turn unbalances me. Is it another clever trick, another way to bait me?

"Teach what?"

"History. Miss Robb left a vacancy."

I cast a skeptical eye. "This isn't about us? A way to get me back?"

He chuckles. It's part of the game. Granting me an answer would be giving in. "Look, I don't know what you've been doing differently but there's a change in you. The kids see it. They're seeking you out."

I sit to take it in. Is he right? Have I made a difference?

If so, why would I stop now? The students have just begun to come to me. For the first time my calendar is full. Students trust me. The word has spread in the halls thanks to...Lisette.

Oh Lisette. Could I restore her faith in me again?

What of Kitay?

Oh, there's still much work to do as a counselor. I don't have to switch positions. I can teach from any chair, even this one. The truth is we're all teachers. It doesn't matter where one stands. It simply requires listening well enough to stand out.

"I decline," I reply.

Hector eyes me incredulously. "But this is what you wanted."

I rest back in my chair. "Right here feels right for now." He tries to make sense of it. "I think that's best for the students. I'm putting them first. Isn't that what you want?"

As he considers it, Vita opens the door, peeking in with an update on the shooting. Apparently, the police found the gun in a student's backpack, hidden in a bag of potato chips. "I prayed for St. Anthony to lead us in the right direction to find it." She kisses the cross on her neck. "The officers would like to speak to you," she tells Hector.

"Thank you." His gaze remains on me as if requiring my permission to leave.

Sensing the tension, Vita flees.

I nod for him to follow. "Hector," I call before he exits.

"If you ever decide to add a class in life skills, something to prep the students for the future rather than the past, I might be interested in something like that. Maybe an hour a day."

"Sure," he says, with a grin.

I return the smile and he leaves as my cell phone rings.

"Lingers!" Jerry says. "How ya doin', baby?"

"Wonderful, except I'm not your baby."

"My apologies *doll*," he says, growing animated. "Great news. I found your aunt, Heather Pratt." He laughs excitedly and my world blooms in color. I choke, caught in its fragrance. "Hey! Where have you been? I tried to get a hold of you last night. Were you out? Cocktails with the girls?"

"Girls?" I cough. "No. I went to bed early."

"You?"

"Never mind that." I attempt to contain myself but the news electrifies me. "Where is she? Do you have a phone number?"

"I have everything," he assures me. "I would've had it to you sooner but there was a miscommunication that stalled everything. Do you know your name isn't Desperation?" He wearily sighs then laughs to himself. "Your birth mother called you something else." My heart quickens. "Remember how I said she got knocked up in high school?"

I disregard his unpolished way. "Yes."

"Well her parents wouldn't let her keep you. But your mother wanted you so much she called you Desire. It's cute, the way your aunt explained it."

"Desire?" Repeating the name I see not stars, but dots, connecting me to a place in the world. I was desirable once. My mother wanted me. She never chose to let me go. My eyes tear up and I say it again. "Desire."

"You got it. That's what your mom called you when she'd rock you to sleep in the hospital," Jerry says. "That's why it was hard to make the connection. Your aunt thought I was joking. She said, 'No, I don't know a girl named Desperation. My sister gave up a child for adoption, but her name was Desire. For short, she'd call her *Desi*.'"

CHAPTER 13

DESI? DESI?
   I gasp, placing a hand on my heart, as the colors grow and shift around me, my world twisting like a kaleidoscope. I'm engulfed by the truth, my world blown to neon bits by one tiny word.

Desi.

Rose was the only one who'd call me that, but she couldn't be my mother. No. No. She was my driver – a confidante, a friend. My mother's name was Elise. That's what Roberta Smith said, not that she's known for honesty. She'd probably say anything for chicken fingers and a milkshake. Had she lied, fabricated the past for money? I can't think of it. I need the truth, even if it pulls me below the surface. Anything is better than another lie. Lies are what led me here in the first place.

"I know someone who called me Desi," I tell Jerry. "But she worked for my family. You said my mother's name was Elise, right?"

"Elise," Jerry repeats. "Yeah. That's her birth name, but that's not what they called her."

"Called?" I grip my desk to gather patience, but the sharp edge in my voice is hard to disguise. "What do you mean? Was that her name or not?"

He stalls, emitting a laugh. "What's going on with you? I found your family. You should be happy."

"I am happy." I'm merely flustered by the thought of being steered in the wrong direction again. I need accuracy, just this once in my life. I haven't time for another blunder. That's why I hired the best – paid the big bucks, turned a blind eye to being blackmailed by Roberta Smith. I tighten my grasp on the phone, jolting in my chair. "Mr. Rich, be clear. What was her name? Her real name?"

"Her real name?" he mimics, like it's no big deal. "Elise," he spits. "But she never went by that. Her family called her Rosalie. Rosalie or...."

"Rose." The revelation is like an arrow tearing through my chest. I close my eyes to see stars, specks of light. They flicker and fade. *Is it like the cartoon?* Kitay's words fill my head and I flash to a sunny day out for a drive on Collins with Rose. I recall holding up my first bra – the one she just purchased – and shuddering.

"I don't know if I'm ready," I said. "They're so small. I could probably tame them with Scotch tape."

Rose laughed, observing from the rearview. "There's that sense of humor. I knew you had it in you."

I struggled with the clasp. "I just think I can wait."

"Now. Now. There's comes a time where every girl has to cover her ta-tas," she said. "It's part of growing up."

"Well what if I don't want to grow up?" Boggled, I tossed the bra and threw up my hands. "Shouldn't my mother be helping me with this?"

Rose said, "That's why she sent me."

The words float to the surface in the present and I inform Mr. Rich that I've heard enough. I obtain Heather Pratt's info and hang up.

Moments later, I tell Vita I'll be out for the rest of the day and possibly tomorrow. She ceases watering a plant at her desk.

"Is something wrong?"

"No, just forward my calls."

"But Ms. Harper's still in the hospital. Who will see the children?"

"If it's an emergency, call me. If not, you know the kids. Your ear is as fine as mine. Take a moment to listen." She fidgets. Her eyes open wide. "Please Vita. It's my family. Something has come up."

She nods firmly, bracing herself. "Then you go. Family comes first."

I warm with a smile. "Thank you."

"Be safe. I worry!" she calls as I head out in a heated run. I don't slow until my heel hits a crack in parking lot pavement. I recover and set off again, my mind matching my hurried pace.

All this time, all these years, Bev Dear had it planned. How could she keep such a secret? How could she dance my mother Rose before my eyes without missing a step? Had she the skill of a ballerina?

I locate my car as Cici pulls into a nearby space on his moped. He must've had it fixed and done some work on his relationship too. Lisette clings to his torso from behind. The sun blinds me, reflecting off his handlebars. I scurry past.

"Yo. Lingers!" Cici calls, breaking away. He hands a black helmet to Lisette. "What's your rush?"

I take the keys from my purse. "Just running an errand. You're late to class. Go check in. There's been a shooting."

He laughs. "I heard. Some tool went all Miami Vice on the juice machine for keeping his change."

"Get to class." My eyes flicker to Lisette. "Both of you. They have the police all over campus. I'm surprised they haven't found you." I step into the car.

"Wait!" He nudges Lisette with an upward sweep of his chin. "Go on, babe. Talk."

She folds her arms. "I told you to stay out of it." She looks polished, a flattering skirt revealing the curves of her body. I'm reminded of her transformation, our shopping excursion on Lincoln Road. We had a magnificent breakthrough that day, talking instead of fighting. How could I ruin it? "She doesn't care about me," she tells Cici.

The words tug at my heart. I ask, "Do you honestly believe that?" She sadly eyes me without a word. For once, I'd prefer the acuity of her tongue. That I could take. "I don't blame you for being mad," I say. "I know you didn't steal the money. I made a mistake." Glowering, she edges closer. Cici pats her back. "I should have believed you." She eyes me with suspicion. "I want you to know I'm sorry."

"Sorry?" She stops in front of me. "What about lesson two? No apologies?" I blink in amazement. My teachings stuck? I hadn't realized she'd been listening. "That's why women earn less, isn't it? We apologize too much. Isn't that what you taught us? Or was that bullshit too?"

"No. That was true."

A step away she maintains her cool, speaking with words rather than fists, a long way from the girl I first met. "You might think I'm stupid, but I remember a lot." I stand my ground, matching her cement gaze. "So why are you apologizing if women already do that enough?"

I think of an honest response. I owe her that much. "Because as women we don't apologize enough *to each other*."

She pinches one eye closed. "Well, I'm not looking for an apology. You can save that for Kitay. That's what you need to make good again." She cocks her neck and Cici comes up from behind, wrapping her in his arms.

"It's gonna be ok, baby," he says.

She shrugs him off. "I'm not a baby. I got this." He lets go, raising his arms in surrender. "Jazz said Kitay's back in Arcadia," she says to me. I confirm with a nod and she frowns. "I looked up her dad's funeral online. I have no one to watch Amelia or I'd be there. Cici has to work later."

"She'll come back."

"Not after you tried to kiss her man. Not without a job." Tears fill her eyes. "What does she have here?"

"You. She has to see you graduate."

"Yeah." She dabs her eyes. "Like that's a big deal."

"What about the class?" Cici suggests. "There's always something more she can learn." He gestures to the moped. "Like hey, Ms. Lingers, how about teaching them some tricks so my girl doesn't trash my wheels next time I screw up."

Lisette snaps. "How 'bout this? Don't screw up."

"Yo, I'm a man. It's biology."

"Not if you want to make chemistry with me."

He laughs. "Ah. You see? That's my girl."

She turns to me with a serious gaze. Her voice goes soft. "Find Kitay. Bring her home for us."

I happily nod, the thought tickling my throat. "I will."

"She's at Hackson Funeral Home in Arcadia," she calls, as I pull out of the lot. "The viewing ends at four." I wave, making a mental note. Perhaps I'll stop en route to my aunt's home in Myakka City. It's along the way. But will she want to see me after the mistake I made? I don't want to make things worse. Oh, I don't know. A friend would go, right?

Heading north, I connect the white highway dots on I-95 before taking an exit to cut across the state. Soon, I'm passing fields of sugar cane, only to realize I haven't phoned my aunt. Bloody hell. I just can't show up. *Good afternoon. I'm your long lost niece. Come again? You're phoning the police? Oh dear.*

Indeed, a call in advance would be best for all parties involved. Then why can't I dial? It should be an effortless task. Simply press the numbers. Even if I'm not a 'numbers' person I can get that right. After all, the digits add up to a family and yes, I've been blessed with traces of the very same thing along the way – a father who loved me and Bev Dear who tried her best – but I was too young, too green to catch sight of a true gift in Rose.

Somewhere along the road I muster the courage to call. "Hello? Heather Pratt?"

"Yes?" Her voice is raspy, yet has a smooth finish.

"This is Dee Lingers." I wait for a signal of acknowledgement – a flicker of enthusiasm – proof she recalls who I am. Nothing comes. "You might know me as Desi." Again, silence. "You spoke to Jerry. Is that right?"

"Yes," she says, her tone neither here nor there.

I swallow my nerves. This isn't going as planned. I hadn't expected angels harmonizing on harps, but something. "Jerry said you spoke about me." Tick, tick, tick. "Jerry Rich."

"Yes. That's right."

"Well," I continue, since she fails to. "I'd like to pay you a visit. I'm heading in your direction and...."

"Now?"

"Yes. Later today. Is that too soon?"

"Oh dear." Her voice cracks. "We weren't expecting company. The kids just left. Father needs his rest."

I inhale and disappointment sets in like a disease,

quick and debilitating, until I try to speak and go blank. What a fool. I should've known. She doesn't know the lady I've become. I'm a faded memory, a niece discarded long ago. A forgotten family secret. Still, there must be some form of curiosity.

The pressure builds in my head, pulsating at my temples as if searching for an escape.

"I understand if you can't meet," I say, but the truth is I don't understand. I'm family – that has to mean something. I can't give up. I've come so far. "It's only, well, you see I've been searching for some time." I sense a tear and I curse myself. "Stop. Damn it. Stop."

"Miss? Are you all right?"

"Yes. I...well...no. I haven't been for some time." It feels good to share it, to be honest even if she is a stranger. "This is silly. I'm ok. I shouldn't have bothered to call. Good day to you." I begin to hang up when she speaks.

"How about sunset?" she asks. "Can you be here then? That's when father and I have dinner."

My heart quickens. "Sunset? Yes." I catch my breath. "Are you sure?"

"I'll set an extra plate."

I hang up and scream with delight, the adrenaline pouring in my veins. I'm going to meet my family! It's no longer a dream, no longer a fragmented picture but the very next dot, connecting everything.

I tremble, tracing the road along a body of water and a barren field where horses feed. White fences frame the greenery, reminiscent of a Grandma Moses painting. Farmhouses hide behind tall trees draped with Spanish moss.

I pass an abandoned gas station when my phone rings. "Hello?"

"Good afternoon." It's Wes, his thick Scottish accent easily detected. "How are you doing on this wonderful sunny day?" The charmer – apparently, ignoring him didn't work. Then again, isn't that always the case with men?

"I'm well," I say. "Busy, but well."

At this point, I'd hang up but he's been nothing but

kind. And admittedly his voice leads me to a smile.

"Did you get the orchid?" he asks.

"Yes. It's beautiful. Thank you."

"Great. Glad you like it." He stalls, planning another delivery, this time in the form of a request. "So have you given it more thought?"

Thought? About what? The last I recall he dropped off the aquarium then admitted he likes musicals. Oh, that's what this is about. He wants me to attend the theater with him. A date.

"I'm washing my hair that day," I tell him.

"Really? I haven't even told you what day it is yet."

"I wash my hair everyday."

"Too bad you're so afraid of getting dirty," he says with a chuckle.

"I'm happy to you make laugh."

"Are you always so difficult?"

I hesitate, considering it. "When I don't know someone...yes."

"Oh give me a break. You know me."

"The only thing I know about you is...." I tell myself to push him away. It's no good to lead him on. The path ends in a forest of prickly overgrowth. I fear being lost again. "I don't like you. That's all I know."

"Good. I like a challenge."

I grit my teeth. "Do you also like being hung up on?"

"Why? Are you hung up on me?"

I take an exasperated breath. "Hardly."

He speaks softly. "I'm playing with you. Don't hang up. I like your voice." My voice? Really? Another line? A hook? Please, I can see it sparkling a mile away. I can't do this. It's too soon. I'm damaged – the wounds are still fresh from Hector. The stitches have yet to be removed. "Give me a chance," he says.

I take a breath and play along; he did send flowers. That should afford him a few minutes. "A chance at what?"

"To be good to you."

My heart opens, just a smidge, allowing a seed of hope to be planted.

Damn it. No. I can't give in. It won't work. Not for me.

"Wes. I really need to go."

"Wait," he pleads. "I'm not a bad guy."

If only I hadn't heard that from every other man who has shown interest. I want to believe he's different, see the good in him. I had Felix. He properly loved me. "But I'm not in any place...."

He cuts me off. "I'm not saying it'll work. But if it doesn't you'll have good things to say about me. I can promise you that. Isn't that enough?" I cave a little but I can't allow him to cloud my mind, not when I have stars in my eyes from the thought of seeing my family. "I can be persistent, if that's what you need," he says.

I drive past a drug store with barred windows, thinking of all the men I've allowed in. My cuts run deep, so deep one more may bleed me dry. I'm frightened but I can't admit it. He'll know I have a weakness, a way in. But if I want someone in my life, someone to trust, I need to be honest.

"I'm scared," I say, the words coming out like static.

"Don't be. I won't hurt you." He pauses, sighing. "That sounds lame. How 'bout this? I'll try my best not to hurt you."

"How do I believe you?" I breathe deeply to calm myself. "You might think I'm difficult, defiant, or whatever you'd like to call it, but the truth is I'm tired. It's exhausting, searching for something good." A tear slides along my cheek. "I'd like to find a good man, but first I need to find the good in myself so I know I'm worth it. I've been told it's not there. I lost it as a girl. I assure you, I've built these walls for a reason."

"That's ok. That's ok. I like walls," he says, making light of it. "You need them to hold up a home." I fight a grin, wiping tears. "Now, what about a door? Can you let me build you one? So I can look inside? I'll find the good in you, Dee. I already see it. It lights up the windows of your eyes."

I fight a grin, wiping at tears. "Oh dear."

"C'mon. One chance?"

I smile. "Possibly. Someday."

"When?"

"Well, perhaps when when you stop hammering me with these questions," I say, with a laugh. Along the road, an alligator floats idle in a blue lake speckled with lily pads. I wonder how it would react if I ventured for a swim? It's safe on shore – no risk. But what's life without the adventure of getting your feet wet? Are you truly alive without a gamble? Isn't that the best way to love, to put everything on the line. "I'll call soon," I say, hanging up before he can question it.

Why did I give him hope? I'm too overwhelmed with the students and this trip. I haven't time for flirty, foolish games. Still, that doesn't stop me from thinking of him. Oh dear. I'm doing it again, giving in, but what's the other option? Giving up?

No.

I'd like to love again.

No. I'd love to love again.

But....

Oh! Stop! Stop!

I tighten my grip on the steering wheel, blinking my eyes to shift focus. Crossing the Arcadia city line, I turn up the classical radio station and think of Kitay. Jasper told me in confidence that she was distraught and appeared sickly when she left Miami. Her father's death only magnified her unhappiness. She couldn't afford gas so he blessed her with the better part of the cash he'd stolen from me. If only I could be such a friend.

I hope she can forgive me.

Up the road I take in a 'hay for sale' sign on the lawn of an antique shop operated in a red wooden house. A series of turns later, I find Hackson Funeral Home situated on a square bed of manicured grass. Sky blue, the building seems like a converted convenience store with tinted plate glass windows and a pay phone near the entrance. Hearses line the half-moon driveway with steel crosses anchoring each end.

I park and say a prayer, heading inside to the vacant receiving area. I sign my name to a greeting book and follow the flowered carpet to an employee in a navy blazer. Short with white hair and neck whiskers, she stands guard at a closed double wooden door. I smile and she opens it, gesturing me to the next room.

"The Fritter viewing ends in an hour," she whispers, handing me a prayer card with Jesus floating on a cloud.

"Is the casket...open?"

"Yes. At the family's request."

I flash to Bev Dear's funeral, her neck draped with so many grand jewels. Her casket sparkled like a treasure chest.

Oh, how it pained me to see her lifeless, painted body. The service seemed more like punishment than a day of praise and remembrance.

Therefore, for father's funeral I chose to have the casket closed. I found it more respectful. When Rose died I understood why she chose no funeral at all. She opted for a celebration of life, asking her roommate Stephanie to spread her ashes on the shoreline of Miami. I read a poem. It relaxed me. I was at peace.

I think of Rose today, entering the viewing room, my heartbeat quickening at the sight of the people. Nearly each chair is full.

Oh dear.

I'm a stranger. I don't fit...don't belong. I wronged Kitay. I should've never come, but how else could I save our friendship? We have something special.

A friendship difficult to make should be equally difficult to break. Isn't that true?

I search for a seat and the attendant gestures to a chair in the second to last row. I thank him, glancing up to view the casket at the front. It's bordered by white carnations and green-leafed plants. One individual in a blue beret faces the casket in prayer.

"Excuse me," I whisper to an elderly man. Failing to move, his knees block the row. I squeeze by him, clipping his toe.

"Ouch. Didn't you see my foot?"

"Pardon me."

The tension rises, reddening his already sunburnt head. "But you stepped on my foot."

"It was an accident."

He turns to the woman beside him. "She stepped on my foot!"

I lose patience, taking a seat. "Well if you were a gentleman you would've stood up. Then we wouldn't have this problem, would we?"

He casts me a stony gaze and I sit down to find others viewing me as well. I awkwardly smile, scanning the room for Kitay, only to see strangers dressed in black. In the front row, Kitay's mother Gladys turns to view me. In a pillbox hat, she nods with the hint of a grin. Confused, I offer the same. I thought she disliked me.

"Charlie," she calls.

The person standing at the casket turns and I realize it's Kitay without makeup. Hair tucked beneath the blue beret, her body swims in a dark jacket and pants. Gladys signals her to turn and look at me. She does and I offer a wave. In tears, she squints as if trying to make sense of it. The air leaves me. I can't handle the view – the way she tries smiling through the pain. Perhaps it's best to leave. I go to move but my heart anchors me to my seat.

"I'm sorry," I mouth.

She seals her lips, her face trembling.

Gladys whispers to two women behind her seat. They examine me, mouths slightly ajar. What is it? What's Gladys telling them?

Turning to the casket, Kitay cries into a handkerchief and my heart burns. She shouldn't be up there alone. She could benefit from a friend, even if it comes in the smashed package of me.

I stand, making my way up the aisle to take Kitay's hand. She doesn't pull away. She squeezes and we remain quiet, the only sound provided by a violin and the whispers of Gladys. *Girlfriend. Girlfriend.* That's what's she saying, that I'm Charlie's girlfriend. That's why she's happy to see me. I'm part of the charade.

I pat Kitay's hand, knowing she heard it too.

Her body goes weak. She begins to fall.

"No. You're a strong woman." I pull her up and she

braces herself. I echo the words she'd once told me. "Everyone hears *their* voices. You can't let them win. Remember?" She tightens her grip as I glance at the casket. Her father seems to be smiling, a few gray hairs plastered across his head. "I'm sorry," I say quietly. "What I did was wrong. I can't take it back, but I would if I could. I never wanted to hurt you." She tightens her grip, her body shaking. Suddenly she falls again. "No," I instruct. She bends at the knees, melting. I act stern like Bev Dear, seeing no other way. "I taught you etiquette. Gather yourself." She chokes down tears and I let go of her hand to reach in my purse. "Here," I say, handing her my red lipstick. "You left Arcadia a girl, but you've come back a lady. You don't need to hide anymore." She turns to me, her eyes brightening more with each blink. "Go on," I implore. "And take off that beret. Show off that beautiful hair. No reason to be ashamed." With a sniffle, she examines the lipstick, glancing at Gladys who cranes her neck to see what's taking place. "You can do it," I say. Then without a moment spared she nods, as if stalling would extinguish her nerve. She brings the lipstick to her lips.

"No!" Gladys rises to her feet.

Kitay doesn't waste time. She quickly colors her lips and pulls off the beret, releasing her blonde locks. The crowd gasps as Gladys approaches.

"Charlie! What are you doing?" Wedging herself between us, she rips the lipstick from Kitay's grip then stares me down. "This is your fault! You're not wanted here."

"That's not true. Kitay wants me here."

"Who's Kitay?" With a nervous laugh she scans the crowd, her hand clinging to Kitay's wrist. "You need to leave. You're ruining our day."

"No," I reply.

"Look at you. You're crazy. You're making Charlie crazy. If his father was alive...."

"Kitay, tell her I'm your friend," I interrupt. She chokes, too overwhelmed to speak. "We need each other, right? Just us *gals*?"

Two funeral attendants in navy coats approach. I look to Kitay for help but she covers her face. Was I wrong to come? What did I do?

Panicked, I place my palms to my ears and listen to the sea. It guides me to her father, blissful in slumber. I'm reminded of Felix, how he'd manage a smile even when he was sick. He said I was his medicine, that I'd keep him alive forever.

A hand grips my arm and I shriek.

"Ma'am, come with us," an attendant says. He guides me down the aisle with a coworker who takes my other arm. The crowd looks on in silent horror as I put my head down in defeat. There are so many things I could say, I should say, but any further disruption would be unfair to Kitay.

Leaving, I turn my head to see her a final time. She appears to have wings, a crucifix of white roses framing her back. I gasp, her fragile eyes reaching for me, suggesting she's stuck. I offer her a smile, an acknowledgement that I understand, until I'm forced to exit.

Reaching my car, I don't dawdle. Any delay may cause second thoughts so I set my foot on the gas and head off to find my family.

As I travel west I pass herds of black and white cows and long rows of oaks until I arrive in Myakka City where my GPS guides me to turn left. Following the directions, I slow for a blinking light on a snake-curved road bordered by a low barbed wire fence. Along the shoulder, a woman rides a horse. The surrounding fields are dotted with hay bales. I see no other signs of life except for a man running on a treadmill on his farmhouse porch. I take a dirt road that ends at a white shell driveway narrowed by ragweed. Slightly ajar, the wooden gate displays a sign festooned with chickens and hearts, along with the name Pratt.

I continue halfway up the driveway – shells cracking under my wheels – when I stop, saturated with second thoughts. What am I doing? What have these people to give? Dog toys, white bones and rubber balls, line the edge of the drive. I view them and reflect on my childhood, a place where pets were never allowed. *They've too many germs. They're too much work. Little Miss Mess, you can barely clean up after yourself.*

Will this visit be enough to fill in the holes? Is that something I can expect Heather Pratt to do? Is that something anyone can expect from anyone?

I drive on in silence, the sun dipping down to create a bright orange light. I imagine a welcoming committee racing out to greet me, family members with pie. Silly to think, but one can only dream of something for so long before it learns to dream on its own.

I proceed to the clearing. The house is simple: small and square with peach stucco walls. Spanish tile lines the roof like waves. A citrus tree provides shade to a lawn gnome with a cone hat.

I park behind a blue pickup truck and exit the car, taking in the view when a mosquito bites me. Slapping it away, I head toward the front door, eyeing a chicken coop enclosed by wire fencing on the left side of the house. I look at the red and white chickens pecking at the ground as I hear the squeak of the Pratt's front door. Footsteps follow and two brindle Greyhounds greet me on the path, keeping a safe distance. A woman calls them from the porch and they quickly retreat.

"You coming too?" she asks me. Tall and plump, she has a pink apron tied over her plaid dress. Her long gray hair is wrapped in a knot that hangs over her shoulder. "Dinner's on the table," she says. "I'm Heather."

I quicken my pace. "Am I late?"

She shakes the question, wiping her white house slippers on a mat by the door. "Shoes off. I just cleaned." She lowers her round spectacles to glance at my heels. "Those hurt?"

"Not really."

She lowers her voice. "Father won't like them. He doesn't care for women who stand on their toes to stand out. God can see you plain as day from the ground." She nods to a space on the porch beside a pair of muddy work boots. "Put them there."

I listen and leaning on a railing I steal a look at her face. Its shape is peculiar, almost square. Her jowls are freckled with spots and her nose is small like a button. She bears no resemblance to me except for her height.

In the home, I'm met by the chemical scent of floor cleaner and cigarette smoke. A large clay ashtray with imperfect grooves sits on a coffee table in front an old-fashioned tele; pastel crocheted blankets cover the couch. I scan the house for something that connects me. Finding nothing, I speak.

"Thank you for inviting me," I say.

"No need for that, honey. You invited yourself." An oven timer chimes. "Oh, that's our bread." She points me to the sofa and heads to the kitchen. I take a seat, silently watched by the two greyhounds spread on the scuffed wood floor near the brick fireplace. A ceiling fan stirs a slight breeze. "You eat chicken, right?" she calls.

"Yes," I reply before considering if dinner came from the backyard. I smile through the thought. A good guest would be grateful. I check my manners only to realize I haven't introduced myself.

I stand upon her return. "Pardon me. I should have properly greeted you." I extend a hand. "I'm Dee Lingers."

She shakes it. "I know who you are." Her eyes examine me as if trying to piece together the past and present. She neither smiles nor frowns, briefly freezing in thought until the floor creaks in another room. It triggers her to focus. "Father must have finished taking a shower." I tilt my head with curiosity. "Henry. Mr. Pratt. My husband," she explains.

"Oh."

"I'm sure this is all very confusing for you. You'll get through it," she offers, with more diplomacy than warmth. I think of Rose. How could the two be related? Mrs. Pratt's smile seems cold, icy enough to slip on – a trait similar to Bev Dear. Had a chill been in my blood all along?

I follow her to the kitchen, the green tablecloth matching the plaid valance on the window beside it. The walls are red with rooster portraits.

I take a seat. Mrs. Pratt cuts into the steaming bread at the counter. "You don't look like anyone in my family," she says, her back to me. She snaps around, a fist at her hip.

"I see your father Stephen in you. Like a beanstalk, he was. And that nose." She shakes her head. "I never thought I'd see the day. I...." She catches herself. "Are you ok with just water?" She nods at my glass on the table.

"Yes."

"We don't allow alcohol in our home. Not anymore." Uneasy, she turns to finish cutting the bread.

"You knew my father?"

She takes the butter from the fridge. "I did."

"Can you tell me about him?"

She sighs, lost in thought. "I was a few years older than Stephen and your mother." She approaches the table with a breadbasket, setting it next to the baked chicken. White corncobs are stacked in a bowl. "Please. Help yourself," she says, taking a seat. "We'll eat in a few minutes."

I place a slice of bread on my plate, prompting her for more information. "What was he like? My father?"

She smiles weakly. "I don't remember much." Her controlled response tells me she's holding back.

"Anything you recall, I'd be grateful if you'd share. I've waited many years."

Heather takes a seat and butters a piece of bread, placing on her husband's plate before buttering her own.

"Stephen played the trombone," she quietly says. "He was a member of the marching band at Desoto High, a few miles down the road. He was artistic." I fill with gold, reflecting on how I feel most at home in a modern art museum or when listening to a symphony. The revelation seems connects us. My chest buzzes with warmth, the pieces forming a whole. "Your mom said he wrote plays. He dreamed of being a playwright. At least, that's what she'd go on about. She'd talk about him to anyone who'd listen." She sighs.

"Stephen," I say, connecting a dot that hadn't been visible before. "And his last name?"

"Mikos. The family was Greek. He was in the same grade as Rose."

"Stephen Mikos." I grow excited. "Is he still close?"

"See? This is what I was worried about. You'd get ahead

of yourself. Remember young lady, some rocks are best left unturned." She callously eyes me before continuing. "His family moved away long ago, a few months before you were born." I picture the sequence of events. It doesn't add up. Where did he go? Who stood by Rose in the delivery room?

"Is he still alive?"

She butters a corncob. "He cut ties with the move. That's how the families wanted it."

"He left her pregnant?" I set down my fork to inquire more but she hushes me when Henry enters the room. He stops to study me, his lined, sunburnt head the color of a cherry. Blue suspenders hold the jeans over his belly. A pack of cigarettes are visible in the chest pocket of his white tee.

"Rose's daughter," he says, the words more of a conviction than a greeting.

I grin and wipe my mouth with a napkin. "Hello." I extend my hand, but he grunts and ignores it, treading around the table. Taking a seat, he bows his bald head.

"Let us pray," he says.

I lower my chin and the three of us clasp hands.

He blesses the food and thanks the good Lord (or Lo-word), along with his wife for preparing the meal. I smile and nod, saying amen when silence finds us.

The first to eat, Henry shoots me sharp glances in between bites of chicken. His wife eats quietly, watching his every move.

"Are you a landscaper?" I ask Henry.

"No. I mow."

"Really? Well, the grass is so manicured I thought it was maintained by a professional."

He nods without a word and Mrs. Pratt interjects. "Henry's a lawn expert," she says. "Instead of turning on the TV, I often sit by the window with a lemonade and watch him do his magic." Henry slightly grins, clearing his throat, and a bout of silence later, I steer the conversation to Rose.

"So what can you two tell me about my mother?"

Henry promptly sets downs his fork, seemingly annoyed.

"Oh honey. She just wants answers," Mrs. Pratt says.

"I told you. No unholy talk at the table. You can talk later."

She speaks uneasily. "But she's come this far. We can give her that much." He casts her a steely gaze until she relents, her face flushing red. "Forgive father," she tells me. "He doesn't like to hear talk of my sisters."

"You get too upset," he says. "Talk about it another time, not over dinner." He puts up his hand to cease the matter and the remainder of dinner is sprinkled with commentary about bass fishing and the Pratt's three grandchildren.

After the meal I help Mrs. Pratt with the dishes. Henry retires to the living room, talking to a friend on the phone about a scalloping trip to Gainesville.

I rinse, and she places the dishes in the washer. "Father's had a long day in the yard. You understand." She looks over her back, accepting a plate with jittery hands. She whispers, "We'll talk when he goes to work."

"When's that?"

"Tomorrow morning."

Tomorrow? Does she expect me to spend the night?

My spirit withers. The thought of waiting even another minute seems long enough to drive me mad. What's so unholy, so unsettling about my past that she can't openly share it? Intrigue rattles my bones.

"Are you certain we can't find time tonight?" I ask. "In a private part of the house or outside?"

"Father watches the news and then we retire. He can't sleep without me in the bed. We'll only be awake for another hour."

Later, I sit beside them on the couch, catching up with current events on the tele. A fire that started at a gas station, a tropical storm – Mr. Pratt says God has plan of action for every story. Mrs. Pratt nods in agreement, drinking a cup of Chamomile tea. When the news ends she leads me to the guest room. To learn the truth it seems I have little choice but to stay.

I call Jasper to tell him that I won't be home until morning. He moans but thanks me for keeping him in the loop.

"I love you," I tell him, the words coming before I can resist them.

He hesitates. "Yeah. About that...."

"Yes?"

"I love you too." I smile, rocking on the bed, cradling the white nightgown that Mrs. Pratt offered before leaving the room. "And I'll love you even more if you get that turtle food on the way back." He laughs.

"Yes. I will," I promise. "Good night."

"Night."

Hanging up, I put on the robe and turn off the light. Still, I don't sleep. I rest my head on the pillow and tap my chest to soothe my heart, listening to the crickets harmonizing with the bullfrogs outside the window. I hadn't realized how much distancing myself from Jasper would affect me. Anxious, I roll on my side, more isolated than ever. I thought this visit would be beneficial. Why do I feel so alone, disconnected? I imagine it to be one big misunderstanding and that my family, my real family, lives down the road in the house with the man running on the treadmill. Right now they're celebrating with music and cocktails, checking their watches, wondering why I haven't arrived. Since I've made contact, all of my relatives from every state have flown in. They're having a grand party, so loud the whole city of Arcadia can hear it.

So why is it so quiet?

I lift my head from the pillow to look around the room. I see toys and dolls sitting in dark silence rather than estranged family members rushing to reunite. Plastic trucks line the wooden dresser and teddy bears hold court by a pink castle in the corner. This must be where the grandchildren sleep. How lucky they are to be limbs on the family tree without vines covering the lies.

Turning over, I swaddle myself with sheets, hoping to sleep. I close my eyes but it's no use. My mind runs a marathon of what-ifs, and I stir all night, the feeling of solitude stinging my heart.

At the first crack of daylight, a rooster crows and I head to the kitchen for a glass of water.

"Desi?"

Taking a drink, I jump at the sink, thinking it's Rose.

Turning, I find Mrs. Pratt in a pink nightgown. She presses a finger to my lips, hushing me before I talk. "You needn't wake father. Come. I have something for you to see."

I set down my glass and follow her through darkness as she lightly treads, careful not to wake the dogs snoring near the fireplace.

We exit through a door in the laundry room that leads to the garage. Mrs. Pratt flicks on the light. "Sleep well?" she asks. I shake my head and she smiles knowingly. "I couldn't either." She leads me past the front bumper of an old red station wagon onto a carpeted space on the other side. It's cluttered with colorful toys and a tricycle with green tasseled handlebars. A toy stove cooking sunny side up eggs on a black skillet is placed beside it. "The children tend to be messy," Mrs. Pratt says. She picks up a rag doll, placing it in a yellow toy box. "We don't mind as long as they stay away from father's tools." In the far corner of the garage she stops at a stack of cardboard boxes just beyond a tool bench. Lifting the top two boxes she sets them down and bends to open the third, labeled 'Christmas.' I peer over her shoulder; her hands dig under the strands of tree lights. "I hide it in here because father won't think to look," she says. "I'm in charge of the tree. I put it up with our grandkids every year." She takes a pleased breath, standing with a silver-ringed photo album in her hand. She becomes misty-eyed. "You see, I miss Rose too. I never had a chance to apologize." She adjusts her round glasses and walks to the tool bench where she makes space, clearing metal gadgets and nails. She sets down the album.

"I didn't come to upset you," I say.

"I know. You came for answers." She opens the album, tracing her fingers along the photos. "I find myself thumbing through this a lot when father is asleep. It reminds me of what life was once like, what I could've done different. Sometimes I wonder where I'd be if I'd have made different choices." She turns, searching my eyes under her blurry lenses. "Are you married?"

"Not really." She squints at me, attempting to understand. "I'm not over the last one. He died." I look away. "I've tried to go on, but I haven't been able to match him."

"Of course not. It's silly to try." Her boldness startles me. "No two loves are alike. That doesn't make them any better or worse. Do you think father is the only man I've loved?"

"But I loved him so much."

"Good." She flips through pages. "Then you understand what a woman will sacrifice at times to make her husband happy."

I contemplate it. "Actually, marriage taught me what I refuse to sacrifice." I try to explain. "For example, my dignity. I'll no longer buy a diaper for a grown man just because he's fond of peeing himself."

She turns to me, bewildered. "Oh dear."

"And I'll no longer allow a man to push or shove me because he says it'll only happen once. I know a push will lead to a punch and that I'll grow to rely on the same tactics as well." She nods knowingly, momentarily looking off in thought. Perhaps her feet have been muddied in the same soil before. "I'm not proud of my behavior. I take full responsibility for it, and I'm trying to make a change." I stand firmly. "Now, what do you have to show me in that album, Mrs. Pratt?"

"Yes, yes." She quickly sifts through the black and white photos, some torn and faded. "I keep the pictures of Rose toward the back," she says, as if they were forbidden, tainted. "There were three sisters." She points to a photo of three girls ranging in age from elementary to middle school. Linking arms, they stand on a shoreline, each in a black one-piece swimsuit. In sync, they kick their legs to the air like the Rockettes. "I was the oldest, then Sadie, then Rose."

"Sadie? Where is she now?"

"No longer with us. She was in a car accident over a decade ago." She sighs. "Our family has a history of alcohol problems, you see. Sadie felt she had it under control. Daddy had the problem too." I flush, considering my liquid blunders. She finger taps a photo containing a mustached man beside a woman with black curls. It's a wedding portrait; the woman wears a long white dress and veil. "Daddy was a mail carrier in Arcadia. Mom was a homemaker. She gave piano lessons for pocket money every Sunday." She traces her finger along her father's black suit. "Daddy loved all three of his daughters, but he had a special place in his heart for Rose. We could all tell." She smiles, reflecting back. "What a fit Rose would have, putting on a Sunday dress. Mom would be incensed but Daddy would just laugh. I'd fight too sometimes, even though I loved to dress up."

"Then why did you fight?"

"I was jealous. I wanted daddy's attention too." Her voice takes a childish tone. "We all did. But he was busy with Rose, teaching her baseball or some other sport. Rose never liked dolls or playing house." She flips the page, pointing to a picture. I immediately notice it's Rose. In a white tee shirt and shorts, she wears a baseball mitt. My heart flutters. "Mom blamed him for the way Rose turned out," she says. Just then, the house settles with a crack, sending a chill down my spine. Mrs. Pratt turns an eye on the door leading back into the house.

"Turned out?" I inquire.

Her body tenses. "I shouldn't be talking about it. I promised Henry."

"Promised him what? What is it?"

"I know it's foolish but he has an old way of thinking." She eyes me with a sense of urgency. "He thinks if we talk about it too much then the grandchildren will catch it." She scans the garage for ghosts, whispering fearfully, "Rose preferred the company of girls."

I hesitate, making sense of it. "Are you saying she was a lesbian?"

"Now, now, lower your voice. We didn't call it that."

"What did you call it?"

"Well, we didn't call it anything. We didn't speak of it."

"My mother was gay?" Remaining calm, I sort the puzzle, finding this piece jagged but perfectly fitting. How'd I fail to make the connection before? Rose had always been masculine, a tad androgynous. How'd I overlook it at her memorial, where her roommate Stephanie lovingly spread the ashes? Had I turned a blind eye? Or did it simply not matter? It was Rose. I loved her unconditionally.

"Daddy thought it was a phase, that it would go away," Mrs. Pratt explains. "Still, Rose would hold hands with girls at school, playing it off as fun. There were rumors that she was doing more but I didn't believe it. I didn't want to think of it. Then one day I saw it for myself at church." She looks down and murmurs, "In the bathroom, I saw Rose kissing another girl. She was only fifteen."

"Fifteen?" I have trouble finding the behavior shocking. "Do you have any idea what fifteen-year-old girls do now?"

She recalls the day. "I had a cold. I needed toilet paper to blow my nose. I didn't mean to see it," she explains. "I only told daddy because I...I didn't know what else to do." Her eyes fill with regret as she resignedly sighs. "Daddy stopped playing sports with Rose after that. He thought maybe she should try other things like cook and sew." I struggle to conceal my disdain. "You have to understand. It was a different time. It wasn't everywhere like it is now."

"But it was. It was just hidden better."

"Daddy loved Rose. He didn't want her life to be hard. He thought he could keep her safe. That's why Rose began to see Stephen. She wanted to make daddy happy."

The truth sickens me. "I can't hear anymore."

She closes the album. "I loved Rose too. I never meant her harm. You have to believe me." She removes her glasses to dry her eyes. "I miss her." She catches her breath. "I wish you could have met your mother. She was full of such humor."

"We did meet," I say. "My family hired her as our driver when I was a teen. You didn't know?"

Her eyes fog with confusion. "Rose left shortly after high school. She never forgave father for making her give you up. She never came back."

I flash to Rose, the way she would replace bad words with something good. We were so happy driving in circles I hadn't realized we were talking in circles too. "Why didn't she tell me the truth?" My eyes water and Mrs. Pratt raises a hand to caress my cheek. "It would have hurt, but I would have liked to call her mother. Just once. Just so she could hear it."

She sadly nods. "She would have liked that."

I step away to gather myself. "Look how ridiculous I'm being. I'm a grown woman. There's no reason to be so emotional."

"It's all right," she says, returning the album to the box. "It's a lot to take in. You should go back to bed. Get some sleep." I refuse, shaking my head. How could I close my eyes so soon after they've been opened? The facts stack upon my heart. My mother Rose was a lesbian shunned by her father. To regain his approval she tried to love a boy, resulting in pregnancy. Her father made her give up the baby and she fled. Is that it? The end? It doesn't compute. Yes, she was angry with her father, but that doesn't explain why she remained estranged from the rest of the family.

"You never tried to find Rose? Not once?" I ask, following Mrs. Pratt back into the house.

She hesitates, keeping her voice low. "We spoke a few times around the holidays. We never visited."

"Not once, all those years?"

"It was for the best." In the dimly lit living room a greyhound lifts his head to yawn. Yellow light peeks through the window. "Henry didn't want to explain Rose's nature to the children," she says. I open my mouth but nothing comes. Only disbelief. "Please. Don't judge him. He's not a bad man. He was afraid."

I resist. "I would have given anything to have a sister."

She takes my hand. "Please understand. It was all around us, surrounding us. He had it in his family too."

"Had what?"

She leads me to the kitchen. The dogs follow, crying at her feet. "Now you hush. You'll wake father," she tells them. "I'll feed you in a minute." She sits me at the table, petting my hand while attempting to explain. "Father won't speak of it, but his brother had a son who liked to dress like a girl." My heart quickens. "At church there is talk he had the *change*." She shivers, the idea too wild to bear. "That's why

Henry was so short at dinner. He read in the paper that his brother died." She massages the small of her neck, growing more upset. "The two hadn't spoken in years. Silly family issues." She sighs. "Father couldn't bring himself to attend the service yesterday. He wanted to...."

"Yesterday?" I can barely get the word out as a million thoughts race in my head. It couldn't be. It couldn't.

Sometimes.

Family.

Chooses.

You.

"The boy. What's the boy's name?" I ask.

"What?" She shakes her head, confused.

"The boy, the one who had the change," I repeat, growing louder. On alert, the greyhounds circle from the commotion. A door creaks open within the house. Footsteps. "What was his name?"

"Why?"

I tug free from her grip. "Please! Tell me."

"Charlie. His name was Charlie."

I gasp. "Fritter?"

Distressed, her speech slows. "How do you know that?"

Henry flicks on the light, entering in a tee shirt and boxers. He stares at us in heated disbelief. "What the heck is going on in here? I'm trying to sleep. I have to work in two hours."

I recite what I know of Kitay's past, my voice muffling the cries of the dogs and Henry telling us to get back in bed. "He was raised in Arcadia. His mother's name is Gladys." Henry ceases talking, the color fading from his face. "His name was Charlie. And...and he had an uncle who kissed him. On Christmas."

Mrs. Pratt raises her hand to her mouth and looks to Henry.

Irate, he points to me with a shaky finger. "You...get... out of my house."

My body electrifies. "You were the uncle."

His face reddens. "I never touched that boy!"

"Father would never think to do such a thing!" Mrs.

Pratt exclaims. "Is that what Charlie told you? He's been a liar ever since he was young. You can't believe him."

The room goes blurry. I focus on the little things – dust on a saltshaker, a crack in a white angel figurine on the counter.

Poise. Presentation. Perfection.

I consider Bev Dear's words, realizing I'm not alone. Life is never perfect. We each bow to a blemish, a booboo – a scar from the past. Some are just more visible than others. A lady can't allow a scrape on her face to bring her to her knees. I must learn to walk with the wounds, find a way to love them. I head toward the guest room to change into my clothes.

Mrs. Pratt follows, her face reddened with anguish. "Why would you come into my home and bring out these bones?"

Henry calls from the kitchen. "Enough with the chit-chat. Get her gone!"

She continues to probe. "How do you know Charlie?"

"Please. Her name is Kitay," I correct. "She's a girl."

She struggles to digest it. "Then it's true. He did have the change." Her eyes worriedly search my face and I take a breath, reminding myself we're not far from the same cut. I was once scared too. She simply requires a lesson.

"I met Kitay in Miami," I begin. "We became neighbors, then friends." She listens intently, nervously tickling the pit of her neck. "Oddly enough, she taught me about life, about myself really. I guess the most important thing I learned is that being a lady requires more than having lady parts. It's about having a heart." She squints to understand but what else can I say? I don't know the entire story of Kitay. All I know is she slipped in my life when I was one foot from the ledge. I didn't will or want her there. She simply showed up right, wanting to be *gals* when I was set to jump. *Then they'd win*, she said, but I didn't know what she meant. I failed to see *they* were there all along – those who don't believe in us, the voices that find us at our weakest in the dark. I couldn't see the truth. I couldn't hear it until, to my ear, I held a woman they once called Conch. Then I truly heard the sea.

Oh dear.

How could I try to alter someone so right from the start? I gave her a new name and new clothes – a new lease on life, but I never asked if she liked wearing a bit of it. I can't go back, but perhaps....

Hurrying to the car, I place it in reverse, spotting a plunger in the back seat. Raising its cup to the wind, the wooden handle glows in the early light as I trek along the foggy road. I turn up the radio, set to the classical station, but all I hear is Kitay.

Family chooses you.

Family chooses you.

Was she right? Had I wasted all this time in search of something that had already found me? I race across the state, my eyes stinging from lack of sleep, replaying what I've recently learned, that Rose had given me up. Yet, in time, she gave up everyone else to be with me. I was wanted, loved. Even if she didn't take on the role of a mother she played an equally important part.

But why did Bev Dear allow it? Had she known it was in my best interest? Did she put my needs before her own? I'd never known her to be so charitable. Perhaps she wasn't as cold as I thought and I owe her more than I let on. She did teach me a thing or two about poise and presentation. The class is better for it. So am I. Why? I suppose because somewhere in all that learning I earned a family.

Say it. "Family." Scream it. "I have a family!"

Oh, how I've longed to shout that for years. So I do and the words lighten my flight, releasing a bevy of black birds across the sky. Anxious to arrive home, I follow their formation. I have much to share with Jasper about my birth parents, Rose and Stephen. I smile at the thought of meeting Stephen one day, if he's alive. If not, that's all right. I had a father. His name was St. Clair. He raised me with Bev Dear, and though he didn't plant the seed he watered me to grow.

So with a splash of perfume to the neck, I cross the bridge to South Beach, making a pit stop at the pet store. The turtles need food, that's the story. I don't even look for Wes. Well at least until I complete the task, pellets in hand. I head to the register, noting that it's empty and look around. Perhaps he has the day off. The thought saddens me. Could he have moved on? Am I too late?

I ring a silver bell at the counter.

"Sorry!" a female clerk calls. "I didn't see you. I was stocking leashes."

"That's perfectly ok. I'm in no...."

The side door opens and Wes emerges, wiping shampoo bubbles from his hand with a towel. "Dee," he says, more pleased than surprised.

"Hello," I say, before stalling. What next? I hadn't planned that far. Should I admit it, that I was a fool, a coward for not taking a chance? Should I tell him I'd like to change and learn to trust again? It shouldn't be so difficult to trust, but it is. I shake the yellow turtle food container. "I'm merely here to make a purchase."

"Yeah?" He grins. "That's the only reason you're here?"

I momentarily look away before I rise to the challenge, swimming laps in his eyes. "Of course. The turtles are quite hungry."

"There are a lot of other pet stores in town that sell the same pellets."

"Well I wanted the very best service."

"I see." He flashes a look to the clerk. "Don't worry. I'll take this customer." She returns a smile before disappearing down the aisle. He heads to the register, playing it professional. "So how are the turtles? Are you changing their water regularly?"

"Yes, with a little help." I hand him the container.

"Help?"

"That boy who was in the shop the other day. Jasper. He's staying with me for a while."

He nods, ringing up the sale. "And your other friend? The one who's good with dogs?"

"Oh. Kitay? She's been through a bit of a rough patch." I become sad, thinking of her at the funeral, wondering if she's back in Miami, if she's safe. "She needs a job," I tell him. "She hasn't had much luck finding one."

"You know, I'm hiring," he says. "Assistant Manager.

Full-time."

"I'll be sure to tell her."

He finishes the transaction and hands me the pellets, brushing my fingers. I don't pull away. I linger until he takes my entire hand. My body shivers. "Dee," he says, breathless.

"Please. I can't."

"Why? What's the matter?"

I'm scared. Be kind to me. Be good to me. Be everything you said you would so I know it's wise to wish for love again. "I need you to be patient." My eyes begin to tear.

"A date. One date. That's all I want," he says.

I warm, agreeing. "One date. And then you'll...."

He interrupts. "And then *we'll* decide where to take it together."

He tickles my fingers and I smile, laughing a real laugh. I haven't had one of those in some time. I'm so caught off guard that I barely hear my phone ring. I believe the sounds – the sirens and whistles – coming from outside are simply a figment of my imagination, residuals of my war-torn heart.

"It's Kitay!" Jasper shouts as I pick-up the phone. I look to Wes, my chest filling with lead. "She's on the roof, threatening to jump."

"Jasper, where are you? Are you ok?" The words come out so fast they blur together.

"I'm fine. I'm on the road, across the street." He begins to cry, and I hear people screaming in the background. "They won't let me on the roof to help."

"No. Stay where you are."

"Mom," he says, a tremble in his voice. "Mom. Come home."

Mom? The words silences all that is wrong, and I take off running, taking Wes by the hand.

No need for a car. No questions asked. Together, we race toward the condo, perfectly in step.

How good it feels, for once, to be headed in the right direction. I sense it in every limb, the magnet of the word mom pulling me to the proper place. Oh, what a mangled canvas, this dear life, but how it can be wonderful when the colors unite, creating a magnificent portrait.

So paint us – a woman and a man – running. Along the sidewalk, by sleek condos and storefronts, we're no more than specks of dust, pigments, reflecting the color of the green in the trees and the blue in the sea. I breathe, picking up traces of heaven, the fragrance of salt water slapping the sand.

By the Savoy entrance a red fire truck blocks the better part of the road. A crowd, barricaded by a team of uniformed officers, looks to the rooftop. The spectators shade their eyes, straining to see Kitay who stands, toes to the edge, ready to jump.

I look for Jasper as the crowd grows, creating more drops, more people to form a funnel. Here to heaven, it's one big splash back to the source. I know it too well, the invitation to fly and be free.

The firemen ready the safety nets and my knees go weak. I can't look. I feel as if I'm to blame with all my talk of jumping. Among the confusion I let go of Wes and cup my hands to my ears, listening for the sea. Where is Jasper? My heart drowns in emotion until his voice floats to the surface.

"Mom, mom!" he calls. Plunger in hand, he runs into my arms, embracing me. "You have to do something. She left a note under the door. She doesn't want to return to her mother. You have to stop it!" he begs.

I rub his back, keeping an eye to the roof, wondering if *they're* up there too – all the voices. I imagine she's outnumbered and needs me to balance the scales. I look to Wes to find he's looking right back. He nods upward, signaling I have to go. The man barely knows me but seems to know I have no other choice, not when it comes to family.

"You need me?" Wes asks.

I let Jasper go with a smile. "Just for support."

"Here," Jasper says, handing me the plunger. "You can do it."

Yes, but how do I get to the roof?

I look up and find the answer in Wes' kiss. Like a monsoon it sweeps along my lips and I realize there's no guide to the sky, no right way to reach heaven. We simply find the right people and they pull us up.

He wraps his arms around me, his nose nudging mine. "Go on. Save the day," he says. "But save tomorrow for me? Dinner? A date?"

The thought brightens my core. "Yes," I say without resistance. I press my lips hard to his mouth then pull back, smiling. "I would like that. I would like that very much." The risk of starting anew puts enough spring in my step to stomp up to the entrance of the Savoy where I find Archibald standing guard.

"Everyone please remain calm," he nervously says, with a police officer by his side. "You'll be granted entrance shortly."

Gathered in a large group on the front steps, the residents, young and old, impatiently push their way toward Archibald, rattling off questions. *What's going on? Who's that woman on the roof?*

I make my way through the crowd, squeezing past the sweaty bodies. I can barely breathe. The humidity combined with residents' heated words raises the sweltering temperature.

Up front, Trixie wipes sweat from her forehead with a rag, threatening the crowd with her cart. "You don't care!" she barks. "She's just another sad sucker to you. You don't give a damn that she's your neighbor. You're more worried about the celebrities on TV!" She rebukes the crowd, rolling the cart toward the toes of the people. I approach and she cracks a smile, allowing me to pass.

"Archibald!" I call, rushing up the steps. "Please. I have to get in!"

The police officer silently provides a boundary with his hand.

"Sorry Ms. Lingers," Archibald says. "We have strict orders, no one can enter without clearance."

"Yes, but tell the officer, tell him that I'm a counselor. It's my job to help in an emergency." I rummage in my purse for credentials as I hear my name from behind. Turning, I find Lisette, above the crowd, bouncing on the shoulders of Cici. To the air, she raises a plunger.

"The woman hood!" she calls.

I nod proudly. "Why, yes, the woman hood," I state to myself. What a mad, confusing place in which to live. But it's worth everything when you have friends and family who support you. I just need to get close enough to Kitay to remind her of that.

I raise my plunger, pumping it in mid-air and returning Lisette's shout out. "I'm a woman!"

To which she echoes, "A woman!"

Not that the policeman cares. He dubiously eyes me, refusing to hear my plea, let alone glance at my business card when I offer it.

Perhaps the plunger is a bit much.

"Ma'am, I need for you to step back," he orders.

"But I'm a licensed counselor."

"Sorry ma'am, I can't let you pass."

I look to Archibald. "Tell him!" I implore.

He flushes, stumbling for the right words. "Yes, she's a guidance counselor at Horizon," Archibald explains.

Holding a walkie-talkie to his ear, the officer pays him no heed, listening to an update from the roof. *The jumper is close to the edge. She's not backing down. Stand by.*

"Please, I can help!" I shout to the officer.

He waves me away. "There are enough professionals handling the matter," he says. "One more person isn't going to make a difference."

"That's not true," Lisette says. Coming up from behind, she takes my hand. "She made a difference to me."

"Me too," Jasper says, worming his way out of the crowd.

"Yo, don't forget me," Cici follows.

I smile, trembling. For Kitay's sake I hide the tension in my heart from the officer just like the first day I stood before the class, unsure of my ability to teach. I was an imposter, a sham. How could I trick them into believing I had a clue about what I was doing? Who can say? Perhaps I hadn't given myself enough credit.

I see myself in each of them now, as if I'm standing here but also in three different places – the ground, the steps, the roof.

"Please let me go up," I plead again to the officer. "I'll get her down alive. I promise."

He negatively shakes his head. "I need you to stand back."

"But you have to understand, I can't lose this woman. She's the one who saved *me*. It's good manners to return the favor."

"Yeah dog. Let Ms. Lingers go!" Cici urges. He rallies the crowd, raising his voice. "Let her go! Let her go!"

"You wouldn't want blood on your badge," Jasper notes.

"Please," I continue, as the crowd chants. Trixie wields the loudest voice of all, fist to the air.

"LET HER GO! LET HER GO!" she shouts.

Eventually, the officer's resistance wanes. "All right. Enough. You want to go?" he asks. Calling me over, he grabs my upper arm, pulling me close to his chest where a gold badge shines brightly. "Go. But I didn't see you. I didn't see nothing."

"No," Lisette states, smiling devilishly. "That's improper usage. You didn't see *anything*."

I beam, washing her over with a quick wink. Then I waste no further time. I ride the elevator to the penthouse floor before taking a small stairwell that leads up to the rooftop patio. Opening the door, my vision is temporarily overwhelmed by the streaming bright light reflecting off the concrete surfaces. I blink and move on slowly, guided by voices. The first I recognize is Gladys.

"There's no reason to jump," she says, keeping her distance behind a metal barbeque grill. "Please. You're being silly." Bending over, the butt of her red plaid dress obscures my view of Kitay who stands on the short wall bordering the ledge.

"I'm not going home!" Kitay calls. "I can't go back to that life. I'm not who I was."

"Oh, stop that nonsense," Gladys says. "You could live with me again, get a job. I'll help you." Behind her, shaded by potted palms, a lady police officer with cropped blonde hair stands guard. Two tall firemen, still as stone, secure the ground by the gray patio chairs. The professionals allow Gladys to take the lead. "You can even work in one of them clothing stores if you like. Come off the ledge."

Kitay begins to cry. "No."

"Please. You don't want to hurt me now. I just lost your father." She quiets, allowing space for Kitay to think. "Charlie? I love you so much. You're my special boy. Charlie?"

"My name is not Charlie!" Kitay screams.

I silently approach, following the concrete path around the hot tub. I look to Kitay, noting her striking blue dress. It ripples in the wind, the color of a clean sea. In her hand she holds a plunger.

"What's wrong with Charlie?" Glady asks. "That's a beautiful name. It's the name God gave you."

"No. It's the one you gave me," Kitay states. "I don't want it anymore." She lifts the plunger like a scepter, a majestic component of the Crown Jewels, addressing her mother regally. "I want you to call me by my true name."

"And what's that, darling?" Gladys asks.

To which, I make my presence known. "Kitty. At least by her friends."

The officer and firemen turn quickly, along with Gladys who shoots me a disparaging look – one that says I'm the reason for this mess. And maybe with all my talk of jumping, that's true.

"You!" Gladys groans, standing upright to fix her dress.

"Her name is Kitty," I continue. Closing in, I grip the plunger to my chest. "I made a mistake. I changed it too. I should've known there was nothing wrong with it. The package was perfect all along."

"Oh spare us the poetic license," Gladys gripes. "You're not welcome here." She turns to the officer. "That woman's not wanted. Make her leave."

"I'm not going anywhere," I say.

"Then I'll have you put in handcuffs."

"Miss, where's your clearance?" the officer asks.

I stand firm. "I don't need clearance." I look to Kitay

who sighs bleakly. "I'm a licensed counselor and I'm...."

"Family," Kitay offers.

Enflamed, Gladys hikes up her sleeves, approaching me. "Lies! Lies! Lies! This woman is not family." She reaches the edge of my nose. "You're nothing but an instigator. You have no business being...."

"Stop! I can't take the fighting!" Kitay calls. She stomps her foot and loses her balance before steadying herself from falling. I freeze from saying another word. Instead, I listen to the sound of the sea. The waves blanket the shouts of the people below and the wail of the sirens. Speaking up, Kitay provides orders, at least to me. "Dee, I need you to take Taser and Tacky. Promise me, you'll take them."

Becoming obstinate, I decide it's best to refuse. I can't allow her a smooth escape. That's not how it works. She'll release the pain and it will wash over the rest of us, drowning the hope that life can get better, that something left in this world is right.

I offer a spiky word, a jagged edge, to capture her collar on the way down.

"I'm not parenting those monsters. I'm too busy with my turtles. Besides, I don't like them. If you want them to have a home, you'll have to live. No one else would stand for their unsightly mugs."

Kitay gasps, covering her mouth.

"You're a mean woman," Gladys hisses.

I smirk. "Perhaps we run off the same tap."

The color drains from her face. "You want Charlie to jump," she suggests. "You're pushing him."

"She was pushed from day one. We're each given a choice which way to go out. Up or down." She eyes me with confusion, her pupils twitching beneath her glasses. "Now, if you'll excuse me, I'm pulling for her the only way I know how." I leave her behind and walk to the ledge.

"Don't come any closer. I'll do it. I'll jump!" Kitay threatens.

I flash to a day where I promised the same thing, where the only answer to losing ground in a hardened world seemed to be slamming into it.

"I don't believe you," I say. "You're bluffing."

The plunger trembles in her shaky hand. "You don't know that."

"Yes I do, because I know if you jump, *they'll* win. That's the last thing you want, isn't it? For them to win?" She gulps knowingly. I reach out my hand. "Here. Lift me up."

Her face tenses. "What?"

"You heard me. It was my idea, this blasted suicide bit. I'm not letting you get credit for it." She stalls, considering it. "My hand, hurry!"

She shakes her head. "No."

"It's what friends do. We stick together," I remind her. "Just us gals." She refuses, and I pull myself up. "All right, but if I jump first, don't use my body for a landing pad. I want to look presentable for the paper. I plan to pucker my lips like a fish right before I fall. That's in vogue, right?" She nervously yelps as I peer over the edge.

"Stop!" the officer calls, but Gladys hushes her voice. Perhaps she realizes I'm the last link left, the only one left to save her child.

On the ledge it all connects – the city and the sea. The cars, the waves, and the people become dots, uniting and coming apart. The city is a mad masterpiece, painted with the passion of a Picasso. Such beauty persuades me to add a stroke of color to it, tinting the sidewalk red to leave my mark.

Is this the end? I lift one foot off the ledge and the exhilaration builds; the thought of the plummet pulsates through me. What a splash I could make, the people forming to provide the perfect puddle.

The police officer sends a message on her walkie-talkie. *There are two jumpers, repeat two jumpers now. Ready another net.*

"What are you doing?" Kitay says nervously. "Don't joke around like that. You'll fall."

"So? If you're gone, why should I live? What do I have left?"

"You have Jasper and Lisette. You have a lot of

reasons."

"So do you," I say.

Saddened, she looks off. "You don't understand. I don't want to go home."

"Don't you see? You *are* home." I brainstorm a way to help her see the clouds will clear, the sky returns to blue even after the rainiest of days. "You can stay with me and the turtles. Jasper too. We have an extra room."

"With you?" Kitay asks. Her voice strengthens with hope.

"Yes."

"Taser and Tacky too?"

I consider it. "If they're gagged and quarantined, I suppose."

"But you don't like them."

"I like you."

"But I still don't have a job."

"I've talked to Wes. There's a job for you at the pet shop. You can save up 'til you can afford your own place. You won't have to leave."

"Charlie, don't listen to that woman!" Gladys calls. "She's not your family. I'm your mother and I love you. You're still my little boy and you need to come home!"

Conflicted, Kitay shifts her focus back and forth between Gladys and me, shading her eyes from the unyielding sun.

"Or stay," I offer, reaching out my hand. "Live with me and I'll love you for the lady you are." She considers it, her eyes reading me. I smile and she carefully takes a step closer, raising a shaky hand. The tips of her fingers touch mine and I jolt, brushed by an electrical shock. I lean back, losing my footing.

"Stop! You'll fall," Kitay pleads. "I'll do it. I'll stay. I'll stay!"

"Wonderful. It's settled," I say, squeezing her hand. Then letting go, I raise my other arm and we cross plungers with a crack. I welcome the rush of victory until the force of the collision troubles my balance. My euphoria suddenly crumbles as my heel slides off the edge.

I sway and my ankle twists.

I fall, grasping the ledge, my legs dangling down.

Kitay emits a thunderous scream, dropping to her knees to extend a hand, but I don't take it. I'm not scared. I can breathe. I can finally breathe, float, taking in what's below me – Bev Dear and all the menacing men. The horns. The pricks. The cuts.

Down on the street, the people seem to call to me. Their voices are so welcoming I believe I can ride the sound waves.

"Dee, grab my hand!" Kitay pleads.

I shake my head no. "I love you!" I tell her. And with that I smile and let go, releasing the weight of the years spent heavy in the thought of seeking a heaven that I couldn't find on earth. I hadn't realized I had to find it within myself. I can give love, and in return, receive it. Life can be good. I can be good, and someday these wings will carry me to my daughter where I'll wrap her like a warm blanket 'til we tingle with love. And Rose can wrap me.

Until then, to live is to find the proper puddle. Get wet. Muddy. Every now and again, take a plunge even when you're not certain where you'll land. So I drop, like water to the wind, faster and faster – the cries of the people cascading upon me like fresh rain.

I raise the plunger high, high, high.

Here I go, a blip on the radar, a headache of a headline. You might not see me. I'm not much to look at. I'm a dot in the sky, a crack in the sidewalk, a blind spot in your eye. But I'm here, whispering that we're all worthy of love, connected as colors in the canvas of life. No need to jump or escape into the light, for light bounces us right back. Just like this net catching me.

Whoosh!

I'm bouncing and bouncing and the crowd cheers.

And tomorrow, I'll go on.

I'll suffer more. I'll love more. Wes and I have a date....

For Desperation never dies!

She lingers.

Take the plunge.

Visit Anthony Paull online!

**For more literary fun check out
Anthony Paull's debut novel
*Outtakes of a Walking Mistake!***

Made in the USA
Lexington, KY
14 September 2013